MIA ZACHARY's
Another Side of Midnight

"Mia Zachary has a winner with
Another Side of Midnight! With a wonderfully
defined heroine, snappy dialogue and
an intricate plot, what's not to love?"
—*USA TODAY* bestselling author Julie Kenner

"Mia Zachary takes chances that pay off
in this edgy, compelling read!"
—*USA TODAY* bestselling author Julie Leto

"Sparks fly when Steele and Stone clash
in this dynamite, double-blind mystery."
—*New York Times* bestselling author Rebecca York

"Steele is…sassy and strong, beautiful and smart
but she also has [a] hint of vulnerability underneath
that smart mouth attitude. Put Steele and Stone
together and you get explosive chemistry…
the pages fairly sizzle…. *Another Side of Midnight*
grabs you right from the very beginning
and keeps you until the end."
—*CataRomance*

"Mystery, hard-balled suspense and a sizzle
that won't quit are a combination that I crave
when I read a romantic suspense. Mia Zachary
delivers my cravings to the max!
This book is definitely a keeper!"
—*The Best Reviews*

MIA ZACHARY

Over the years, award-winning author Mia Zachary has penned really bad poetry, even worse song lyrics, adolescent short stories and overly descriptive class papers. Her first completed contemporary manuscript placed second in Harlequin Books' 2000 Summer Blaze contest.

She's written four Blaze novels since then, including the bestseller *Afternoon Delight*; "Spirit Dance" in the paranormal anthology *Witchy Business*; and *Another Side of Midnight*, her first romantic mystery. Go behind the scenes of the Midnight agency at www.SteeleMidnight.com.

Mia lives in Maryland with her husband of seventeen years and their beautiful little boy. Visit Mia online at www.miazachary.com for excerpts, reviews, articles and more!

ANOTHER SIDE OF
MIDNIGHT

MIA ZACHARY

HARLEQUIN®

TORONTO • NEW YORK • LONDON
AMSTERDAM • PARIS • SYDNEY • HAMBURG
STOCKHOLM • ATHENS • TOKYO • MILAN • MADRID
PRAGUE • WARSAW • BUDAPEST • AUCKLAND

If you purchased this book without a cover you should be aware that this book is stolen property. It was reported as "unsold and destroyed" to the publisher, and neither the author nor the publisher has received any payment for this "stripped book."

ISBN-13: 978-0-373-19893-1
ISBN-10: 0-373-19893-0

ANOTHER SIDE OF MIDNIGHT

Copyright © 2007 by Mika Boblitz.

All rights reserved. Except for use in any review, the reproduction or utilization of this work in whole or in part in any form by any electronic, mechanical or other means, now known or hereafter invented, including xerography, photocopying and recording, or in any information storage or retrieval system, is forbidden without the written permission of the publisher, Harlequin Enterprises Limited, 225 Duncan Mill Road, Don Mills, Ontario, Canada M3B 3K9.

This is a work of fiction. Names, characters, places and incidents are either the product of the author's imagination or are used fictitiously, and any resemblance to actual persons, living or dead, business establishments, events or locales is entirely coincidental.

This edition published by arrangement with Harlequin Books S.A.

® and TM are trademarks of the publisher. Trademarks indicated with ® are registered in the United States Patent and Trademark Office, the Canadian Trade Marks Office and in other countries.

www.eHarlequin.com

Printed in U.S.A.

Dear Reader,

A funny thing happened while driving home from lunch with girlfriends one day. A kick-ass heroine and a complex premise attacked me and didn't let go of my imagination until the story had unfolded onto the manuscript pages…. Now here it is three years later and I could not be prouder to introduce you to the hero and heroine of my first mystery novel.

Steele Mezzanotte has a new P.I. agency, a showgirl's body and a sharp-edged attitude. Born and raised in Vegas, street smarts and a smart mouth have always kept her in control of any situation. That is, until Cameron Stone walks into her life. Drop-dead gorgeous, with a lot of Scots charm, the enigmatic "problem solver" has a habit of disappearing, but he'll always return to Sin City. And to Steele. Because the only thing that comes between a rock and a hard case is love…the greatest mystery of all.

Let me know if you enjoy the story as much as I loved writing it. I love to hear from my readers!

Mia

As a writer I know how important words are. And yet I can't seem to find the right ones to express the breadth and depth of my gratitude to those friends who have kept the faith when my own wavered. This story is dedicated to Mom and Lisa, who believed from the beginning and to Rachel and John who loved it to the end. Thank you from my heart. I'm also very grateful to Marsha Zinberg, Birgit Davis-Todd, and Kathryn Lye for standing by this project from the first premise and pitch. Thank you, ladies!

CHAPTER ONE

Lady Luck Strikes Again

LAS VEGAS, BABY. My kind of town.

Home to five different Cirque du Soleil shows, about 197,000 slot machines, over thirty-six million annual visitors, who knows how many Elvis impersonators and, of course, one Lady Luck.

However, as luck would have it, I'd spent the past half hour in a hot car, my digital camera poised near the small opening at the top of the tinted window. One of my best friends had let me borrow the Toyota from her used car dealership. My beloved Harley Davidson Softail motorcycle isn't exactly conducive to surveillance.

Downtown, the casinos are smaller than on the Strip, the hotels cheaper and the atmosphere more nostalgic than glamorous. "Glitter Gulch" is where you'll find the Golden Gate's ninety-nine-cent shrimp cocktails, the annual World Series of Poker at Binion's Horseshoe and Vegas Vic, the forty-foot neon cowboy. However, once you move past the four main blocks of interest, downtown feels meaner, gritty and weather-beaten.

The February temperature was a balmy eighty degrees, which meant it was over one hundred in the Toyota's driver seat. And I wasn't exactly sitting here for the fun of it. Waiting across from a run-down bar like a paparazzo anxious to snap photos of a clandestine meeting wasn't my idea of a good time, but it is part of my job.

My name is Stella Mezzanotte—midnight star in Italian—and I'm a private eye.

Damn, I like saying that.

Which was why I was roasting my ass outside of the Polar Lounge. At the moment I was following a client's girlfriend of two months because he thought she was messing around on him. Well, duh. With clown-red hair, capped teeth, collagen-filled lips and saline-filled boobs, did he honestly think she'd be genuine about her feelings?

People lie about anything and everything, especially when it comes to relationships. I hate these cases. I usually end up finding out things my clients don't really want to know and then nobody wants to pay for bad news. But, until I get full ownership of the agency, I'll take almost any case that comes in my door.

My mind was drifting toward a heat-induced nap when something—or rather someone—caught my attention.

The man walking out of the Polar Lounge was all kinds of gorgeous, but there was something else about him… An aura of quiet violence. This guy wasn't bulging with muscles under his dark T-shirt, but he had strength.

My instincts told me he wasn't afraid to use it. And yet beneath his military-short, dark blond hair was one of the most sensual faces I'd ever seen. Fascinated by the powerful, confident way he moved, my finger instinctively triggered the camera shutter. When he glanced over at me, I noted the intensity of his light blue eyes.

"Hey! What the hell are you doing?"

Oops. I'd been so focused on the golden god I hadn't seen Scarlet's boyfriend cross the street. Rat yanked open my car door and made a grab for the camera.

"Hands off, pal. I'm just getting some exterior shots for a story I'm doing on the bar." Lame, I know, but it was all I could come up with since I'd been taken off guard.

"Sure you are, honey." This time he tried to grab me.

Big freakin' mistake.

My real name is Stella, but everyone, except my parents, has called me Steele since I was nine years old. After I bluffed him out of his pocket change playing stud poker, my Uncle Vin used to shake his head and mutter, "That girl's got nerves of steel."

I need them in my line of work. In the end we all agreed to part ways: Scarlet with a torn handbag and an ex-lover; Rat with a bloody nose and sore balls; me with a headache and a broken camera lens. I did manage to save the image storage card, though. So, even though it was an affair to forget, my client would get proof and I would get paid.

Good thing since now I was out a three-hundred-dollar Sony Cybershot.

Mission accomplished, I slid into the Toyota and cranked the air conditioner to "arctic." Then I looked down, cursing when I saw Rat's blood on the hem of my favorite T-shirt, the powder-blue one that read Spoil Me and We'll Get Along Just Fine.

Some days I love my job. This was not one of them.

I'D JUST LEFT one bar and was headed for another, this time in my father's restaurant across from the University of Las Vegas campus. Mezzanotte's offers authentic Tuscan recipes straight out of my Nonna Angela's *trattoria* in Siena. The *pappardelle primavera* and the *bistecca alla fiorentina* are to die for. It's a family business. My father, Paolo, and my brother Raffaele run the kitchen while my mother, Vivian, acts as hostess.

Since I have no life outside of work—much to my mother's disappointment—I help out at the bar a couple nights a week.

Thursday nights are pretty slow, especially since Papa refuses to do gimmicks like karaoke or wet T-shirt contests. It took a lot of convincing to get him to put a TV above the bar for the sports channels. Tonight there was a decent crowd, though, enough to have me pouring drafts and shaking drinks at a regular pace.

I'm good at tending bar. I flirt a little so the guys keep thinking and keep drinking. I make the cocktails strong enough to earn a reputation without depleting the inventory.

And I'm normally a good listener, even when I'm really keeping an eye on the liquor levels for a row of customers.

But not tonight. Oh, I was getting the job done but my mind wasn't engaged. Tonight I felt… Itchy. Like my skin was too tight and my nerves were exposed. None of my customers needed refills, so I was absentmindedly watching the NFL Pro Bowl game when I heard a voice behind me.

"I don't suppose you've got a McEwan's Ale about?"

A hot shiver danced down my spine. The Scottish accent was pure just-out-of-bed Sean Connery. Hearing it, I started thinking about getting *into* bed. When I turned around, though, I looked straight into the face of the golden god. Stifling my sexual reaction I studied him, trying to figure out what he was doing here.

I don't believe in coincidence and I never get this lucky when it comes to men in bars.

The guy had broad shoulders and a massive chest beneath a forest green shirt open just enough to reveal a navy T-shirt. His forearms looked as if they'd been sculpted from Carrara marble and his large, blunt-fingered hands… I was getting all kinds of ideas about his hands.

His face had wide planes and interesting angles, with heavy brows that accentuated a coldly compelling blue gaze. The only soft things about him were the slight curl of his dark-blond hair and a deliciously sensual mouth. He was watching me with the barest hint of a smirk.

His eyes hinted that he'd seen the dark side of life and had laughed in its face, that he had secrets and no intention of sharing them. He had the air of a hunter, both patient and persistent. And like any prey, I felt the thrill of danger. All the way down my body.

"Sorry, no McEwan's. See anything else you might like?" I cocked my head and gave him a playful look.

"Aye, something's caught my interest."

I leaned my forearms on the bar, briefly drawing his attention to the lettering over my breasts. "Well, catching is one thing, keeping is another."

He resolutely kept his gaze on my face. A real gentleman, this guy. "It's a bit soon to play for keeps."

But apparently he did want to play. So did I. If the game got out of hand, I had a borrowed car and one hell of a right hook. What I didn't have was a date for Valentine's, as Mom had been reminding me all evening.

"You mean it wasn't love at first sight that made you trail me all the way from downtown?"

His mouth lifted a fraction of an inch and he nodded to admit he'd been busted, but there was no hint of apology. "Why were you taking my photo?"

"I wasn't. You just got in the frame." I grinned and gave him the once-over. "You're kind of distracting."

"As are you." His lips curved a little more and I found myself anxiously awaiting his smile. "What was a sweet lass such as yourself doing there anyway, eh?"

"A job. Why were you there?"

"A job." He returned my deadpan expression in kind then reached across the bar to offer his hand. "Cameron Stone."

"I'm Steele Mezzanotte."

"You don't look like 'steel.'" He smirked, as most guys do. I've got my Papa's bone structure, my Mom's curvaceous figure and, so I'm told, an innate sex appeal all my own. No matter how smart or how tough she is, nobody takes a pretty girl seriously.

"Yeah, well, looks can be deceiving."

As his large, calloused hand closed over mine, energy—unexpected and potentially lethal—shot through my palm. It reminded me of when I was five and stuck a knife into a wall socket. Every nerve in my arm vibrated with sensory overload and I caught my breath. A little shaken, I dropped his hand and stepped back. I felt myself blush as I cleared my throat.

"What can I get you instead of the McEwan's?"

"Surprise me, why don't you."

"I just might." Letting a slow grin spread across my face, I was suddenly feeling very lucky, indeed….

However, I woke up the next morning alone in a hotel suite, unsure of which was worse, my hangover, my heartache or the trouble I had gotten into this time.

CHAPTER TWO

The Waiting Game

THE PORCH LIGHT was on. A sign of invitation, welcoming him for his efforts these past couple months. He smiled in the darkness.

He'd been careful to park around the corner, but still close enough to get a clear view down the street to her house. The sun was stealing over the mountains in the distance. He had to leave soon. Some early-bird neighbor might notice a strange car and it was almost time for her morning run.

A dog barked nearby, startling him. But he continued to watch the house, wondering which room she slept in. Wondering if she slept naked. He pictured her long dark hair fanned across the pillow, her blow job-worthy lips parted slightly as she breathed.

He shifted in the driver's seat. The thought of her mouth always got him hard.

Letting his mind stretch further, he imagined she did sleep naked, her bare skin slick with sweat, the bed sheets twisted around her long athletic body. One hand would part her thighs while the fingers of his other tangled in her hair…

He wanted to hear her voice, if only a single word. Reaching for his cell phone, he dialed the number from memory. Anticipation had his heart racing, his body tense. He ought to speak this time—

"Huhlo?"

He closed his eyes, savoring the sleep-roughened rumble of her greeting…then disconnected the call. The time wasn't right.

Soon.

But not yet.

CHAPTER THREE

Through a Glass Darkly

BLINKING AGAINST the late spring daylight, I checked the bedside clock. Christ, did that thing really say five-fifty? I reached for the phone to stop the damned ringing.

"Huhlo?" My voice sounded as raw as it felt. I must have been screaming in my sleep again.

Silence greeted me in return. The heavy menacing kind that made the fine hairs on my skin stand on end. I sat up, wide awake now. I couldn't hear so much as an inhaled breath, let alone any identifiable background noise. But I knew someone was on the line. Waiting. Intimidating.

Just like the other calls.

And, again like the others, my caller ID didn't register a number. The line disconnected abruptly, leaving me to hang up with an ineffectual bang. Shafts of early May sunlight streamed across the bed but I was shivering, the sheet twisted beneath me damp with sweat. The sun had barely risen, but going back to sleep wasn't an option.

I swung my legs off the bed and padded down the hallway to the kitchen in nothing but my panties. Twinges of pain had me glancing down. The bruises on my ribs were as muddy as day-old coffee and the one on my face probably didn't look much better. Both of my jobs seem to make me a regular target.

The freezer yielded a half-empty bottle of Armadale vodka. I hate taking any kind of medicine. A double shot in my orange juice would hold off the worst of the pain and wash away the aftertaste of uneasy sleep. I'd been dreaming, the kind of dark, restless nightmares that leave a metallic taste in the mouth.

A few minutes later, I had three slugs in me—one from an old bullet and the other two from the vodka. I stood there in my gradually lightening kitchen, feeling the alcohol begin to warm my blood. One of these days I needed to quit drinking. Not today.

Back in the bedroom I threw on a T-shirt and bike shorts, sunglasses and a baseball cap. I used to run track in high school. There are probably still some ribbons and trophies in my parents' attic. I usually do between three and five miles, depending on my route. But my heart wasn't in it—I'd barely covered a mile—so I turned around.

After a quick shower, several ounces of hair goop and a half hour with my professional-grade ionic blow dryer, I started on my face. Normally I just wear moisturizer. But I was going to need some of Mom's stage makeup tricks to disguise the black eye I got last night.

My dad's place is not a dive, I swear. But with the restaurant being right across from UNLV, on weekends the bar clientele includes a lot of students blowing off steam… Sometimes in my direction.

Getting dressed only took me about five minutes. I hate having to think about clothes, so for everyday I just pick from my fifty pair of jeans and a hundred T-shirts. I slipped on the one that read, Have A Nice Day Elsewhere, grabbed my backpack and helmet and headed for work.

Traffic along Las Vegas Boulevard—otherwise known as the Strip—sucked, as usual. Caught by one of the city's many lethargic traffic signals, I braced my feet on either side of my Harley. The sun beat down on me from out of a pale blue cloudless sky, piercing the dark glasses shielding my eyes. The temperature already felt like eighty-plus degrees.

Sitting next to a diesel-belching tour bus didn't help.

Still, as I glanced around me, a chill slipped down my spine.

I'd been feeling all too exposed for the last two months. The caller, my telephone whisperer, might be in the next lane. Behind the wheel of the Nissan with the tinted windows? Or maybe he was the bald guy in the Chevy staring at me funny….

Or maybe all of these people were normal human beings just trying to get to work on time.

As I drove past the glory that is the Venetian Resort Casino, with its Doges Palace entrance and replica of the Grand Canal, my thoughts turned wistfully to the old Sands Hotel that it had replaced. The Sands was "A Place in the Sun" in the days when Frank Sinatra and his Rat Pack played here. And I do mean played.

The Sands is also where my parents met. Papa tended bar while my mother hoofed across the stage in a twenty-pound headdress. Mom was a Copa Girl. They had drinks with Sinatra once. But that's another story, one my father never gets tired of telling. And somehow I never get tired of hearing it.

My folks are still happily married, but the Sands was leveled in a controlled implosion. It was a hell of a final show. Ground broke for the Venetian less than a year later. Who knows how long that will stand before it makes way for something new?

The city is constantly demolishing and rebuilding itself bigger, better and brighter. I was born and raised here—what happens in Vegas, stays in Vegas, as the advertising goes. Depending on who you ask, this is either the most incredible or the tackiest place they've ever seen.

What Las Vegas really is, is glitz and glamour for its own sake. If you take it too seriously, you miss the whole damn point.

I navigated past another bus and hung a left onto Paradise Road. After circling a couple of times, I found an open parking space. I took off my helmet and scratched my fingers through my hair to mitigate the heat, adjusted my black leather backpack and casually strode across the parking lot.

You name it; this strip mall has it. There's a bank, a travel agency, a pawnshop, an attorney and a business services franchise. Midnight Investigation Services is on the corner, the name etched in gold script letters on the window. I get a flutter of both pride and anxiety when I see the place. It's only been mine for about six months.

Although I'd been licensed for just under a year, I'd worked as the secretary in my Aunt Gloria's investigation agency for three years before that. Not long after my life disintegrated because of a cowardly, self-centered decision...

Gloria Diamond, a blackjack dealer turned private investigator, had divorced Uncle Vinnie years ago, but I'd still considered her family. Nobody understood me the way she had, being a hard-assed, soft-hearted Italian girl herself. When I'd dropped out of UNLV my sophomore year, Aunt Gloria had talked me into helping around the office.

I'd mostly answered phones, typed reports, made coffee and paid attention. Then her two-pack a day habit caught up with her and suddenly I was taking over the casework. Gloria taught me what she knew, cut corners where she could and sent me to community college for the rest. But I still had a lot to learn, and now I have to do it without her.

When she died last year, Aunt Gloria left me the agency. She also left me the strip mall and the associated rental income in trust. According to her philosophy, a gal needs "fuck-you" money in a man's world. Smart woman, that Gloria. She'd believed in empowerment and independence. But she'd also believed in earning it.

As long as I keep the place running in the black for a year, I'm set. As long as no one ever finds out how far Gloria went to get me licensed... Otherwise, it all goes to my cousin Rick, who won't hesitate to sell everything and lay the money on the nearest craps table.

Opening the front door to the agency, I gratefully stepped into the air-conditioning. The large reception area is decorated in "soothing but elegant tones of cobalt, maroon and cream." Whatever. It gives clients a place to sit.

My secretary, Jon Chase, was typing furiously and staring at his computer screen. He's about six feet tall with a lean build, sleepy brown eyes, thick hair and a great smile. In a word? Hot. In another word? Gay. This, of course, was a heart-breaking shame to every heterosexual woman who met him.

He looked up and raised one perfectly arched brow. Then he added a glance at his watch. "Whoa. Are you aware that it's not even nine o'clock yet?"

"Just get me some coffee, will you." I have to remind him on a regular basis who employs whom around here.

"Well, aren't you just a delight this morning." He handed me a stack of envelopes and some message slips. Then he did that tsking thing when I peeled off my sunglasses. "I hate to tell you, Steele, but black and blue is so not this season."

Guess I needed more makeup. "Dad needed help at the restaurant last night."

"And to think bartending doesn't come with hazardous duty pay."

"Were there any calls besides these?" I kept my gaze on the phone slips and made my voice as casual as possible.

"Two hang-ups on the machine and a woman who didn't want to leave a message."

The aborted calls shouldn't have bothered me. But they did. "Has anybody stopped by?"

Jon looked at me, his expression curious. "Nobody outside the usual suspects—the mailman, that cute UPS guy. Why? Are you hoping for someone in particular?"

"Nobody outside the usual suspects."

I trudged down the hallway, past the kitchen and bathroom, to my office. When we redecorated, I'd let Jon have his way with the paisley love seats, glass coffee tables, potted bamboo and Impressionist art out front, but my office was off limits.

Framed posters of exotic beaches hung between the floor-to-ceiling bookcases. The armchairs and couch were leather and my walnut partner's desk takes up the far corner. I'd only agreed to the bright blue carpeting for the sake of Jon's "visual continuity."

My helmet and backpack landed on the couch with a dull

thump. Pulling the window shades kept the bright daylight from drilling a hole into my brain. I visited each of the electrical outlets in the room, recharging the pieces of my portable office. Then I collapsed onto my suede desk chair. The best place for my head seemed to be in between my open palms.

But, I had work to do. I picked up the mail and sorted through it. Credit card applications went into the trash along with dating service invitations. My mother thinks I don't know she secretly signs me up for that crap. I separated the bills from the few payment checks and thank-you notes then started a letter of my own.

The last time I was face-to-face with my oldest brother— five years almost to the day—I was only nineteen. Stupid, scared and selfish as only a nineteen-year-old can be. I've had to grow up since then. Vince still won't see me or take my phone calls. I understand, and so respect his wishes.

If you keep picking at an old wound, it never heals. But I hate the idea of having no contact with him at all. I write once a week without fail and haven't missed a week in all the time he's been gone. It's the very least I owe him. And, no matter what it costs, I've always kept my promises.

CHAPTER FOUR

Somebody's Got to Do It

A FEW MINUTES LATER, Jon slid my favorite mug—the one that read I'm Only Here To Annoy You—across the desk.

"Coffee-coffee-coffee." I took a sip and moaned out loud.

"I made you espresso instead of latte. You look like you could use the extrastrength caffeine." Tilting his head, he crossed his arms. "Soo, what's the story with that eye?"

I swallowed another mouthful before answering him. "One of the customers didn't take too kindly to her boyfriend gluing his eyes to my chest every time I delivered their drinks. When she said something, he took a poke at her. I swung on him. After that it got a little ugly."

"*Ugly* is not the word for it." Jon sighed dramatically. "With your looks, you could be a showgirl—"

"I tried that. Then they asked me to sing."

"Or a model—".

"I thought about that, too. For maybe a minute."

"But, no. You have to go around beating up drunks and spying through bedroom windows."

"Lucky for you and your sense of job security, huh?"

He rested a hip on the edge of her desk. "Oh, please. *You've* been lucky to have me these past three months. How many people did you fire before I came to your rescue?"

"About a dozen," I mumbled into my coffee mug. "But don't let it go to your head. You're the only secretary—"

"Administrative assistant."

"Whatever. You're the only one who didn't complain about the part-time hours, the salary or the amount of work. Speaking of which, shouldn't you be typing something?"

He made an exaggerated snap with his fingers and stood up. "Thanks for the reminder. I have to finish writing chapter twelve."

Scowling, I waved my hand at the files on my desk. "I meant something business-related."

"Oh, right. Because we have *so* many cases right now. On the other hand, Savannah and Brick are at a critical turning point in their relationship."

"The trials and tribulations of a Southern belle and her Yankee lover." He smiled as I affected a drawl with practiced ease. I even managed the Georgia mountain dialect he tries so hard to repress. "How's the book coming along?"

"They were undressed and fixin' to fall into bed when you walked in. Let me tell you—"

"Don't. Just don't." I stabbed my index finger in his direction. "I keep you out of my love life. You leave me out of yours."

"Sweetcakes, you don't have a love life."

There's nothing like the truth to end a conversation. And, besides, I hate it when he calls me "sweetcakes." I scowled at Jon's back as he swept out, then propped my boot heels on the desktop. I hadn't had a serious relationship in over five years, not since Bobby died... I didn't want to think about him.

And I hadn't gotten laid in exactly two months, two weeks and four days. But I didn't want to think about *him,* either.

Instead, I turned my attention to the files clogging my in-box. Private investigation is the business of information. Your client needs to know something and your job is to find the facts. People love the idea of Sam Spade, Mike Hammer, Thomas Magnum and *Charlie's Angels.*

Reality is nowhere near that glamorous.

It's hours of sheer boredom while you wait and watch and wait some more. It's days of tedious fact checking and double-checking. And it's paperwork. Lots and lots of paperwork. I have a system for it, though you'd swear otherwise. It involves nearly illegible notes on yellow legal pads or scraps of paper shoved into my pockets.

When I'm ready to type up a report, I shuffle the paper around on my desk like an abstract collage until I make some sense of it. Conventional? No. Organized? Hell, no. But I'm not a linear thinker and it's not pretty when I try to be.

After dropping my feet to the floor, I drained the last of my espresso and grabbed the first folder to draft a status report. *Insert client's name into document template. Briefly recap case. Inform of progress. Advise how to proceed. Save to hard drive. Repeat as necessary.*

I'd reduced the stack by half when the intercom buzzed. Jon was on the phone, using his business voice. "A Mrs. Cavanaugh is here to see you."

Who? I frowned and capped my fountain pen before flipping the page of my calendar. There weren't any appointments scheduled this morning and I would have been happy to leave it that way. Then I glanced over at the pile of bills. Not enough to bury us, but enough to make me sigh.

Due to the steady increase of infidelity, bad parenting and civil litigation, there's a greater than ever demand for private investigators. Just not this one. Jon says it's because we need a Web site.

"Okay, Jon, give me a minute to get professional, then send her back."

I rummaged through my backpack for a compact. Dabbing pressed powder onto my eye didn't help much. Screw it. I pulled my arms out of my T-shirt and turned it around so that the slogan was on the back. Then I yanked the spare navy blazer off the door hook and combed my fingers through my hair. Picking up my legal pad, I tried to project an air of expertise.

Because of my looks, most people think I only have enough brainpower to keep me breathing. While I have no qualms about using their assumptions against them on a case, it works against me when meeting new clients. But as my visitor walked in, I knew my appearance didn't matter.

Her shoulder-length brown hair had expensive-looking gold highlights. She wore a lavender business suit and matching heels. Diamonds flashed at her ears, neck and wrists. She actually wasn't much smarter than she looked, but I liked her anyway. Always had.

"Maria DiMarco." I came from behind the desk to take her hand. "I haven't seen you in forever."

"It's Cavanaugh now. Mrs. Gray Cavanaugh." Her breathy, childlike voice rushed from between pale pink lips, but her tone had an undercurrent. Something flickered in the back of her eyes. Then she smiled, looking like the girl I remembered, and indicated my shiner. "Still raising hell, huh, Steele?"

I grinned back at her and shrugged. "Somebody's got to."

At St. John the Evangelist High School, Maria had been the princess of the popular crowd while I'd been in trouble more often than I'd stayed out of it. Our second year, I'd chosen peer tutoring over detention when the principal caught me smoking in the girls' bathroom.

At first Maria and I had nothing in common except our Italian heritage and American History class. But over time we had become good friends. That lasted until I'd started at UNLV and we lost touch, as people do when they leave childhood behind.

"I didn't realize your aunt wouldn't be here when I called. I'm sorry, Steele. I know you two were close."

Like that, I remembered the last time I'd seen Gloria. She'd needed a hospice, but she'd opted to stay home and go out on her own terms. We'd been sitting on the patio, toasting the sunset with twelve-year-old scotch and a twenty-five-year-old male nurse… That was Gloria. A bad girl to the end.

"Thanks. I miss her."

Maria looked around, a slight frown pulling her brows together. "So…you're doing this stuff now? I mean, do you think you'll be able to help me?"

"I'll do my best. Why don't we sit down."

Maria seemed nervous, in no rush to get started. She was twisting the rings on her left hand. I didn't have to take a wild guess at the problem. This town provides plenty of work in the marital discord department.

I settled against the couch, wanting to put her at ease. "It's been a long time. What have you been up to?"

"Daddy finally let me be part of the family business." Her lips curved, but the feigned emotion didn't get close to her eyes. "I put in a couple of days a week at the Palazzo Napoli. I'm the events planner for the hotel."

"That's great. How is Big Frank?"

"Good. He's, uh, okay." She dropped her gaze for a second. "How's your family, Stella? I hear your brothers are working at Mezzanotte's now."

I shifted in my seat. "Just Rafe and his wife. You remember Laura Caporetto? She was a year ahead of us. Anyway, they help run the restaurant side. Joey's still a cop. He's doing good."

Neither of us mentioned Vince.

"And your folks. Are they as cute as I remember them?"

"Yeah, they still can't keep their hands off each other."

Maria nodded and kept twisting the big-ass solitaire and matching band. With most investigations, you find out a lot more by shutting up than by asking a lot of questions. So, I nodded too and waited for her to tell me why she was here.

She sat and fiddled for another minute or so, then cleared her throat. "You know, my father didn't want me to marry Gray the first time he asked. Daddy didn't think he was good enough for me. Of course, nobody I chose ever was." Maria gave a humorless laugh. "I really loved Gray, though."

I leaned back against the couch, having picked up on that past tense verb, but not wanting to comment.

"The wedding was beautiful. We had a five-tier silver foil cake, a chamber orchestra and dinner with three hundred of our closest friends. Then we spent two weeks in Hawaii for our honeymoon. Daddy gave Gray a job managing the Palazzo's casino. I thought we were happy…."

Listening to the slight catch in her voice, I watched her face. I had a pretty good idea what was coming. I didn't have to wait long.

"I think…maybe…Gray's been, um, unfaithful."

Maria looked at me, her expression bewildered, gauging my reaction. I guess she expected me to be as shocked as she was. Nine times out of ten, if you think your man is cheating, he is. So I made a sympathetic humming noise and didn't try to dismiss her fears.

"At first it was just a feeling, you know? He's constantly on his cell phone and doesn't say who he's talking to. He started dressing differently." Maria shifted her gaze and focused on the carpet. "For a while he was really affectionate, almost too much, but now he's completely disinterested in… You know."

I hummed again. "What made you decide to hire an investigator?"

"Well, Gray's been going up to Reno on business. Daddy's thinking of buying a place up there. I called the hotel one time." Maria took a deep breath. "The front desk told me Mr. and Mrs. Cavanaugh had already checked out."

I winced. I couldn't help it. Guys can be so damned dumb.

"Yeah. I guess I should have seen it coming, considering… But I guess the wife really is the last to know."

Did I mention that I hate domestic cases? Despite the amount of business they've brought the agency. The first one I ever took without Gloria was a freaking disaster. I wasn't too sure of myself so I kept in close contact with the client as I followed the husband. First he met his lover for lunch. Then he took her to look at rocks and I don't mean the geological kind.

My client was pissed; the husband never took her to expensive restaurants or bought her jewelry. She showed up at the motel I'd followed them to. The client ran into the room, the girlfriend ran out and, to make a long, stupid story short, I got shot in the ass trying to break up the fight.

Since then, I set off metal detectors at the airport and I keep my mouth shut until after I write up my case files.

"What would you like me to do, Maria?"

Her eyes and voice hardened unexpectedly, erasing her vacant appearance. "I want to know what's going on."

"I'll find out for you one way or another. But if Gray really is cheating, you've got to promise not to pull any of those movie-of-the-week theatrics, okay?" The look she gave me was totally uncomprehending. "No taking matters into your own hands."

She agreed and asked me to get hard evidence for any future legal action. After jotting her contact information onto the standard contract, I had to decide how to handle the financials. Gloria had used a sliding scale that depended on how much she thought a potential client could afford. With the shades drawn, there was still enough light in my office to illuminate the facets of Maria's diamond jewelry.

I named a figure that included my time, mileage, expenditures and front-row tickets to Cirque du Soleil at the MGM Grand.

She accepted the terms without blinking. "Whatever it takes, Stella."

Damn. I should have added enough for dinner and drinks before the show. "Tell me about Gray."

Maria's lips curved and I could hear the wistfulness in her little girl voice. "The first time I saw him, I thought he was the most beautiful man I'd ever seen. Not handsome. Beautiful. Gray has incredibly expressive amber eyes and a face that should be on magazine covers."

That was nice, but it wouldn't help me pick him out of a crowd. "Maybe you could bring me a picture?"

"I should have a recent one." She reached for her wallet and removed several pictures from one of the pockets.

As she sorted them, a rectangle fell onto the sofa between us. It was one of those four-pose strips you get from a photo booth. I had a quick glimpse of a much younger Maria kissing a guy with long blond hair. I noticed his *Spirits Dancing* concert T-shirt before she slipped the pictures back into her wallet.

"Here." She handed me a snapshot taken on the gangway of a cruise ship. "This is from our vacation last year."

I studied her husband's image, trying to commit it to memory. He was tall with sandy hair and a goatee, a lean build and an angular face that I wouldn't have called either handsome or beautiful. Gray Cavanaugh looked…slick. He was too attractive, too stylish, too everything.

I handed the picture back and went over to my desk. I rifled the bottom drawer for one of Gloria's checklists. She'd called the one for domestic cases the Cheat Sheet. After grabbing a clipboard, I returned to the couch.

"Okay, so tell me. What kind of car does Gray drive?"

Maria tucked a strand of hair behind her ear. "I bought him a white Mercedes, but I don't know the license number."

"No problem. I can get that myself. Is there any property other than your main residence?"

"Why do you need to know that?"

Because if he kept an apartment, he didn't have to pay for hotels. Out loud I said, "So I know where I'm most likely to find him."

"Oh. Well, we'd talked about buying a vacation place but I didn't get around to it."

I made a note to do an asset search anyway and look for rental properties. "What about his work schedule?"

"He usually takes the noon-to-eight. But one of the other managers has been sick recently, so Gray's working some graveyard shifts. I'm not sure of his schedule this week, but I'll find out for you."

"That would be great." I scribbled more notes as she told me about his routine and habits. "Okay, tell me about any hobbies."

She shifted, recrossing her legs. "Gray's been spending a lot more time on his golf game lately. He plays eighteen holes on his days off. We've got several memberships. Aliante Golf Club, of course, but also Spanish Trail and Red Rock."

Uh-huh. The Canyon Gate Country Club property, where the Cavanaughs lived, was home to a championship private course. I was back to thinking how much I hate domestic cases.

Then Maria pulled a thick envelope out of her purse. "This should cover the first week of your time."

I ran a thumb over the bundle of fifty-dollar bills before shaking hands with my newest client.

It's like Gloria always used to say—as long as there are sins and cynics, I'll have a job.

CHAPTER FIVE

No Easy Answers

ONCE MARIA LEFT, I stripped off my blazer and turned my shirt back around. Then I walked out to the reception area and handed Jon the contract and a copy of Maria's cash receipt. "Start a new file, please."

He sets up manila folders with hard copies as well as entering data into the case management program. If I can look something up for myself, it leaves him more time to write his romance novel. Jon glanced at the receipt.

"She paid in advance?"

"That's just the retainer." I grinned as I handed him the envelope. "Drop this at the bank before you go to lunch."

He rifled the thousand dollars the same way I had. Then he cocked his head to one side and wiggled his brows. "I'm taking ninety minutes for lunch. And I'm ordering the lobster salad from El Pescador."

As many times as we've played it, neither of us seems to tire of this routine. "You're taking an hour for lunch, pal. And you're paying for your own lobster."

"It's only thirty minutes, Steele. You can unshackle me from my desk for that long."

"Nope. We've got bills to send out."

He gave me a sly look from under his dark lashes. "I'll bring you back some Tandoori chicken from Shalimar."

Ooh. He was playing hardball. Growing up in a restaurant made me pickier than most when it comes to quality, well-prepared food, and Shalimar was named best ethnic food in the *Las Vegas Review-Journal*. I relented on the ninety-minute lunch, just like he knew I would. Say what you will, but the man knows how to stay on my good side.

Alone again, I called up a blank document on my laptop and started typing up my impressions for the Gray Cavanaugh file.

Kept husband? Got his house, his car and his cash from the wife, got his job from the father-in-law. Maybe he married for love, maybe not. Probably cheating just to prove he's a real man.

Follow-up for work and golf schedules. Check background (basics should be enough), credit statements (past three months) and cell phone bill (frequent numbers and times of calls).

A few minutes later, I got up and wandered into the kitchen. Yawning, I waited impatiently for the water to gurgle and blurp out of the ten-gallon jug and into my oversized plastic cup. I'm not trying to be trendy. Las Vegas is the fastest growing city in North America, which puts a lot of demand on the desert environment.

All the golf courses around here don't help.

I do my part by only drinking the bottled stuff. It's imported from some natural spring in Pennsylvania. I guess you'd say I'm a closet environmentalist, saving the world one cup at a time. Then again, I never remember to separate the trash on recycling day.

As I walked back toward my office, the hairs rose on the nape of my neck. The air seemed oddly still. I was no longer alone. Remembering this morning's dream and the subsequent phone call, my heart hiccupped in my chest. There was a phone in my office. My nine-millimeter was stashed in my desk drawer. The emergency exit was through the storeroom. Which would be quicker?

My fight-or-flight instinct froze with indecision. Shit. All three choices were too slow and it was too late to hide my reaction. Nothing to do now but fight. Whipping around, I saw a hulking silhouette. His features were hidden by the glare through the front windows. I tensed as he came closer, bracing for whatever happened.

His presence was somehow primal, unnerving. And familiar. It ought to be, as often as I'd studied his digital photo.

I released the breath I'd been holding. Flinging out my left arm, I aimed the full cup of water at his face.

"Hey! It's—"

I put everything I had into the punch that followed. When my right fist connected with his chin, I felt equal parts satisfaction and pain.

"It's me, damn it!"

I bent over to grab my cup with a shaking hand as the adrenaline slowly filtered out of my system. "I knew who it was."

It's not like I could have forgotten him. A guy doesn't walk into your life, turn it upside down and then disappear without leaving an impression. I thought I'd gotten past it. If not forgotten, at least moved on. I was wrong.

Okay, maybe it hadn't been the first time I'd gone to bed with a guy and woken up by myself. But it had been the first time I'd cared.

After the nuclear meltdown that had been Bobby Mattingly, I hadn't dated much. Two years passed before I accepted a dinner invitation. Another year before I had sex again. I'd slept with a couple of guys since but hadn't let it get serious. Then I'd met Cameron and lightning struck.

So I figured I could be forgiven for expecting more than his morning-after note. *S, You're amazing. I'm sorry for this. Something's come up and I have to leave immediately. I'll call when I can. C.* He hadn't bothered to come up with an original kiss-off line. Obviously, I hadn't been *that* amazing.

After wiping a hand over his face, Cameron raked back his wet hair. "I guess you're surprised to see me, eh, love?"

I flinched. "Don't call me that. I'd be more than happy to hit you again."

Not exactly true. He had a cast-iron jaw and my hand already hurt like hell. It had been worth it. I hadn't heard a word from him in two months, two weeks and four days. But who the hell was counting, right? Why be "surprised" about that?

What really ticked me off was my other reaction, which was purely physical. His damp black T-shirt stretched tightly across his shoulders and chest. Faded blue jeans skimmed over what I knew to be long, muscular legs. And I'm a sucker for long, muscular legs. He moved toward me and I had to fight my natural reaction—internal combustion in the face of an alpha male.

Cameron Stone is a lion of a man—six foot three or four, golden and gorgeous. In a word? Dangerous.

"Are you having a go at me because you lost the last fight?" He reached toward the tender skin beneath my eye.

I ducked his hand and crossed my arms, tapping a finger against the cup. "No, I'm picking a fight with you because your note wasn't exactly the Valentine I'd hoped for. While I appreciated breakfast, Stone, I would have appreciated an explanation more."

"Stella, love—"

"Don't call me that." He'd used the *L* word twice now. Even out of context, it was awkward, unsettling, and so very wrong.

Unable to avoid it any longer, I looked directly at his face. Wherever he'd been, whatever he'd been doing, his features now had edges hard enough to suit his name. He'd let his hair grow and his Celtic skin was deeply tanned. His light blue eyes still had the power to both captivate me and put me on my guard.

He looked really good, damn it.

I tried to forget how often he'd made me smile that night, the way my heart had raced when our fingers touched, or how eager I'd been for him as midnight became morning.

His eyes warmed considerably as he'd looked at me and asked, "Where have you been?"

"Right here, waiting," I'd answered.

The intense sunlight hurt my eyes. That's why they were tearing up. I swallowed hard, struggling for control. The level of my anger would reveal the depth of my feelings, and damned if I was going to allow that. I had questions, lots of them, but I also had some pride. So I kept things as simple as possible.

"Where the hell have you been?"

"As I said in the note—"

"*Something came up.* That was the best you could do?" I let my tone slide down into the sarcastic range.

His mouth flattened. "Aye, something came up. It was rather urgent and I had to take the first available flight."

"Where to?" I tipped my head, intrigued. Stone didn't strike me as the kind of man who ran from trouble. But, then again, what did I really know about him?

He continued to look me right in the eye, not an apology in sight. "I can't give you any details."

"Can't? Don't you mean 'won't'?"

"Can't. Client confidentiality and all that."

He shrugged, one of the cockiest gestures I'd ever seen. Either he was using confidentiality as an excuse, or he was adhering to it out of expediency. Professionally I understood, but personally it set my temper off.

"Fine, no details. How about a broad overview? It's been almost three months, Stone. What kept you from calling once this *something* was finished?"

His hesitation only lasted a nanosecond, long enough for me to realize he'd already decided how much not to tell me. "This is the soonest I was able to contact you."

Asshole lying jerk bastard.

"Nice to see you, Stone. Feel free to drop out of my life again." I turned my back on him, heading into my office.

"Not so fast."

Before I could take more than a step, his arm banded around my waist. He leaned back against the door frame, turning me in the space between his thighs. The thrill of being so near him again struck me like lightning. I felt the sizzle in every nerve of my body as repressed desire added to the heat of my anger.

I could have knocked him on his ass, had him flat on his

back in less than a heartbeat. That's what I told myself, anyway. But I didn't because, knowing Stone, he'd have thought it was foreplay.

"Let me go."

"I did that once and didn't much care for it."

I laughed harshly, not about to fall under the spell of that sexy brogue. "You've got it backwards, Stone. *You're* the one who left."

"I know. Believe me, I didn't want to." When I pushed away he didn't stop me. I moved toward the opposite wall, putting distance between us so my body would stop humming. "But I'm back, Stella. I'm here now. And I'm wanting to work things out."

Crossing the space between us, he cupped my shoulders, sliding his calloused hands up and down my bare arms. He held my gaze calmly, his pale eyes clear and candid. I knew better. There's nothing open about Stone except his blazing sensuality. Seriously, he's a natural-born charmer.

But I was in no goddamned mood to be charmed and feeling emotionally unprotected did nothing to improve things. So I ignored his oh-so-sincere assurances. "The only thing we need to work out is when to file—"

The little bell over the front door chimed. I frowned, startled to realize that it hadn't made a sound when Stone came in. Jon started down the hall, then stopped dead in his tracks. His expression hardened as he looked at us—Stone still loomed over me, grasping my elbow.

Jon drew himself up to his full height and struck a menacing pose, muscles flexed, eyes watchful. "Who's this?"

I'll be damned. A knight in flaming armor.

But, instead of an Uzi, Jon had a takeout container under his arm. It ruined the effect. Right now, I needed to defuse the situation or I'd be picking carpet fibers out of my lunch.

"This is Cameron Stone." I slipped from his grasp and took a step back. "He's—"

"I'm her—"

"—leaving now."

Stone shot me a look, but thankfully didn't finish his sentence. "Aren't you going to introduce me?"

I squared my shoulders, irritated by his unspoken censure. "This is Jon Chase, my secretary."

"Administrative assistant," Jon cut in, glancing from me to Stone and back again. He had yet to move, apparently still gauging the threat.

Stone nodded in greeting, though his focus stayed on me. "We've some things to discuss, you and I. A proposition."

I snorted inelegantly. "I'm still trying to recover from your last one."

That brought Jon closer to my side. He stood just in front of me, making himself an obstacle. When I tapped his shoulder, he turned his head but didn't take his eyes off Stone.

"I thought you were taking a long lunch."

"It can wait." Jon didn't seem ready to shift out of action-hero mode. "Should I ask why he's wet?"

Stone spoke up. "*He* is wet because I gave her a bit of a start when I came in."

I looked over and caught his faintly amused expression. Damn it, couldn't he at least pretend? Jon was acting more jealous than Stone was.

"I'm fine. Really. I just wasn't expecting the ghost of mistakes past." I darted my eyes in Stone's direction, then held my hand out to Jon. "Can I have my food now?"

He handed over my chicken and a small plastic bag. "I got yours first. Try to remember this when I'm up for a raise."

"I'll make a note of it," I replied in my least sincere voice. "Go get that lobster."

"I'm not hungry." Jon eyed Stone some more even though he was talking to me. "If you need anything at all, I'll be right at my desk."

"Nice to've met you." Stone held out his hand.

Jon ignored the gesture.

Stone let his hand fall to his side. "I'm sure we'll cross paths again."

That did not make me happy. It sounded like a threat to my mental health as well as a casual promise to my secretary. Jon walked away, but not before giving me a look that warned he'd be asking a lot of questions later. Let him ask.

There was no easy way to explain Stone.

CHAPTER SIX

A Matter of Trust

"YOU CAN GO, TOO."

Stella pierced Stone with a green-brown glare, angling her head toward the front door. Then she turned on her heel so swiftly that her braided hair swung in an arc. Cameron admired the sway of her bum before following her down the passageway. With little effort, he recalled the satin feel of her bare skin and the sinuous muscle beneath it.

He glanced about, registering the agency's layout and exits from habit. He walked into the last office just as she went round the desk, set her meal down and flung herself into the chair. He studied her, replacing memory with reality. Hair as dark as a raven's wing with wide hazel eyes beneath straight brows, a classic nose and a full mouth that begged a man to kiss it.

And that bloody shiner. The anger had hit him out of nowhere, as if he could feel the impact of that fist against her cheek… He'd seen quite a few people die over the years, some of them by his own hand. And yet the sight of her barely concealed bruising made him ill.

He forced his gaze away, schooling his expression to mask the sudden rush of feeling. Looking around, he made note of the motorbike helmet, technical books and utilitarian blinds along with the watercolor canvasses, delicate glass paperweights and flowering plants.

"You're just as intriguing as I recalled."

"Flattery will get you nowhere, Stone. Why are you still here?"

He hated having his back to the door, but he took the visitor seat, gingerly crossing his left ankle over his damaged knee. "As I said before, we need to talk."

"So talk." She flung up her arms in resignation before opening the polystyrene container. The room filled with the scent of grilled chicken, garam masala and lemon.

He nodded toward her food. "I don't suppose you're sharing that?"

"No." She took an exaggerated bite, closing her eyes and humming with gusto. "Why did you come back?"

He couldn't tell her, couldn't possibly explain how he'd left the Bellagio with the oddest sensation of the light going out of the room. He hadn't much experience with light. A relationship was something he never thought he'd have. In his line of work truth and true emotions weren't to be allowed. No ties to hold him back, no assets to compromise him.

Yet there was something about Stella. For the first time in years, he'd felt…

He'd begun making arrangements while waiting in the Vegas airport's international terminal for his flight to Bogotá. He hadn't wanted to leave in the first place. But Nick Anson, head of the Nighthawks, had needed him and the job had been one he couldn't refuse. A matter of a life or painful death.

Unfortunately it had taken longer to come to the final end of things than anticipated. He, Ice, Loco Vaquero and Blueman had spent miserable weeks in the jungle dealing with the Liberation Front rebels. The ordeal had only strengthened his resolve to return to Stella. He'd begun several times to ring her up, but even so he'd known an impersonal call wouldn't do.

He'd wanted—no, he'd needed—to see her again.

"I'm here for a job… Among other things."

"Uh-huh. Obviously I missed something before. What exactly is it you do?"

"I…" Cameron smiled briefly. "Eliminate problems."

She laughed at his careful phrasing. "What, you're some kind of enforcer for the Scotch mafia?"

"Scottish, actually. Scotch is something you drink. But, no." He dropped his foot back to the floor. "I'm a risk management specialist, mostly negotiations and recoveries."

She set her fork down with a snap. "I wouldn't have pegged you for an insurance agent. They usually don't disappear in the middle of the night."

Cameron knew what she wanted and he resisted giving it. He was very much his own man, had been since having to leave the Special Air Service behind. There had been other women, of course, but he'd made the rules clear from the start. He'd come and gone as he damned well pleased. Until now.

Until her.

His natural aptitude for unconventional warfare was discovered during his Army training. Each time he'd put his dark gift to use, it had cut away a bit of his core and it showed. Given the life he led, he looked like ten kilometers of bad road and well he knew it.

Yet somehow she'd recognized him, as he had her. The instant they'd touched, he felt it. Like that split second before impact when you knew the bullet was coming, but couldn't do sweet fuck-all about it. Souls colliding as bodies merged.

Anyone outside of his best mate would think he'd gone barmy, but he was sure about himself and Stella. He'd seen that same certainty in the eyes of his parents when they looked at each other, right up until they were killed. Therefore now that he'd returned, he had every intention of staying on. Whether his wife liked it or not.

"Well?" Stella crossed her arms and glared at him.

"I'm what you might call a conflict consultant."

"Consulting could mean anything or nothing."

Clever girl, his Stella. That was precisely why he'd set up

his company in that manner. The less known about what he did, the better for all involved.

"When one person's agenda conflicts with someone else's, they call me. That's why I'm here. Frank DiMarco called me."

CHAPTER SEVEN

Money Changes Everything

Now, I HAVE TO ADMIT, that stopped me. On several levels. Frank DiMarco is Maria Cavanaugh's father. And, like I said before, I don't believe in coincidences. Stone was here because Big Frank had called him, not because he wanted to see me.

Son of a bitch.

Fearing my look actually would kill him, I stared down at my lunch. The Tandoori chicken, jasmine rice and spinach paneer were neatly separated on lettuce leaves. Little tomato rosettes and parsley sprigs garnished the meal. It's the details that count, both on my plate and in my job.

When Stone reached over to steal a piece of chicken, I shoved the container toward him. My appetite was gone, but my interest was aroused. "Big Frank called you. Is he the 'conflictor' or the 'conflictee'?"

Stone took a bite before answering. "DiMarco would be the conflictee. He's out a good sum of money."

"From which business?" Maria's father owns a couple of small hotel casinos and some adult entertainment clubs on the Strip.

"The Palazzo. About four hundred thousand dollars was stolen over several months. An inside job."

Normally people tiptoe around a man whose nickname is "Demon" DiMarco. Stealing four hundred grand is more like stomping. I shook my head in disbelief. "Why not go to the cops or the Gaming Board?"

He swallowed a mouthful of rice and spinach. "DiMarco doesn't want the publicity. More importantly, he wants the money back. Which leads to my proposition. We'll work together, sharing information—"

I interrupted with a bark of laughter. "Oh, like you've been such a wealth of knowledge in the past. Forget it."

"As I recall, Stella, we're damned good together."

I recalled, too. In vivid, true-to-life color with high-definition surround sound. Then I remembered the elegant and expensive silence in the hotel suite the next morning. And the silence ever since.

My anger hummed so close to the surface I felt sure he could hear it. I picked up one of the mouth-blown paperweights I keep on my desk, rolling the crystal globe between my hands. Judging its weight to be about three pounds, I wondered how hard I could throw it.

"I work alone."

"Let's see if this sparks your interest, then." He wriggled an eyebrow. "The thief is Gray Cavanaugh."

I thought back to the picture of Maria's husband, not surprised somehow. Then I thought about the timing of Stone's arrival. "Big Frank hired you to trail his daughter?"

"No, but he did recommend a local investigator—that would be you—who might be a good resource. Following Maria provided a convenient excuse to see you again."

I ignored that as best I could. "Does Frank think she knew about the embezzlement?"

"He believes she would protect her husband."

She might. But I remembered Maria's tone when she mentioned finally being in the family business, her suppressed outrage over the affair. "I'm not too sure about that."

"Why? What did she discuss with you?"

"I can't tell you. Client confidentiality and all that." I focused on the paperweight, paying exaggerated attention to the swirling ribbons of colored glass inside. Then I sent Stone a smile, big on sarcasm and low on sincerity.

He wiped his fingers on a napkin. He leaned back in his chair and gave me a considering look. "If you don't think Maria would cover up for Cavanaugh, I'll hazard a guess she came to you about Gray's bit on the side."

I shrugged, answering without answering.

He went on. "I've a notion this woman is not only his mistress, but his accomplice. Together, we'll find her that much faster."

Although I was dying to know how Cavanaugh had grown the balls to rip off Big Frank's casino, that wasn't what I'd been hired for. I didn't know nearly enough about Cameron Stone, but I seriously doubted he needed my professional help. And it was just too unlikely to think this could be personal.

"I can find the mistress on my own without wasting time and money solving your case, too."

His cool gaze mocked me. "I shouldn't think money is an issue, considering your assistant can afford lobster for lunch."

Good. I'd been wondering if he'd picked up on that. The agency may not look like much, but he didn't need to know we were struggling.

"What do you get out of our partnership?"

He responded with a cool smile. "I'll have the pleasure of your company and ten percent of the recovery. As my 'local resource,' twenty percent of that could be yours."

Twenty percent of ten percent of four hundred grand. A nice round eight K figure.

He smirked at me. "Ah, now you're wondering if you'd be better off with or without me, Nevada being a community property state."

"Without, Stone. No doubt about it."

He dropped his gaze and his voice took on a husky quality. "I didn't really ask before. How've you been, Stella?"

"How have I been?" The sudden show of interest had me parroting his question.

"Are you seeing anyone?"

I set the paperweight on the desk before I threw it at him

after all. "You're kidding, right? I mean, you're not exactly in a position to ask."

"Am I not?" When he finally looked up, the color had shifted in his eyes again. "You're certain of that, are you?"

I leaned back in my chair, clenching my jaw and trying to clamp down on my feelings. Did he actually think he had any kind of claim to my life? After the callous way he'd treated me? My hurt, resentment and confusion warred with my anger. As usual, I let anger win.

I remembered that night—the champagne, the flowers and the Bellagio's dancing fountains lit up below our window. I'd believed in magic that night. The way he'd looked at me, the unspoken message in his touch, had made me think we were on the verge of…something.

Then I'd reached out for a man and stroked a vacant sheet instead. The pillow under my head had still smelled of citrus shampoo and male sweat. But I'd known even before I saw his note that he hadn't run out for coffee and a paper. I felt my blood pressure rise and changed the subject.

"Let's get back on track."

A professional mask replaced his expression. "Right, then. DiMarco hired an independent auditor to go over the finances. As the casino manager, Cavanaugh has authority to sign markers or IOUs. There were a few questionable transactions."

"Yeah, like what?"

"He signed off several markers as paid. However, they don't have corresponding bank deposits."

I rested my chin on my fist. "So, when his girlfriend didn't pay her debts, he 'forgot' to take the money from her account, huh?"

He shook his head slowly. "She didn't have an account to take from. Apparently the application for casino credit was approved without ever being verified."

"Gray okayed the marker on both ends while his girlfriend cashed out the chips. All under his wife and father-in-law's noses. Dumb ass. If Big Frank is sure that Cavanaugh's been embezzling, why hasn't he confronted him?"

"As I said, this must be kept quiet. Casinos never want to let on about losses, especially from employee theft. However, DiMarco is adamant that this be managed as swiftly as possible. Find the tart and we should find the money."

"There is no 'we.'" Not when I wasn't sure of what was really going on and he'd given me no reason to trust him. "If you figured that since I'd be following Cavanaugh, you could tag along, think again."

His lips curved into a confident grin. "Come now, love. We'll be bumping into each other, constantly getting on top of things. Better to share what we're doing and get comfortably into position, I'd say."

Could he put any more innuendo into that line of reasoning? I swear, everything was sexual with him. "Don't get any ideas. I'm not going to sleep with you."

"Happy to hear it. When I take you back to bed, I fully intend to keep you awake."

I let that pass, though it wasn't easy. Stone was one hell of a lover. But I didn't want the complication right now. At least, that's what I told myself. Then his gaze raked my chest and he winked. I looked down to see my nipples standing at attention. Dammit. Damn him.

He stood up and reached for his wallet, then handed me a business card. It was bright white with only his name on the front. On the reverse were three telephone numbers. "My mobile phone, my pager and my answering service."

Tossing the card onto the desk, I dismissed him with a look. "I've got work to do. You can find the door."

The glacial blue look he shot me was heavy with unspoken words. I'm a gambling woman, so I was willing to bet I didn't want to hear them.

"Ring me once you have Cavanaugh's schedule. We'll coordinate from there." Stone walked out.

It wasn't until a couple minutes later that I realized I hadn't actually agreed to work with him. We both should have known better. Impulsiveness had gotten us into trouble in the first place. But I love a good mystery and the agency could use an injection of cash….

So, here I was, headed for trouble once more.

CHAPTER EIGHT

The Business of Information

JON WAS BACK in my office so fast you'd think he teleported. He'd probably been lurking in the foyer, waiting for Stone to leave. I was already waiting for him to leave again, too.

"So, who was our unexpected visitor?"

I must have reacted to his odd tone because Jon smiled and plopped down on the chair Stone had occupied. "Start talking, girlfriend, and don't skimp on the details."

"I'm not your girlfriend and there's nothing to tell."

"Puh-lease. I have eyes. I saw *him* and I saw the sparks." He leaned his elbows on my desk, his brown eyes intent. "Now, who was that divine creature?"

"Stone is…"

My voice trailed off. I tapped my pen on the blotter, struggling for a description. He wasn't my lover or my friend. He was an impulse I'd quickly regretted, a mistake I wouldn't mind repeating, but also a problem I needed to resolve.

"Stone is none of your business."

Jon pouted, an expression that managed to look adorable on him instead of infantile. "You're no fun. At least give me a vicarious thrill and tell me he's as good as he looks."

I pictured Stone naked and sweaty and smiled. "Better."

"So you are involved." His voice sounded flat for a second, but then he camped it up as usual. "Here I've been teasing about your nonexistent love life, and all the while you've had this big, sexy secret."

Yeah, but sexy or not, our relationship was staying a secret. I arched my left brow. "Are you done?"

"Not even close. When did you meet him? Where did you meet him? What did—"

"Skip traces," I blurted.

"Excuse me?"

To stop Jon from pursuing the subject of Stone, I'd get him to search the proprietary information databases. Locating people is time-consuming, often frustrating but also a large part of the job.

I handed Jon a couple of manila folders from my *Do Something* pile. One client was looking for child support from her scumbag ex-husband; another was searching for his birth mother; and the third wanted to find a former boyfriend from the class of 1952.

"See if you can at least find current addresses. Anything else you come up with would be great."

"You want *me* to find them? Me, a mere secretary?"

"Administrative assistant," I retorted.

Jon gave me a look. "You're not completely off the hook, Steele. I'll just bide my time until you confess all the sordid details about Cameron Stone."

"Skip traces."

I opened the top drawer of my desk to put away Vince's letter. I'd finish it later. Catching sight of a particular court petition, I hesitated. Now was as good a time as any to take care of that. But after less than a second's hesitation, I decided to wait and see what happened. I locked the drawer on the letter, the petition, my gun and my past.

Moving around the office, I unplugged my gadgets and chucked them into my backpack. I never leave without making sure I have supplies for any situation. Cell phone, pens, notepads and new digital camera landed among the detritus. Bandages, GPS locator, lip gloss, high-powered binoculars, condoms, protein bars, electronic data organizer— that kind of thing.

Bag ladies haul less stuff around than I do.

"Where do you want me to start?" Jon was still skimming through the files.

"The deadbeat dad. Ryan's mother is working two jobs, so keep the cost down, please."

He looked up with a gleam of amusement in his eyes. "I never would have guessed you had a soft heart."

That's why I surround it with the toughest armor possible. The damned thing keeps getting me into trouble. I sent him a cool glare. "It's better to milk a client with repeat business than to hit them with one big bill that they won't pay."

"Uh-huh. Sure."

I picked up my backpack and helmet. "Quit lounging around and get back to work."

Jon casually got to his feet like it was his own idea. "Where are you off to?"

I filled him in on my schedule as we walked down the hall. "I'm stopping at Dreyer's office to pick up some papers he needs filed. Then I'm going to run by a claimant's house to see if he's up to anything his doctor says he can't do. I doubt I'll be back."

"Okay, I'll lock up. Call in for messages before I leave." He slid behind his desk and logged onto the Internet. He opened the first file, apparently eager to get started.

"Oh, and Jon?" I turned, halfway out the front door, not looking at him directly. "About earlier. Um, thanks."

I think he knew I wasn't talking about my lunch. He kept his expression neutral, though. "Don't get all mushy on me now, Steele. I won't know how to handle it."

Moment over. I sneered at him and left.

I WALKED PAST the Ticket to Paradise travel agency next door and waved to Lisa and Isabelle. They discount my trips on the rare occasions I leave the state. In exchange, I run background checks on their new boyfriends.

I have the same sort of barter arrangement with Barry

Dreyer, the attorney on the other side of the travel agency. He's helping me with a velocity issue. One more speeding ticket and I max out the number of points on my license. In return, I listen to the endless stories about his kids.

His eyes lit up behind wire-rimmed glasses, deepening his laugh lines. "Stella! I'm glad you could drop by. I've got new pictures."

Sometimes I think Barry and his family live at the Sears portrait studio. He married later in life and never expected to have kids, let alone twins. I wasn't sure how it was possible, but the boys already had their father's overbite and receding hairline. Combine this with their mother's narrow chin and close-set eyes and you had two less than attractive toddlers.

"Here. Look at these."

Barry proudly handed me a couple of five-by-sevens. I shuffled through images of the boys in various poses and forced a smile.

"Great pictures. I like the composition and the lighting." If you can't say something nice, compliment the skill of the photographer.

"Yeah, I've got good-looking sons, don't I?" He accepted the pictures back, beaming as he put them away. "Let me tell you what those two did yesterday—"

"Gee, Barry, I'd love to hear about it, but I've got to get going. I just came to pick up the Complaint you want filed."

"Oh, sure. Let me see where Elaine put them." He went to the credenza and rifled through some stacks of paper.

Barry doesn't have a paralegal anymore. He kept dating them and then he married the last one. He hasn't hired another. I guess Kim doesn't want history repeating itself. Instead, Barry keeps a secretary and pays me to file suit papers and serve subpoenas for him. My monthly bill is cheaper than a full-time employee or a divorce.

"Listen, Stella, I've got something else for you. A little more interesting than filing."

"Yeah, what's that?"

"Estate stuff. I need you to do an asset search. The widow is very merry and wants everything she married the old guy for." He watched me closely as I scanned the documents.

It took me a minute, but then I jerked my head up. "Uh, it looks like there's a few things missing."

"Yeah," Barry scoffed. "Just a few. As the estate's Personal Representative, I can engage experts to ascertain the value of the assets. I already got letters of administration for you. We just need to do a retainer agreement."

After signing some forms and making copies of what Barry had in his file, I shoved the papers into my backpack and told him I'd get something for him as soon as I could.

"I appreciate this, Stella. Come back when you have more time. I'll tell you my plan for the twins' birthday party."

Nodding politely, I decided I'd rather hear about dental surgery. "Sure, Barry."

I left his office and walked across the parking lot, thinking about the other attorney I needed to visit soon. Although Douglas Holbrook was one of the most successful, well-respected lawyers in Nevada, my hopes for righting an old wrong faded with each passing year.

Or maybe it was my resolve that was weakening. The cost of my mistake had been higher than I could have imagined. Trying to correct it would cost me everything I had left.

With difficulty, I shook off that line of thought and started the Harley. Seeing a break in the traffic, I pulled out onto Paradise and headed north. When the road ended, I drove up the Strip for a mile or so before making a left on Lewis Avenue. I parked in the public garage and walked the block down to the Regional Justice Center.

As soon as I entered the building, two overweight and overly eager security guards went on high alert.

"Hold it!"

"Stop right there, miss!"

I barely stopped myself from rolling my eyes. "Do we have to do this every time, you guys?"

Not until the metal detector, handheld scanner and manual search of my backpack failed to reveal any incendiary devices was I allowed inside. One of these days I'll start carrying a purse and briefcase and avoid the hassle.

After waiting in line for ten minutes, I filed Barry's papers with the District Court on the third floor. I slipped the time-stamped receipts into a folder in my backpack and headed back out into the heat. I think Walter and Ted were glad to see me go. Must have been the bitchy T-shirt and black eye that set them off.

As I bounded down the steps, the opening notes of Sinatra's "Fly Me to the Moon" began to play. I dug out my cell phone.

"Midnight."

I love saying that. Cool, succinct and kind of mysterious. But wasted on my secretary.

"It's Jon. Mrs. Cavanaugh just called with the schedule she said you wanted. She also gave me the tag number for the Mercedes."

"Great. Hang on while I get a pen." I planted myself on one of the concrete benches and found a notepad. "Okay, just give me the next twenty-four hours."

"She said he's working from eight tonight until four in the morning, then he's off the rest of the day. He's supposed to play golf at the Red Rock course. Tee-off is at eleven. I'll leave the rest of it on your desk."

"Fax it to the house, too, will you?"

I scribbled down a few more messages and reminded Jon to turn off the espresso machine before he left. After we disconnected, I bounced the phone in my hand, procrastinating. I didn't have to make the call. Cavanaugh was an average, everyday infidelity case….

Except for the missing four hundred grand. Nothing ordinary about that. Reaching into the zippered pocket of my backpack, I pulled out Stone's business card. Three phone numbers, but no address.

Yeah, I know what you're thinking. I'm a private eye; I'm

supposed to have access to all sorts of data. So why hadn't I tracked him down before now? Why hadn't I located him through vehicle registration, income or property tax records or something?

Because there hadn't been any records to find. Stone's not a U.S. citizen. Apparently he didn't live, work or drive here. The guy was a ghost. So, not wanting to pass up an opportunity, instead of dialing Stone's cell phone or paging him for a call back, I punched in the number for his answering service.

"Canongate Consultants."

Hmm. This might be promising. I decided to pretend not to know where I was calling. "Can I talk to Cameron Stone, please?"

"I'm sorry, he's not available. May I take a message?" The girl sounded young, with just enough of an accent to let me know she was originally from the East Coast.

"When will he back?"

"I'm sorry, I don't have that information."

I leaned back on the bench, adjusted my sunglasses and pushed a little. "Well, maybe I can drop by. I have something for him. Where's his office?"

"Like I said, he's not in right now." She was starting to get an attitude, but I gave her points for control.

"Will he be there tomorrow?"

"I'm sorry. Mr. Stone is not available. I'd be happy to take a message." She didn't sound either sorry or happy, and her East Coast roots were showing.

I wasn't getting anywhere nor was I likely to. I stood up and grabbed my bag, ready to leave. "Fine, just tell him Steele called and—"

"Oh! Is this Ms. Mez-zuh-knot?"

I frowned and answered cautiously, not knowing what to expect. "It's pronounced Met-suh-no-teh."

"If you'll give me your message, I'll use the emergency access."

She acted like Stone was some kind of government

agent. I could just imagine her punching codes into a red hotline phone. "I just want to give him some information. You don't have to—"

"Yes, Ms. Mezzanotte, my instructions are to contact Mr. Stone immediately anytime you call."

What the hell was this about? I felt both flattered and pissed off. Did Stone really think he'd be forgiven just because he made a show of his current—and, I was certain, temporary—availability? I tried not to be impressed.

"The message is, 'I have Cavanaugh's schedule.'"

"Okay. You have Cavanaugh's schedule. I've got it. Is there anything else, Ms. Mezzanotte?"

Yeah, there was a lot more. But nothing fit for even Bronx-born ears. "No, that's it. Thanks, um…what's your name?"

"I'm Jamie. If there's anything else I can help you with, don't hesitate to ask."

"Thanks, Jamie."

I hung up and dialed information, asking for the reverse directory. After giving the operator Stone's telephone number, I got an address in return. One more call to information got me a main switchboard. It was in an office building on Rainbow Boulevard—one of those anonymous, multicompany executive suites. Another dead end in my ghost hunt.

I stuffed the cell phone in my backpack and hiked back to the parking garage to get my bike. Knots had formed in my neck and shoulders and Stone was to blame. The man had been back in my life for less than three hours and already he was driving me crazy.

I didn't need some secretive Scotsman messing with my head, or any other body parts. Holding in the clutch and twisting the throttle, I let the growl of the Harley's 1450cc twin cam engine express my frustration. As I pulled out of the parking garage, I squealed the tires.

Just because I could.

CHAPTER NINE

Trouble in Paradise

As I WAITED TO MAKE a turn on Freemont, I looked over at the Experience on my left. The Freemont Street Experience is a roofed pedestrian thoroughfare that runs four blocks to Main Street. By day, the ninety-foot canopy offers shade and background music to tourists going into the stores and casinos. Once the sun goes down, though, the Experience is, well, just that.

You have to be subjected to the two million lightbulbs and 540,000 watts of sound to believe it.

I made my turn and drove southeast for a while, thinking about the Cavanaugh case. It can be hard to tail somebody on a motorcycle, so I was going to need another set of wheels. About fifteen minutes later, I'd parked the bike and was wandering around the Vegas Metro Motors lot, waiting for Anna to finish with a customer.

She, Nikki Lopez and I met in French class our freshman year at University of Nevada. We've been best friends through nights out clubbing, nights in playing poker and days spent shopping. More importantly, we've been friends through Anna's broken engagement, Nikki's unexpected pregnancy and Bobby's death.

Friendship has often been the key to our emotional survival. That and food.

Anna rushed over to me, bright red curls flying and a huge smile of welcome on her face. She grabbed me in the kind of hug I tolerate from very few people. I even hugged her back for a second. Her light brown eyes sparkled as she looked at my Have A Nice Day Elsewhere T-shirt.

"You're wearing the one I gave you. I can't believe I added to the collection, but the message is just so you. So, what have you been up to, Steele? You look a little pale. Are you sleeping okay? You should add some iron to your diet."

I couldn't help but laugh. "Take a breath, will you? I'm fine. No salt, no artificial color and I even bought some organic vegetables last week."

"Oh, that's great! Good for you." She went on to tell me about the produce at a new whole foods shop over on West Charleston.

Anna is a naturopath, a holistic and organic Earth Mother type. Her hair falls to the middle of her back and the only makeup she wears is beeswax lip balm. She doesn't need anything else. Her freckled skin glows from good health and a positive attitude. Basically, she's my exact opposite in temperament and outlook.

Anna says we get along because of cosmic balance, karma and the fact that we're reincarnated sisters from ancient Mesopotamia. I love her anyway.

"So, Steele, I'm guessing you need a car?" Anna slid me an exaggerated glance. "I've got the sweetest little Corvette around back."

Interested, I cocked my head. "Oh, really?"

She wriggled an eyebrow. "400 horsepower V-8 engine, 6-speed transmission, leather sport bucket seats, speed-sensitive power steering and a seven-speaker sound system."

I rubbed my chin, checking for drool, and started to ask what color it was before I caught myself. I'm a big fan of the *Magnum, P.I.* reruns, mostly for the episodes when Tom Selleck takes off his shirt. But real private investigators don't drive Ferraris. Or Corvettes, damn it.

"I'm just keeping watch on a guy claiming disability and a cheating husband. Better stick with a nondescript, late model sedan."

"Boring." Anna grinned.

"Beyond."

After storing the Harley in the service garage, Anna helped me pick out a metallic gray Honda Accord that ought to blend in just about anywhere. Anna gave me another quick hug. "Don't forget about the iron. You have to take it with lots of vitamin C and some chelated zinc."

"Yes, dear." Anna will make somebody a great wife someday. In the meantime she keeps trying to save me from myself. Whether I want to be saved or not.

I tossed my helmet and backpack on the passenger seat and left in air-conditioned splendor. I played with the radio, finally choosing 97.1 KXPT, a classic rock station. After turning left onto Eastern Avenue, I drove back toward North Vegas to check on a guy who'd filed a dubious workers' compensation claim.

A friend at a big insurance company sometimes throws work my way. Kenny Asher had filed for total temporary disability from an injury on his job at Rose Trucking. He'd used all the right buzz words—slip, fall and twist. However, the insurance company, Fidelity Reliance, still wanted him investigated.

There was a For Sale sign in front of one of the townhouses. I cruised past slowly, a prospective buyer checking out the neighborhood. Fortunately Asher's house was an end unit, so the second time around I parked a little ways down the street where I had a partial view of the back as well as the front.

What a freaking mess. If I were looking to buy, it wouldn't be any of the houses in sight of Asher's place. The yard was a patch of burnt grass decorated with rusted tools and children's toys. The paint had peeled and one of the upstairs shutters was hanging loose.

As I watched, there were no signs of life. Odd, since the kids should have been home from school by now. I took my digital camera out of my pack and snapped a couple of shots. Then I settled in to wait. I figured I was good for about two hours since I hadn't had much to drink. Surveillance is much easier for guys, if you know what I mean.

After about ten minutes, an older woman came out of the house next door to water the flower boxes. I got out of the car. She had a slight figure, with hair and nails as well manicured as her lawn. Despite the statewide push toward xeriscaping—plants with low water requirements—her small patch of grass was green and perfectly trimmed.

"Good afternoon, ma'am. Sorry to bother you, but I saw the sale sign…"

She eyed me up and down. I probably should have changed my shirt. Oh, well. "You're thinking of buying the Jacksons' house? It's a good choice. They've kept it up nicely and the inside was recently updated. Heather did the wallpaper herself."

I held back a smile. There's nothing better in this business than a nosy—I mean, well informed—neighbor. I nodded toward Asher's house. "Yeah, it looks a lot better than that place."

Her lips pursed in disapproval. "Yes, well, he's never been the neatest of home owners."

"Have you lived here for long, Miss…"

"Mrs. Sharp. My husband and I moved in over twenty years ago."

"Then you know the neighborhood pretty well?"

She gave me a look that matched her name. "Young woman, I suggest you tell me what this is about. Because you certainly aren't buying anything and neither am I."

Aunt Gloria used to say, "If you can't dazzle them with bullshit, then give honesty a try." I offered Mrs. Sharp my hand. "I'm from Midnight Investigation Services. I'm looking into Mr. Asher's work injury."

"Work injury, huh?" She took my hand in a weak grasp. "I thought perhaps he'd been laid off again. Mr. Asher seems to have a terrible time with supervisors who don't like him."

Her tone said more than her words. Apparently Kenny was the type to blame everybody else for his screw-ups. "Did his current supervisor like him?"

"I doubt it. There aren't many people who do. I just don't

know how Beth puts up with him. She's a lovely girl and so good with the children."

Mrs. Sharp happily agreed to take my card and call me if she saw Kenny push, pull or lift anything heavier than a beer can. The lady really did not appreciate his weeds encroaching on her rosebushes. I got back in the car, pulled a steno pad from my backpack and jotted a few notes that I'd include in a later report.

This one might take a while. Asher is probably a chronic couch potato. Talk to people at the trucking company. Find out if he's filed for workers' comp before. Start thinking of heavy things to have delivered to the house.

By now it was getting close to rush hour. Since I'd tended bar until two this morning, it was time to call it a day.

One of my favorite songs came on the radio. I turned up the volume and sang along. Badly. I can high kick in four-inch heels but, despite my mother's best intentions and a year of voice lessons, I can't carry a tune in a bucket.

I sing anyway.

I WORK IN Sin City, but I live in Paradise.

Not many people know this, but the unincorporated township of Paradise is separate from the city of Las Vegas. The Strip, the University of Nevada and McCarran International Airport are all located within the township's confines.

I turned onto Skyland Drive and slowed down in case any of the kids were out playing. My neighbor, Dave Ginsberg, waved to me as I pulled into the driveway. He was walking a busty blonde to her car. Probably another cheerleader since that's the only type he seemed to entertain. I hoped this one didn't go to UNLV… Dave really needs to start carding his dates.

My house is a twenty-year-old single story with white stucco exterior and a gray tile roof. It's got three bedrooms, a pool in back and desert landscaping in the front. Unlike Mrs. Sharp, I've got the xeriscape stuff. That means gravel, rocks, cacti and no grass to cut.

After making sure the doors were locked, I secured Anna's Honda in the garage. Accords aren't exactly high on the car thief Christmas list, but I wasn't going to take my friend's generosity for granted. I set my helmet on an empty shelf and walked in through the laundry/utility room door.

I love my house. The only problem is I don't spend enough time here, so I haven't done much with it. I've bought some things for my bedroom and the home office, but I eat in the kitchen and rarely entertain. Maybe, one day when I've got absolutely nothing better to do, I'll ask Jon to help me decorate since he did a pretty good job with the agency.

I walked to the far end of the house to the spare bedroom that's set up as a home office. I dumped my backpack by my desk and booted up the computer. While I waited for it, I grabbed the fax Jon sent and checked messages on the answering machine.

"You may have won a free vacation! Just call this number—" I hit the erase button.

The next message was from my mother. "*Cara mia,* don't forget Wednesday night. We're scheduled for seven o'clock, so don't be late. *Ti voglio bene,* Stella."

Ah, the mother/daughter bonding ritual. Mom decided a while ago that we don't spend enough time together and that I need to get in better touch with my feminine side. So once a month we share a series of spa treatments. Last time I let her talk me into the Blush Pink Pedicure.

But I didn't admit I liked it.

"Hey, Steele, it's Joey. I need you to go shopping with me. Tina's birthday is coming up and I don't have any idea what to get her."

Neither did I, so I'd hint around when Mom and I went to the spa, Indulgences. Santina Otenyo owns the place. Tina was the best thing that ever happened to my brother so I'd make sure he got her something really…expensive.

There were no other messages, so after checking my e-mail and finding mostly spam, I went back down the hall to my bedroom. Peeling off my socks, jeans and T-shirt, I rooted around in the dresser for a clean swimsuit. I changed into the bikini, twisted my hair up and headed for the kitchen.

Opening the fridge, I checked to see if the steak I'd pulled from the freezer this morning had thawed. Then I grabbed a bottle of spring water and walked through the living room to open the French doors to the pool.

After baking in the Nevada sun all day, the concrete was hot under my feet. I tiptoed over to set my water down in the shade of the patio roof. Then I took a few steps and made a shallow dive into the crystalline water. The pool was warm but still cooler than the air. It felt wonderful.

I stroked down to the far end, rolled and swam back. After the first five laps, I hit my stride, pushing myself to cut through the water and beat the timer in my head. I'd just about completed my personal race when I noticed a dark blur at the edge of the pool. Startled, I almost swallowed a chlorinated mouthful.

Only a human being casts that large a shadow.

Had my creepy caller decided to show up in person? My heart tap-danced in my chest. My arms and legs began to tremble. Anxiety burned in my gut. Treading slowly beneath the surface, I felt like an idiot for staying underwater and I couldn't stay under much longer—I was running out of air.

To hell with it. If I was going to die, it wouldn't be from drowning. I leaped up, dragging breath into my lungs and loose hairs off my face. I swiped the water from my eyes so I could identify my assailant—

One totally aggravating Scotsman.

He squatted down, offering his hand to pull me out. I ignored it and headed for the ladder. Stone followed me to the top end of the pool and waited. I couldn't believe this. I don't see the guy for almost three months, then suddenly he shows up twice in one day. I climbed out and stood facing him, amazed that any water dripped onto the patio. It should have evaporated right off my skin.

"What the hell are you doing at my house?"

"Here's a fine welcome, then." His blue eyes slowly roamed my body with exacting attention to detail.

I fought the urge to squirm. My body remembered the way his hands had once followed the path his eyes now traveled. It took a lot of willpower for me not to put out signs saying, *Thank You For Visiting. Please Come Again.*

Then his mouth widened into a mischievous grin as he admired my chest. I glanced down. The transparent nature of my white cotton swimsuit was my undoing. Guess those signs were visible after all. I raised my chin and met Stone's gaze head-on. Let him look; it wasn't like he'd never seen my breasts before. But damned if he'd get to touch.

That's what I told myself. Repeatedly. However, the soft light of evening emphasized his golden good looks and I could feel his innate sensuality drawing me like a lodestone. Standing half-naked and yearning before him, he had me at a disadvantage. But, as much as my mind protested, my body didn't seem to mind at all.

CHAPTER TEN

Wet and Out of Breath

CAMERON SAW THE DESIRE beneath her anger and knew he had only to reach for her. If he drew his fingers along the slick-wet surface of her skin she would heat to his touch. He smiled. In half a moment he'd have her in his arms and out of that bit of a bikini. Stella knew it as well.

Which was precisely why he kept his hands at his sides. They'd come together so damned fast before, and though the red-hot impulses were obviously still present, he intended to proceed with caution this time.

"I asked what you're doing here." She swept past him, snatching up a towel from a pile on one of the chairs.

"You called me. I came."

Stella sent him an odd look, a brief furrowing of her brow, then her mouth thinned in disbelief. "So, that's how it works. Wish I'd known sooner."

"From now on—"

"I left a message, Stone, not an invitation." She turned her back to him and picked up the water bottle from the table.

"You left part of a message." He tipped his head, correcting her. "I'll need the rest of it, since we're going to work together."

"I never said I'd partner with you." She set the water down with a bang.

"I don't recall hearing you refuse, either."

Her nostrils flared in a way that shouldn't have been sexy, but was. She glared at him in silence. He could almost hear the synapses firing as she struggled between accepting his offer and throwing him out on his arse. He knew his backside was safe when she rolled her shoulders in a kind of shrug.

"Wait here while I change."

"Don't bother on my account. I rather prefer you wet and out of breath."

He only just managed to keep a grin from his face as spots of color appeared on her cheeks. When he dropped his gaze, he noticed the very feminine, pale pink lacquer on her toes. He looked up to see Stella glaring at him, daring him to comment. She stalked toward him and he quite wisely stepped aside. The French door slammed behind her, rattling the glass.

Cameron bent over to rub the ache in his right knee. Hurtling the low brick wall into her back garden had set it to throbbing. Straightening, he helped himself to her water and glanced at the door. It would be much more pleasant inside. He stepped through to the living room.

Only it didn't look as if she did much living in it. There was a single ratty armchair with a wee folding table beside it, near the fireplace. A few cheap bookcases filled with videos and DVDs stood next to a large-screen plasma telly that sat directly on the floor.

He took the four stairs past a decorative rail to the next level. Peering about, Cameron noted that while the open kitchen boasted professional-looking cookware hanging from a copper rack and an impressive display of food-prep gadgets on the counters, there was no table in the dining area.

Eating alone, was she? Or simply eating elsewhere?

As he set the empty water bottle on the counter, he frowned at the butcher's block. It held an expensive-looking chef's knife set. He lifted one from its slot, hefting the weight of the professional carbon steel blade, then slid it back in place. All of the slots along the bottom row were empty. Odd, that.

He wandered into the bare foyer, listening for Stella, then moved along the hallway. The first room on the right was her bedroom, had to be. A queen-size mattress stood against one white wall with a plain wooden night table at the left-hand side; a single dresser sat near the closet. A quick glance into the lav revealed a lone toothbrush in the holder.

It would appear she slept alone as well. Cameron smiled briefly. Even as he acknowledged a sense of relief, he recognized that Stella's life seemed to be as empty as his own. All the more reason they should give their relationship a try.

He moved toward the armoire, his curiosity piqued by the glass orbs and picture frames arranged on top. They were the only personal touches he'd seen in the house so far.

A black-and-white photo showed an attractive couple— must be her mum and dad—standing at a bar with Frank Sinatra. The second picture was of Stella with two other girls, a redhead and a brunette, on a beach somewhere. The third showed her standing in front of her office beside a brassy looking older woman, however the sign read Diamond Detective Agency.

The last photograph intrigued him enough that he picked it up for a closer look.

Stella posed up front, clutching an American football, with her three brothers standing round her. She looked quite disheveled, young and carefree and grinning like mad. The younger two lads looked annoyed and mischievous while the oldest's eyes were focused on something other than the camera. His halfhearted smile failed to mask the aggressive intensity of his gaze. The photo must have been taken *before*.

"Give me that."

Stella reached for the photo and tore it from his grasp. Her attitude up 'til now had been prickly. At the moment she seemed genuinely furious…or was she merely defensive? As she set it back on the armoire, he caught a flash of sadness in her eyes before she turned on him.

"You don't follow directions worth a damn."

"Never have done, actually. It's saved my life a time or two." He wasn't supposed to know about her brother and so kept his sympathy to himself.

She shoved at his upper back, pushing him toward the door. "It won't save you from me if I catch you in here again."

He swept his gaze over the snug jeans and damp cotton top she'd put on and grinned. "I promise not to go near your bed without a proper invite."

"Don't hold your breath." As they approached the foyer, she thrust a sheet of paper at him. "Here. This is Cavanaugh's work schedule for the next couple of days. He's got the grave-yard shift tonight, the same tomorrow and Wednesday."

"Thanks." He folded the note and tucked it into his hip pocket. "Nice place you've got. Bit sparse on furnishings, though, eh?"

"I don't want you to feel welcome."

The look on her face was dead serious. He hadn't expected her to forgive and forget after the way they'd parted, but the fact of the matter was he'd come back for her. And if that meant a proper courtship, so be it. He sighed and slid his hands over her waist, gently tugging her toward him.

She tensed, resisting his touch, but didn't struggle away. She challenged him with her gaze, rejection darkening her eyes. And yet he saw the flush of color on her cheeks, felt the sudden catch of her breath. Stella had a tough shell but underneath, he knew, was a molten core.

Not that she was soft, far from it. She'd like as not thump him for saying so. It wouldn't be easy to win her over, but he'd have a go at it all the same. She was more than worth the having.

He reached up to free her hair and then stroked his fingers along the side of her neck. "I'm no damned good at this, Stella. But, I'm willing to try. Now that I've returned, I want to pick up where we left off."

CHAPTER ELEVEN

Simply Irresistible

WE'D LEFT OFF IN BED, naked and insatiable for each other.

I didn't want to pick up from there. I wanted to back up several steps, both figuratively and literally. Things were moving too fast again. But I stayed where I was, even grasped his biceps, enjoying the feel of hard muscle and hot skin under my hands.

When Stone dragged his right thumb across my lower lip, I gasped, barely resisting the urge to take it into my mouth. Faint lines of amusement bracketed his eyes, though his expression remained predatory. He looked like a man who wanted a woman and knew he could have her.

I bit his thumb.

He chuckled but wisely moved his hand. "You're a fiery woman, Stella. Wicked sweet. And damned if I've not missed the feel of you."

My pulse fluttered as his big hands slid down my hips to glide over my butt, pulling me closer to the erection testing the zipper of his jeans. As they flattened against his chest, my breasts ached with a need echoed in my womb. His heat seeped into me, warming me in too many places.

Closing my eyes, I inhaled the faint citrus smell of his hair and the purely male scent of his skin. My hands caressed the taut muscle beneath his shirt. I rubbed up against him like a cat in heat, while his hands seemed to touch me everywhere at once. It wasn't enough.

Dark greedy desire permeated every fiber of my being. Yes, it was stupid, risky even, but I wanted him. It had been like this from the first moment we'd met. Something about him ignited my basest need for hot, wild sex. He slowly lowered his head and, eyes still shut to everything except the anticipation of the moment, I turned my face to meet his kiss.

Instead he nuzzled his soft lips against my temple and growled in my ear. "You've a way about you. Makes me want to strip you bare, to feel your heat and your passion. Remember how it was between us? Like capturing lightning in a bottle."

I almost moaned aloud at the images replaying in my head. He's got the kind of voice that lends itself to seduction, a blend of smoky resonance and rich brogue. It's one of the reasons I'd fallen for him in the first place, one excuse for what happened…

"It will only be better this time, Stella."

He lowered his head and I finally got that kiss. I'd braced myself for—hell, I'd counted on—a hot, urgent plundering that would fan the burning need inside of me and have us going at it on the foyer tiles. Instead, Cameron took me off guard, brushing his mouth slowly, oh-my slowly, over my lips.

The sweet thrill of his touch, combined with the spicy taste of him, seduced me. I could feel long unused parts gearing up for action but he resisted when I tried to take the lead. Although it's so not my personality, I sat back to enjoy the ride.

Slanting his mouth over mine, he enjoyed my lips as though they were something precious, cradling the back of my head with unexpected and unwarranted tenderness. Which thoroughly confused me. I raised my palm to his chest and pulled back, then realized that placing my hand over his heart was a mistake. The strong, steady beat was a false promise of durability and commitment.

Stone didn't relinquish his hold on me. "Let me have you, Stella. Let me make you my own."

That did it. I broke free, staring at the floor while I tried to collect myself, and instantly missed the feel of him. If I were honest, I might admit that I've missed him all along. But I'd eat the engine out of my Harley before I told him so. The last man who'd attempted to possess me, make me his, hadn't lived to regret it.

"I did that once, but didn't care for it." I'm a pretty good mimic, so I got the accent down cold, but my voice wasn't bass enough for a perfect imitation. Stone recognized his own words anyhow.

"Is it over, then?" His tone was colored with as much defiance as disbelief.

Stone's personality was magnetic, hypnotic, overwhelming. I didn't want to be his, not at the risk of getting lost in his shadow. My gaze settled on his left arm. The short sleeve of his T-shirt revealed the tattoo on his triceps. The winged dagger with *Who Dares Wins* etched below it said a lot—and reminded me how little I really knew about him.

"Let's be honest, Stone. It never really began."

Finally I looked up at his face. I've seen photographs of glaciers in Alaska, formed by weight and weather and time until the core turns a bright, frozen blue. Stone's eyes are that color. I wanted to look away but wouldn't allow myself the cowardice. "We're strangers who shared an incredible night once, who now have to work together temporarily, and that's all."

His gaze narrowed, hitting me like twin blue laser beams, cutting through the surface bullshit to the core I'm so damned careful to protect. His expression challenged me, dared me, invited me to open up and make something real of whatever game we were playing.

Suddenly I was almost overcome with the need to lean on him, to curl myself against his big body and take comfort from his warmth and strength. But I killed the thought as soon as it emerged. I've worked hard to shut myself off, to not need anyone and to take the hits alone so that no one ever paid for my mistakes again.

I looked away, reaching for the front door and yanking it wide to usher him out. He hesitated for a second then moved resolutely forward, brushing against me as he passed. Suddenly, he whipped around. His arm shot out and before I knew it he'd plastered me to his side. There was no tenderness in this kiss, just the silent insistence that it was a beginning, not the end.

He let go just as abruptly then turned away. He swaggered down the driveway without once looking back. I stood watching him go, dazed, until I realized my fingertips were tracing my mouth. Annoyed with both of us, I slammed the door and headed for the kitchen.

As I chose a shot glass from the cabinet and pulled the vodka out of the freezer, I wondered what the hell I was doing. I'd made a mistake with Stone. But which one had it been? Letting him get close, letting him matter or pushing him away?

Probably all of the above.

CHAPTER TWELVE

Damned Small World

WHO THE HELL was this guy?

From the new vantage point he'd found on the Paradise Park Community Center roof, he adjusted the focus of his binoculars. He had to get a better look at the son of a bitch kissing her. Civilian now, maybe, but hard-core military at some point, by the looks of him. Like some of those head cases back in the joint. Like he'd once been.

Oo-rah.

What was he doing at her house? Jealousy churned like acid in his gut and prickled along his skin.

He wanted to be the one kissing her…rubbing that fine ass, filling his hands with those pretty tits and squeezing… Not hard enough to hurt, though. That was part of the discipline, part of the control.

His breath was ragged as he smiled with anticipation. Maybe once it got dark, he'd jump over the wall like that other guy had and pay her a little visit.

G.I. Jerk finally let go of her and turned to leave—

He dropped the binoculars.

The smell of hot tar filled his nostrils as he scrambled to pick them up. No way. No freakin' way. It couldn't be…. The evening temperature had cooled but he was still sweating. He barely zoomed in on the guy's face before he got into his car.

That was Stone, all right. The man who'd made him disappear.

What a goddamned small world.

CHAPTER THIRTEEN

The Last One Got Away

WHO THE HELL *was* this guy?

Jon drummed his fingers in frustration on the desktop. So far, his attempt to find any information on Cameron Stone via the Internet had turned up a New Zealand college student, a cellist/composer, an Ottawa schoolteacher and a gay porn star. He bookmarked that last one for some other time.

He'd have to wait until he went back to the agency tomorrow to check the criminal databases, but he'd hoped to find something—anything.

His gaze sought the silver frame next to the computer monitor. The original portrait out on his living room wall was much larger and had better clarity of detail, but he liked the softness of this small picture of Steele. She'd fallen asleep on the couch in her office. He'd stood watching her and then hadn't been able to resist capturing the moment.

Jon picked up the frame and angled the photo to the lamp. As always, the artist in him critiqued the work—he would have preferred indirect lighting instead of the stark sun that illuminated her face, her hands closer to her chin rather than curled near her heart. But considering this was a totally candid shot, he loved the results.

She looked beautiful, of course, but her face was a study in contrasts. There was a stillness about her that she never had when she was awake. Even so, tension marred her expression. She was relaxed in sleep, but far from peaceful. A couple minutes after he'd taken the picture, she'd woken up from a bad dream. He'd never seen anybody look so afraid.

That incident—along with her too often occurring bruises—stirred up an unexpected and unwelcome protectiveness in him. Steele thought she could take care of herself. And she usually could. But this afternoon, she'd been pissy and antagonistic to Stone.… A possible sign of someone out of her depth.

Jon carefully replaced the picture frame and continued cyberhunting. On the twenty-second page of "Google results" a small reference caught his eye. He leaned closer to his laptop screen.

WHO DARES WINS—*a site dedicated to the…*
…SAS patrol… Andy Ryan (released from Abu Ghraib), Steve Consiglio (killed by enemy fire), Cameron Stone (escaped to Syria), Julian Lane (died of hypothermia)…

What were the chances this was the same guy? Jon clicked on the item to read the full story. Apparently during the first Gulf War, an eight-man British patrol—Alpha One Nine—was dropped behind Iraqi lines with a mission to destroy Scud missile launchers.

Everything that could go wrong, though, did. Communications failed, storms closed in, their helicopter never came and the enemy discovered them. In the end, three of the team died while four others were captured and tortured.

The last one got away.

That SAS soldier had trudged two hundred miles on foot, suffering from sleep deprivation, hunger, thirst and the desert's extreme environment, arriving in neutral territory eight days later. Then, as soon as he made contact with his regiment, he'd tried to go back for his comrades.

Jon read the rest of the article, then several others he was able to find. Leaning back in his chair, he thought about the tattoo he'd seen on Cameron Stone's left arm and wondered if Steele knew who she was dealing with.

CHAPTER FOURTEEN

Lies Always Follow

PAIN STABBED *at my side while I prayed for the strength to hold my weight against the door.*

Please, God, let it hold.

He hit the other side like a boom of thunder. The force of the impact shuddered along my body and I started trembling, nauseous with fear.

"Nobody will ever know. Do you hear?" He rammed the door again.

My bare feet slipped on the carpet. Hot tears slid down my cheeks as the wood around the door frame began to crack.

Oh, God. Oh, God.

And then it went quiet. What was he doing? If I could make it to the window… The bedroom door crashed in, knocking me to the floor.

"I'll kill you, bitch. I will kill you."

And I believed him.

Not just his ominous tone or the strength in his hands. No, I believed the look in his eyes. It was callous, calculating, terrifying on the face of a man who claimed to love me.

He hit me again just because he could. Jagged shards of pain ripped a gasp from my throat. He'd cracked one of my ribs this time.

"You're not going to ruin me!"

He had murder in his eyes. When I drew in a painful breath to try and yell for help his hands gripped my neck. He stran-

gled my effort and squeezed tighter until the only sound was in my head, a shrill insistent ringing...

Ringing. The phone.

I groaned, rolling over slowly, still ensnared in the heart-pounding fog of my nightmare. Swallowing hard, I tried to get my stomach to stay where it belonged. The surreal feeling of both reliving the past and anticipating the future made me want to puke. So did the feeling of being watched....

The number was blocked from my caller ID, further putting me on alert. Hand shaking, I reached over to answer.

"Hello?"

I closed my eyes and concentrated, straining to listen beyond the emptiness. Nothing.

And just like that my fear flared into anger. I'm not weak anymore and I refused to ever be a victim again. Kicking off the sheets, I swung my feet onto the floor and leaped up, stalking away from the bed. I was sick of this bullshit and said so. Loudly.

"Talk to me, dammit! Stop playing around and tell me what the hell you want!"

More nothing. More freakin' head games. Then, unexpectedly, I heard a rasp of sound. "Nice panties. A thong?"

I froze. So did the breath in my lungs. I turned in a sluggish circle as my heart galloped beneath my ribs. Because my brain had just registered the difference between night and shadow on the window glass. I dragged in enough air to voice the only thing I could think to ask.

"Why?" I whispered.

"Lies always follow you. Vince forget to tell you that?"

The line disconnected. But hearing my brother's name was the impetus I needed to move. Dropping the cordless phone, I slammed the curtain and window aside then rammed the screen out of its track with my shoulder. Before the aluminum frame had even clattered onto the concrete patio, I was jumping to the ground and running alongside the pool.

But within seconds I realized the futility of giving chase. Whoever had been peering into my bedroom was gone, having disappeared over the walls into any one of the neighboring yards. I stood there, tense, confused and unarmed, the cement cool under my bare feet, listening for some sound of retreat.

I didn't hear anything except the light breeze rustling the palm fronds.

I don't know how long I stayed rooted to that spot, wondering if he was still watching and hoping that if he was, he saw the pissed-off and defiant look I'd plastered onto my face. Assuming it was the same guy, tonight was the second time he'd called in as many days. And now he'd invaded my home. For some reason he was escalating the threat.

And I hate like hell being threatened.

I crossed my arms, rubbing my shoulders, as I realized how chilly it was wearing nothing but sleepwear. Leaving the broken screen for later, I jackknifed back through the window, making sure to lock it. Still cold, I pulled my terry robe off the back of the bathroom door and went to my office.

I stood in front of the wall safe, debating. I only unlocked this door once a month for target practice with Joey. After a couple of minutes, though, I chose 80 proof over firepower. Crouched in the living room armchair, I swallowed big mouthfuls of orange juice-laden vodka. I thought about the voices in my sleep and on the phone.

Then another voice, my brother's voice, echoed in my memory. The words were almost the same as in my dream. *No one ever has to know,* he'd said.

Except maybe someone did.

I BEAT THE ALARM CLOCK, first figuratively since I hadn't been able to sleep anyway, then physically since I felt like hitting something. I've never been one to face the new day with a dazzling smile. The best I could manage this morning was a disagreeable snarl.

I got dressed and did some stretching to warm up and work out kinks the armchair had given my back. I fast-walked down my street, studying every car I passed, braced and anticipating the unfamiliar. Out on the main road I quickened my pace, my feet slapping the asphalt in a steady rhythm as I ran past cluster after cluster of beige stucco houses.

The tension unknotted from my muscles, the stale air of a restless night cleared from my lungs. I hit my stride when I reached Paradise Park and turned onto the grass-bordered path. Oxygen rushed freely through my body until I finally achieved an endorphin high. But I kept pushing. A mile passed, then three, five. By the time I returned to the house, I'd managed to outrun some of my uneasiness.

At a time in my life when nightmares haunted me even during the day, when darkness crept further across my soul, Aunt Gloria had smacked me across the back of the head. Hard. Though her eyes had been sympathetic, her attitude was no-nonsense when she got in my face.

Are you gonna to spend your life folding, or are you gonna try to stack the deck in your favor? Get off your ass, girl, and go shuffle those cards.

When I walked into the agency an hour after my run, I was eager to perform a dovetail riffle. I was also willing to deal from the bottom of the deck if I had to.

"My gawd, aren't we just bitchin' today?"

I stared Jon down, using my best don't-mess-with-me scowl. "Is the coffeemaker on?"

"When is it not? I'll bring you some in a minute."

He came out from behind the reception desk, but instead of going toward the kitchen, he looked me up and down. "Hm, yes, I see what you're going for. A sort of Lara Croft meets Electra, right?"

"Move already." I started past him.

He took his life in his hands by blocking my path. Jon propped one hand on a trim hip, the other palm cupping his cheek. "I love the casual, flowing hair, the dark eyeliner and red lipstick. Très sassy, darling. It whispers *you know you want me.* And yet, the gray-and-white camo T-shirt, black jeans and infantry boots bark *so not going to happen.*"

"Are you done?"

He made Ls of his index fingers and thumbs, creating an imaginary camera shot. "All in all, though, I'd say the bags under your eyes make this ensemble 'feisty' instead of 'fierce.'"

I struggled against a grin. It's really hard to maintain a hostile attitude when he gets his gay on, as Jon calls it. "Bite me, Mr. Blackwell."

"Don't you growl at me, honey. Not when I found that deadbeat dad for you." The look on his face could only be described as smug.

My brows shot up in surprise. I'd only given him the file yesterday. "You're joking."

"He wishes." Letting Jon have his moment, I listened as he explained how he'd skip traced Randy Grissom. "Apparently he's living with a friend in Boulder City to hide his address and he's getting paid under the table to avoid a paper trail."

"So what gave him away?" I set my backpack on top of his desk.

"Well, there was a small notation in the file about his gambling problem. Like most addicts, Grissom's a creature of habit and superstition. He still plays Jumbo Jackpot video poker at the Fiesta Rancho casino every Friday night."

"Wow. Nice work. Give his wife a call and tell her the good news. Then I've got something else for you." I handed Jon the Kingman file from Barry and rested my elbow on the desk while he flipped through it.

"Oh, goody. A scavenger hunt… The widow's name is really Bunny?"

I smirked. "She was an exotic performance artist before Cookie Kingman made an honest woman out of her."

Jon looked up. "Bunny and Cookie? You can't be serious."

"Kingman owned a bunch of successful bakeries, as well as some high-end real estate, a fleet of luxury sports cars and a rare coin collection."

He snapped the file shut. "So then what am I supposed to be looking for?"

"The money."

"Excuse me?"

"It looks like Kingman sold off all his assets not long before he died."

"No kidding?" Jon frowned. "But even without getting her hands on the estate yet, Bunny should have been able to afford the best lawyers in Nevada. Why pick Barry?"

"Don't let his pudgy exterior fool you. Barry is one of the nastier Great Whites in a legal ocean of sharks. Bunny is going to need a guy like him if she hopes to pry any cash away from Cookie's kids."

"If there's any to be found." Jon glanced over my shoulder at the same time the front bell chimed.

Turning, I watched Maria glide across the foyer toward me. She was carrying a tiny purse and an oversize manila folder. The sea-foam color of her suit perfectly complemented her burnished curls, pale pink lips and little-girl voice. "I'm so glad I caught you! I have the papers and things you asked for."

Maria's eyes took on the flinty edge I'd noticed yesterday. She slipped a sheaf of papers carefully marked *credit card statements* from the expandable manila folder. "I couldn't find any of Gray's recent cell phone bills—apparently he started paying that one himself."

The papers were held together with a binder clip and so neatly stacked it was hard to tell how many there were. Small, brightly colored document flags marched along the right-hand edge of the pile. Flipping the pages with my thumb, I saw Maria's meticulous script noting the dates and amounts paid.

"Why don't you come back to my office and we can—"

Maria shook her head before I could finish. "I don't have time, Steele, sorry. I only allocated ten minutes to drop these off. I have to meet with some gynecologists about holding their annual conference at the Palazzo. If I'm late, it will throw off my entire schedule."

"Oh, okay."

"As you'll see, I've already highlighted the recurring numbers. Some of them I recognized as our friends or his golf buddies. But I called some of the other numbers and a woman answered this one."

Her voice broke as she pointed and I noticed her eyes were damp with unshed tears. "I guess she had caller ID because she said, *Hey, lover,* instead of hello."

I made a sympathetic noise. I also wondered why she was paying me so much when she'd already done a lot of the work. "I'll read through everything and call if I have any questions."

"Find her, Steele." The edge was back. "I want to know who this little bitch is that thinks she can steal my husband."

"Don't worry about this, Maria. I'll look into it."

The door chimed again as she left. I guess I should have given her a hug or patted her arm or something since we're old friends, but I'm terrible at that stuff.

"Phew. I hope she took her meds this morning. By the end of the day, she's gonna be exhausted from all of those mood swings."

Jon had said it as a joke, but I understood too well to smile. "Maria always was kind of emotional, but after her mother committed suicide… Well, everybody changes after losing someone they love."

I took the folder from him and hefted my backpack, aware of a different weight on my shoulders as I walked away. In my office, I dropped the pack onto the sofa and dragged myself to my desk. I stuffed Maria's folder into the Cavanaugh file. It hung out on both ends, but I'd already dismissed the case from my mind when I added it to my overcrowded in-box.

I unlocked my desk drawer and removed the letter I'd started yesterday. After a time, I reached for my fountain pen, rolling it between my thumb and fingers as I gazed, unseeing, out the window. Needles of anxiety pricked my stomach. I didn't want to do this. I didn't want to lift the rock covering the hole into which I'd buried my guilt.

I flinched, remembering what Vince had done. And what I hadn't done. And, as always, the stab of memory led me to the deeper pain of a shame I couldn't turn away from. I thought about loss and change and irrevocable decisions. I had lived my childhood for Vince's approval; loved my cool, rebellious yet overprotective brother with my whole heart. Few things die harder than heroes.

Before, I could talk to Vince about anything and I knew he'd listen. He's the only one who knows my secrets. At least, I'd thought he was. Hanging my head, I fiddled with the pen some more, smoothed an invisible crease from the paper. Did I really want to do this? No. But with a heavy sigh, I slowly completed the last paragraph I'd written yesterday then scratched today's date beneath it.

Although I didn't mention all of the phone calls, and I downplayed last night's incident, I told Vince about what happened. The facts, but also my fears. It wasn't fair to burden him with those but no one else would understand. Besides, what was a little more guilt added to those regrets I already owned? I started a new paragraph, then paused for so long that ink bled into the paper.

God knew there was no easy way to ask.

I had no right.

But I had to know if Vince had told anyone the truth about the night Bobby died.

CHAPTER FIFTEEN

Games People Play

GLANCING AT MY WATCH LATER, I scrawled my name across the finished letter and stuffed it into an envelope along with a prayer. Gray Cavanaugh was scheduled to tee off in less than seventy-five minutes. But when I left the agency, I took the extra time to walk to the retail postal business at the end of the strip mall.

Yeah, I could have left Vince's letter for the mail. But I didn't want Jon to see the institutional facility address on the envelope.

Out in the parking lot, I tossed my backpack into Anna's Honda and hit the road. For once I left the radio off, preferring the silence in my current mood. I headed west on Sahara Boulevard for about eight miles or so, and then made a right onto Canyon Gate Drive. Then I ran into a problem.

A guardhouse bordered by taupe stone archways fortified the entrance to the Estates. Dammit! I'd known Maria lived in an exclusive neighborhood, but the fact that I needed a way in had slipped my mind when I saw her earlier. I'd blame my late-night visitor for the lapse in my memory and my professionalism. But finger-pointing wouldn't help me now.

Reaching into my backpack and thinking fast, I pulled up to the security gate. A middle-aged man with a belly as round as his bald head marched out to glare at me. Thick black brows hovered over his distrustful brown eyes. He glanced around the interior of my rental car before swaggering up to the front to check the tag.

Gee, I think my military attire and fading bruise made Security Officer Lancer suspicious.

Back at my open window, he leaned down to give me a baleful stare. "Morning, miss. Can I help you with something?"

"Hi, there. I'm supposed to take some important documents to Mr. and Mrs. Cavanaugh." I flashed an envelope full of blank paper I keep in my backpack in case of emergency lying.

"The Cavanaughs are expecting, uh, you?"

I consulted a small clipboard of phony delivery addresses I also keep handy. "Yep. It has to be signed for by ten o'clock."

Lancer retreated into his little fortress and did some reconnaissance. After carefully consulting a sheet of paper, he came back out with a clipboard of his own. He held it up to make sure I saw that his was bigger.

"Your name, miss?" On the off chance that he asked for ID, I told the truth. "Okay. It looks like Mrs. Cavanaugh sent your name down last shift. Go ahead." He raised the gate and saluted me through.

I waved back and smiled, though I was actually a little pissed off. Some kind of trained investigator, huh? My client had been better prepared than I was.

As I drove through the community, it was hard to keep my eyes on the road. This was a whole different world. I know I sound like some über-bubbly real estate agent but, looking around, I really was tempted to use words like *stunning, gorgeous* and *spectacular.*

Obviously no one ever heard of xeriscape out here. The manicured golf course and acres of lush emerald foliage sprawled in stark contrast to the olive and umber mountains in the distance. I caught glimpses of glittering ponds, waterfalls and swimming pools between the houses as I drove past.

In a word? Nice.

Okay, that's an understatement. The homes were absolutely palatial. You could tell these were custom designed. Unlike my neighborhood, none of the Mediterranean-inspired structures looked alike. I turned onto Championship Circle and slowed down to check the house numbers. Three doors down from my target, I parked on a slight curve so I had a good view.

It should only take about ten minutes to get from the Canyon Gate Estates to the Red Rock Country Club. I checked my watch. There was still a good forty-five minutes until tee off, so I unhooked my seat belt and waited for Cavanaugh to leave the house.

Damn good thing I'd been so early. Gray jogged out the front door less than five minutes later. He was dressed in a casual blue plaid shirt and khaki slacks, but he didn't have any golf clubs with him. Maybe they were in the trunk already. Maybe he planned to stop by the pro shop and buy new ones. Maybe.

Whistling, he bounced the ring of keys in his hand like a man looking forward to a good time. Personally, I think golf is about as exciting as watching grass grow. Who could get excited about smacking a little ball with a stick? Then again, my suspicious and non-sports-oriented mind could have been working overtime.

In any event, Gray slid into his white Mercedes and started the engine. This was a quiet neighborhood with members-only traffic. The residents probably know each other's cars and most visitors would be driving high-end vehicles. But he backed out of his triple-wide driveway without so much as a glance in my direction.

I snapped my seat belt in place but waited a few seconds before pulling off after him. There was no way to lose him on his own street. Just as I passed by the Cavanaughs' house, though, a silver Lexus came out of another driveway and cut me off. I hit my brakes—then dropped my jaw.

Cameron Stone leaned across his passenger seat and grinned at me before taking off after Cavanaugh.

Son ovuh bitch.

I hadn't told Stone about the golf match. Obviously we had an Oxford Unabridged versus Merriam-Webster's definition problem. *Working together* was supposed to mean doing things my own way and filling him in on selected details sometime later.

Frowning mightily, I circled back to the Estate entrance. After Security Officer Lancer logged my departure, I hit the gas so I could keep the Mercedes in view up ahead. I cursed the silver car with the Scottish nuisance between us. Especially when we reached the intersection and Cavanaugh pulled a fast one.

I'd expected him to turn right on West Sahara, giving him a straight shot to the Red Rock course. Instead Gray turned east, in the complete opposite direction. My suspicious mind had been right. Unless he shocked me by going to a different course, golf was not on his agenda today. I cursed cheating husbands and pseudo-partners alike as the three of us cruised south.

Trying to follow Cavanaugh while staying out of his sight and maneuvering past Stone at the same time was not easy. I slid into the right lane and got maybe a car length ahead of the Lexus. But then Stone pulled into the left lane, passing me and two other cars so that he was in front again.

Hearing the muted tones of "Fly Me to the Moon," I reached for my cell phone. "Midnight."

"You know, love, we're both going to end up in the same place. There's no need to race."

"I'm not racing, Stone. You are."

"I seem to be winning, as well." He didn't try to hide the trace of laughter in his brogue.

"Bite me."

"I have actually, as I recall. Right on your—"

I hung up and hit the accelerator. We continued to play road tag along Durango until Cavanaugh signaled a left turn. Stone made the light. I didn't. But I made the turn anyway and ignored the blare of car horns. Hoping the sound hadn't caused Gray to look behind him, I hung back a bit.

Stone was right. Why race when he could do the work and I just had to keep *him* in sight. Except I had no idea there were so many silver and light-gray Lexuses…Lexi…Lexus-brand cars on the road. I lost him for a minute and then had to double-check I was following the right car.

Eventually I caught up as Stone followed Cavanaugh onto the Strip. The traffic moved so slowly I could count the number of lightbulbs in the billboards outside of the casinos.

Cavanaugh turned at Harmon Avenue, drove about a block and then pulled into the lot of the Happy Traveler Hotel. It was a garish hot-pink stucco building with outside access to the forty or so rooms. The kind of place that probably had condom dispensers in the bathrooms and coin-operated vibrating beds.

Classy. Gray obviously knew how to treat a girl right.

After making sure he'd parked, I continued on past. I drove to the strip mall next door and chose a space in front of Madame Verushka's. The psychic reader's business seemed to be slow. I could only hope it stayed that way and no one came out to ask why I was loitering.

My cell phone rang as I rolled the window down a few inches. One look at the number told me who was calling. A quick look at the motel parking lot told me Stone had found a space not far from Cavanaugh. "What?"

"Don't bother getting your future told, Stella, love. I promise you I'm in it."

Arrogant jerk. That was for me to decide. Later.

"I have work to do, Stone. So do you. The target is on the move, or whatever you military guys say."

Cavanaugh was out of his Mercedes. Dropping the phone, I pulled my camera from the backpack. He looked out at the main road and smoothed a hand over his hair, then patted his pants pocket. As he walked toward me, I adjusted the zoom focus and took a practice photo.

When Gray got closer, I turned my head but kept him in my peripheral vision. Oblivious to everything but his purpose, he went into the glass-fronted business office. It was on the corner of the building so I had a clear view of the transaction. Cavanaugh shook his head when the clerk tried to hand him a key, pointing to a different one instead.

Maria's husband must be a regular guest.

He came out a few minutes later and stood in front of the hotel's coffee shop. Gray looked at his watch, paced a few feet, then rolled his shoulders. He fiddled with the room key, paced back and looked at his watch again. Suddenly a huge grin broke out on his face and he stepped off the curb.

I captured the instant with my camera. Now I understood a little better what Maria saw in him. Gray Cavanaugh wasn't all that, in my opinion. At least not until he smiled. I turned my head to see a cherry-red Mustang turn into the lot and slide in next to the Mercedes.

The engine had barely died before a curvy young woman who kind of matched the sports car threw herself into his wide-open arms. He bent slightly to scoop her up. The next thing I knew they were sharing a kiss that wouldn't have been out of place in a porno movie. All lips and hands and hips.

I took several more pictures, trying to clearly identify them. It wasn't easy with their tongues tied together like that. Eventually they came up for air and I got some good photos. The girl was very cute. She had a sweet face with big eyes, a button nose and a wide smile. The body underneath her red baby-doll top and black slacks looked well-padded, but in a healthy way.

She was the complete opposite of Gray's slender, delicate and refined wife. I figured that must be part of her appeal. She had the pale freckled skin of a true redhead and, evidently, the clichéd earthy passion of one, too. She might not look like a golf caddy, but Gray sure seemed to enjoy the way she handled his balls.

When they parted, he gave a perfunctory look around as he pulled her fingers off his zipper. However, I seriously doubted that he saw me or Stone or anything else. His attention was focused on his "date." Gray led her back to the Mercedes, unlocked the trunk and pulled out a black nylon gym bag. I did glimpse a set of golf clubs before he shut it again.

All the while the girl had been rubbing against him and

squeezing his butt. Not exactly unfamiliar behavior. I now had proof Gray was cheating and, unfortunately for Maria, I didn't think this was a one-time thing. With his arm over the girl's shoulders, Cavanaugh led her into the passageway between two of the lower level units.

As I lost sight of them, my cell phone chimed. "Yeah?"

"See anything, love?"

"Not at the moment—"

"Hang on. They're on the upper landing. The view is better from my angle." Stone's charming voice made the statement into an invitation.

I declined, still not warmed up to the partnership idea. "They have to come back to their cars at some point."

"Suit yourself."

We hung up and I settled in for who knew how long. I ran through my mental grocery list. I watched a dark-haired maid in a uniform the same color as the stucco push a heavy laundry cart. Shifting in my seat, I rolled my window down another inch to try and catch a nonexistent breeze. I killed some more time.

Da da da-da-da...

I should probably give Stone his own ring tone. He was starting to ruin Sinatra for me. "What now?"

"We could be in for a bit of a wait."

"Maybe."

"Cavanaugh and his skirt might stay up there for hours."

"So?"

"So, why not come over and wait with me?"

"I'm not that bored yet."

Another twenty minutes passed in a haze of still air and idle thoughts. Stationary surveillance is my least favorite part of the job. You really can't get involved in much. As soon as you try to balance your checkbook or do a crossword puzzle, the chances are high that something will happen.

It's kind of hard to explain to a client how you missed the money shot because you weren't paying attention. So I watched people come and go from the coffee shop. I munched on a protein bar. I washed it down with a small sip of water. Fifteen more minutes evaporated from my life expectancy.

Giving in to the inevitable, I picked up my cell phone and hit the recall button. It only rang once before Stone answered.

"On your way, are you?"

"Now, I'm bored."

"Such flattery, Stella. How can I stand it?"

I grabbed my backpack, got out of the car and made a show of looking out at the road. Then I wandered toward the back of Madame Verushka's lot, strolled behind the cars parked at the motel and finally came up to the Lexus. Opening the passenger door, I was greeted with a smile and a shake of the head.

"You could simply have walked over, you know."

"I was trying to be inconspicuous."

The engine was off but surprisingly cool air hit me as I slid onto the leather seat. Glancing over my shoulder, I saw a battery-operated fan propped on the rear bench. The oscillating blades created a nice draft. Heaven. When I wiped the back of my hand across my forehead, Stone reached in the small cooler at my feet and pulled out a half-frozen bottle.

Maybe having a partner wasn't such a bad thing after all.

He offered me the water along with a slow once-over. "You look hot."

So did he. I tried not to notice. "Thanks. For the water, I mean."

His sensuous mouth curved into a slow smile. I guess he'd noticed me not noticing how his khaki shirt stretched across his broad shoulders; the way his dark blue jeans were painted onto his muscular thighs… I took a long swallow of icy water and cleared my throat. "It's been almost an hour already. How much longer do you think they'll be up there?"

"Don't know, really." At my restless sigh, he cocked his head and regarded me curiously. His clear gaze scanned my face and for some reason I felt more naked than when he'd looked at my body. "Care to talk about anything?"

For just an instant, I was tempted. I'd barely closed my eyes last night; each time I did I was forced to relive the past. Dreams never forget. No matter how much the waking mind wants to. It would be such a relief to confide my fears, to talk and talk and talk…

"Nope."

He studied me without blinking then turned away, draping his left wrist over the steering wheel. We sat in silence for a while, then he broke the quiet. "What do you reckon Cavanaugh had in that hold-all?"

I shrugged. "A change of clothes, I guess."

"Ah, boring that. Use your imagination."

I tried to shake off my mood and play along. "It's probably clothes for her. Sexy underwear from Victoria's Secret or Frederick's of Hollywood."

"Like those bits of lace and satin you wear?" He slid an interested glance my way. "Could be. I think our Gray is more the adventurous sort though."

Getting into the game, I wriggled my eyebrows. "Maybe he has her dress up in a nurse's outfit or a schoolgirl uniform."

Stone chuckled. "I'll wager it's kinky corsets and whips so Caitlyn can paddle his bum."

I tried to picture that cute little cheerleader in a black leather teddy and spike heels, but failed miserably. Laughing out loud, I was about to suggest that Gray was the one wearing the white blouse and school-plaid skirt, when my breath caught. Narrowing my eyes, I turned to look at Stone.

"Did you say *Caitlyn?*"

CHAPTER SIXTEEN

About a Fortnight

AH, WELL. There went any hope of lowering Stella's tension level. Cameron angled his body toward her.

She looked tired. No, more than that, deeper than that. She looked haunted. The faint bruise beneath her eye was a mere shadow of the older, darker injury at the back of her gaze. He'd been so pleased to hear her laugh again, that rich, spontaneous chortle he'd remembered from months ago, and was damned sorry to hear it cut short.

"The car is registered to Caitlyn Folger of West Cheyenne Avenue. Height five feet three inches, weight one hundred thirty pounds, date of birth June 22, 1983. No outstanding traffic tickets."

"And you know this how?"

He shrugged. "I asked Jamie to check out the license plate on the Mustang."

Stella arched her left brow. "I thought she just answered your phone."

"Jamie's my right hand, as it were. I hadn't realized just how indispensable she was until she went on strike for a week." He smirked, though he'd been less than amused at the time. "She's a lovely girl, smart as hell. Brilliant, really."

Stella turned to look out her window. "Is she here in Vegas, too?"

"Not yet. I've told her I want her with me, but she's loath to move away from New York."

"Too bad." Her voice had a bit of an edge, the corners of her mouth wrenching with the sarcastic reply.

"Jealous, Stella?" He modulated his tone, made the question teasing instead of hopeful. "Don't be. You're the only woman for me."

"Yeah, right."

He looked away and clenched his fingers against his thigh to keep from reaching for her hand. It was daft to expect her trust so soon, yet he resented the lack of faith. They sat in silence for a moment, facing apart and rapt in the unspoken. He didn't make a habit of sharing confidences—it went against both his nature and his training. He was ruthless, efficient, fearless and therefore in great demand.

The nasty games he often played had opened a circle of entirely the wrong sort of acquaintances, the kind of men who valued nothing more than money and a sense of power. Jamie's father had been one ambitious bastard. He'd not thought twice about endangering his young daughter's life.

Cameron knew for a fact, though, she'd featured in Michael Barrett's last thoughts as the light withered from his eyes.

He cleared his throat against the tightness that always accompanied images of a bruised and bloody twelve-year-old sobbing into his shoulder. "Jamie was kidnapped as a girl. Went through a bit of an ordeal. I was fortunate enough to find her."

From the corner of his eye he saw Stella turn back toward him, knew she was watching his face. "What happened, Cameron?"

"She was…hurt…but still alive." He shook his head, refusing to say any more, but never regretting the things he'd done to rescue Jamie.

"You kept in touch with her."

He smiled a little, remembering the crayon drawings and handmade birthday cards and the call the day she'd turned eighteen, asking for a job. "I don't know how I'd manage without her."

Her sigh was quiet, but he heard it nonetheless. "I under-stand—"

"No, you don't." How could she when he didn't himself? He looked Stella fully in the eye. "I care about the girl, she's dear to me. But Jamie works for me, nothing more. You and I—"

"I guess Gray's really enjoying himself." She jerked her head in a gesture toward the hotel.

Right, then. Not the time or place. He scratched the side of his neck. "Aye, I'm sure he is."

"No, I mean the whole situation." Stella pulled one leg up, tucking her ankle beneath the opposite thigh. "Not only is he screwing the girlfriend, he's also screwing over the wife who keeps him on a short leash."

"How's that?"

"All but one credit card is in Maria's name. From what I've gathered, she owns every asset they have—" she ticked off on her fingers "—the house in Canyon Gate, all of the insured artwork, the time share at a Telluride ski resort, both of the Mercedes and the boat out at Willow Beach Marina. It's all hers."

He shifted in his seat, easing the pressure on his knee. "Unless they divorce. The lot of it would have to be divided between them if…" He paused, recalling Cavanaugh's expression. "Well, that'd explain it, now wouldn't it?"

"What are you talking about?"

He leaned his forearm against the wheel. "You've just said. It's all hers. If they were to split up, Gray would only be able to get his sticky fingers on whatever was purchased during the marriage, not anything Maria owned before. That must be why he stormed out of the solicitor's."

"When was this?"

"I followed Cavanaugh to the firm of Thomas, Crown & Associates. It would seem the firm specializes in posh divorce cases."

"Let me rephrase the question. *When* did you have time to follow Gray? You just came to my office yesterday."

She spoke with her jaw clenched, her eyes going as dark

as her expression. He tensed, bracing for the firestorm of her temper.

"Exactly how long have you been in town, Stone?"

"About a fortnight."

"Two weeks." She continued to stare, her gaze boring into his skull, then deliberately turned away.

In the course of his life, he'd faced down wild-eyed enemy soldiers, ruthless drug dealers and cold-blooded killers with utter disregard for his own safety. He was a right bastard, as hard-core as they came, in the midst of combat.

But, knowing he was in the wrong, he was suddenly afraid to confront a woman half his size.

"Why didn't you call?" She spoke softly, her voice tight with hurt, her fingers braided in her lap. Anger would have been preferable.

"I…"

He felt like a complete arse. How could he explain that he'd never felt anything like this before; that he'd been uncertain if what he remembered was real. And he wasn't about to admit to whatever he was feeling when he wasn't sure.

He inhaled sharply. "I dunno really."

She nodded once and grabbed for the door handle. "I'll keep the name of that divorce lawyer in mind. Thanks for the information."

He did reach for her now. "Stella—"

She nodded toward the upper floor of the hotel. "Here comes Cavanaugh and his girlfriend."

CHAPTER SEVENTEEN

What Were the Odds?

"IT'S TOO LATE, Stella."

He had that goddamned right. I needed to get out of this car, away from this man. Not only hadn't he apologized, I doubted he knew what he was supposed to apologize for. The first few weeks after he left, I'd jumped for the phone like some high school sophomore....

Stupid. Beyond stupid.

"I have to get back before they come downstairs."

"Leave it for now." Stone cupped his hand over my wrist, firmly enough to stop me but not exerting any pressure, denying me an excuse to smack him one. He fastened his seat belt and started the ignition. "If we don't go now, they'll realize we've been waiting."

I still could have opened my door and stepped out, slamming it behind me. But he was already easing out of the parking space. Fuming to have lost my chance at escape, I snapped my own seat belt and crossed my arms. "Gray's going to recognize your car anyway since you were parked right near him."

"That's why we're going to follow the girl. She won't have seen us arrive. And besides, unless he's got another bit on the side, I doubt he'll be of much interest the rest of the day."

He drove us out of the Happy Traveler's lot, down the street about thirty yards and turned the Lexus so he could follow in either direction. We sat in icy silence, except for the purr of the engine and the hum of the fan, and waited.

What was I supposed to say anyway? Did I even have a right to feel this irritated and hurt? It's not like he owed me anything... Except common courtesy, some basic respect...

The cherry Mustang pulled onto Harmon Avenue and headed east. Stone hesitated, waiting for Cavanaugh to leave too. After a few seconds, though, he took the chance of being spotted and followed Caitlyn. I glanced over my shoulder to see that Gray's Mercedes was still parked in the same spot. It looked like he was talking on his cell phone.

Up ahead, Caitlyn made a left on Paradise Road. Stone followed her past the Hard Rock Hotel and then my office. As we went by the now-closed Desert Inn Golf Course and continued north, he cleared his throat. "Where do you suppose she's going, then?"

"I dunno really." I spit the words out, slouching down in my seat.

"You're upset."

I hate when men state the obvious in that ultra-logical tone of voice. "No, shit, Sherlock. Maybe you should go into the detective business—"

Too late, my brain told me to shut up. Damn it, I knew better than to give a guy the leverage of my emotions. It left me vulnerable, a circumstance I couldn't tolerate, one that shouldn't even exist, considering how short a time Stone had been in my life.

I stared out the window as we drove by the Convention Center. Oh, the Coffee Fest Trade Show was coming to town. I perked up—no pun intended—and made a mental note of the dates.

"I'm sorry, Stella."

The quiet sincerity in his voice surprised me. I tilted my head, silently transferring my attention, waiting to hear what else he had to say.

"Our...situation. It's a bit unusual...."

I'd have to keep waiting, however. When I turned to look at him he was obviously distracted. Following his gaze, I saw that, two cars ahead, Caitlyn was turning on Riviera Boulevard. I frowned and glanced back at Stone. He wore the same expression.

What were the odds…? Maybe she was actually going to the Riviera, or further on to Circus Circus or the Stardust. But then she signaled a right turn into the driveway leading up to the Palazzo Napoli and put an end to my speculation.

"I'm not much one for coincidences, are you?"

"Nope." Shaking my head, I was thinking hard.

What the hell was Caitlyn doing here? All sorts of wild ideas flashed through my mind, everything from simply visiting the Terme Sarteano spa to blackmailing the unsuspecting wife. The only thing I knew for sure was that Maria was definitely not going to like this.

As Stone navigated the twisting curves of the driveway, the blinding-white façade of the hotel emerged from the palm trees and flower-heavy foliage. It's a near-exact replica of the Galleria Umberto in Naples. However the Palazzo's soaring Renaissance grandeur is at least twice the size of the original, which claims to be the largest glass-roofed arcade in the world.

Everything is bigger and better in Vegas. It's a rule.

Stone followed the Mustang into the underground parking garage, hanging back a little now that there were fewer cars to hide behind. He drove slowly past several parking sections to what I remembered was the designated employee lot. Finally Caitlyn turned into an empty space.

"Keep going." I pointed, indicating a set of ornate bay doors against the far wall. "That's the closest elevator. Drop me off over there and I'll follow her up."

Stone reached behind him and felt around. Finally he pulled my backpack from the rear floor. "Ring me on your mobile when you're ready to leave. I'll fetch you from round the front."

I got out while Caitlyn weaved through the vehicles toward

the building. I lingered to give her time to get closer, speaking loudly through the open car door. "Okay, honey, I guess I'll see you later then."

"Hmm. I rather like you calling me that. Although, I seem to recall you moaning the name—"

I slammed the door shut and waved goodbye as Caitlyn walked past me. I followed her through the entrance to wait for the elevator. When it arrived, I let her go in first and made note of the button she pushed.

Caitlyn looked at me. "Which floor?"

"Oh, the lobby, thanks."

Like many people, she glanced at the silver medic alert bracelet next to my watch. I've worn it ever since the cure for an ear infection almost killed me, instead. Then she looked at me again before averting her gaze, as if whatever was wrong with me might be contagious.

I moved behind her and leaned my back against the wood paneled wall. While pretending to watch the glowing numbers above the doors, I studied Caitlyn from the corner of my eye. She looked a lot younger up close. Her face and body still had the round softness of adolescence and she kept snapping her gum.

If Jamie hadn't gotten hold of her birth date, I'd think Gray was doing something illegal instead of just immoral.

When the elevator opened, I waited for her to step out. I walked a few feet in the opposite direction then turned to see which way she went. One of the clerks greeted her as she rushed across the lobby's mosaic floor. Caitlyn ducked behind the front desk and disappeared through an unmarked door.

Shifting the weight of my backpack, I affected an impatiently-waiting-for-someone stance so I didn't look like I was spying. It seemed pretty obvious that Caitlyn worked here but I needed to make sure. About five minutes later, she came back out wearing a suit jacket and name tag and took her place behind the reservation counter.

Could this get any more complicated? Not only was Cavanaugh stealing from his father-in-law and cheating on his wife, he was committing both sins right under both of their noses. Gray was either really ballsy or just plain stupid. Until I found out otherwise, I chose to believe he was stupid.

After calling Stone for a ride, I started toward the front entrance. The Palazzo is laid out like a Greek cross with equal-length arms. Polished granite arches led people into the shops, restaurants, lounges and gaming halls. At the center was a huge glass-and-steel dome that connected the vaulted glass ceilings of each wing.

Walking under it, I gave a passing thought to the location of my sunglasses. It was too damned bright in here, especially after a night without sleep.

The *ding-ding-ding* of a hundred slot machines caught my attention as I approached the main casino. Like Pavlov's dog hearing the dinner bell, my palms itched to play a couple hands of blackjack or fondle the dice at a craps table. I'd worked here a few years ago as a "prop" and fondly remembered the excitement of gambling with someone else's money.

The tables were calling me….

"Stellaaaahh!"

I startled at hearing my name bellowed, à la *Streetcar Named Desire*, and turned toward the voice. Pseudo-Stanley did it again, his anguish echoing off the marble walls and floors. I rolled my eyes and smiled. Headed straight for me, with arms wide open, was Frank "the Demon" DiMarco.

In all the years I'd known him, I never asked what he did to get his nickname. Personally? I think he made it up. Big Frank wrapped me into a bear hug greeting before I could avoid it. After I finally patted his back in return, he loosened his grip. I settled my backpack more securely onto my shoulder.

"Hi, Mr. DiMarco."

"Lemme look at ya, Steele. Heey. Beautiful as ever."

"You look great yourself."

He's a handsome man, with dark olive skin and only a few strands of gray highlighting his short, dark hair. He's built like the former linebacker he was, ropy muscles evident beneath his shirtsleeves and the slightest of paunches above his belt. His twinkling brown eyes boasted lashes that a showgirl would envy and his smile—like his personality—was big and friendly.

"Not that I'm complainin', Steele, but what brings ya to the Palazzo here?"

I kept my gaze from straying to Maria, who had hastily followed her father to my side. "I was just in the neighborhood and—"

"The Centrina executives are waiting," Maria interrupted quietly, but her body language was loud and clear. She was not thrilled to see me.

"I'll be there in a minute. So, Steele, whatcha up to? I still can't get over you bein' a P.I. You workin' any undercover cases?" A chuckle rumbled from deep in his chest.

"Mr. DiMarco, you know I can't—"

"The executives, Daddy—"

Frank shook off the tentative fingers she'd placed on his arm. "In a minute, Maria. Ain't you two gonna say hello?"

She acknowledged me with an automatic smile. "Hello, Steele."

"Hey, Maria."

"I think they want to get on with the meeting, Daddy."

"In a minute." Big Frank narrowed his eyes, staring first at his daughter then at me, and back again. "You don't look surprised to see each other."

My attempt at looking innocuous was a hell of a lot better than hers. Maria's pretty little welcome smile froze right to her teeth. It didn't take Frank long. His belly laughs and self-deprecating shrugs hide the computer chips in his brain.

"In the neighborhood, huh, Steele? Ya know, when you girls used to have sleepovers, I always knew when you was plannin' to sneak out and meet boys." He turned to his daughter. "Somethin' you want to tell me about?"

"Um, no, Daddy." She glanced over her shoulder, seeking escape. "We should probably—"

"Robert can handle them. That's why I hired you an assistant with a degree in business management."

As faint pink color stained Maria's cheeks, I deliberately stared behind her. "I think the Centrina folks are getting impatient, Mr. DiMarco. We can catch up some other time. I've got to be going anyway."

"Yeah, okay. Maria, go on over and apologize for keepin' them waitin' while I say goodbye to Steele here."

For a nanosecond, I saw something—frustration, resentment?—flicker in her eyes and I actually thought she might challenge her father. But then she dropped her gaze and quietly complied. "Bye, Steele. Keep in touch, okay?"

"Sure, Maria, I'll see you around." Even if she hadn't darted a hard stare in my direction, I wouldn't tell her father anything.

She nodded and walked back to the corporate types. They seemed anxious to finish talking business and take their expense accounts into the casino. As soon as she was out of earshot, Big Frank rushed me like the ten-yard line was in sight. "Is my little girl in some kinda trouble, Steele?"

I avoided his question, instead looking around the lobby. "I like the new sofas, Mr. D. They really—"

"It's that husband of hers, ain't it? I knew that son of a bitch was trouble from the first time he came sniffin' around." He ran a beefy hand over his face. "Maria finally knows it now, too, huh?"

"Listen, it was great seeing you but I'd better go." I took a step sideways, preparing to move around him.

Big Frank sidestepped as well. "I guess Maria didn't want to come to me, I gave her so much grief over marryin' the bum in the first place. So, what's she gonna do?"

I shifted the other way. "How's your tennis game? You were just starting to take lessons the last time I saw you."

He blocked me again. "Shoulda known the guy couldn't keep it in his pants. She asked you to tail him, huh? What else did ya find out?"

Since we were already dancing, I decided to mention one of his nightclubs. "I went to Element with some friends a few weeks ago. The place seems to be doing well. There was a line around the corner."

"You're smart, Steele. Ya got a good head on your shoulders." He grinned at me, his tone persuasive. "That's why I kept encouragin' Maria to pal around with ya. Hoped some of it would rub off. You know how she is. Can ya blame me for wantin' to protect her?"

I smiled back, acknowledging the compliment, but said nothing. I'm a damned good card player and he knows it. He wasn't going to lull me into giving anything away.

"A'right, a'right. I know when to say when. At least she had enough sense to hire you. But, just so ya know." He crossed his arms over his chest and lowered his voice. "Cavanaugh's not gonna be a problem much longer. I'm takin' care of this, okay? I already got a guy. So you just write up somethin' for Maria, close the book and let me handle the rest."

My temper sparked but I kept my voice light and friendly. "I like and respect you, Mr. DiMarco. But we'll get along much better if you don't tell me how to do my job."

He narrowed his eyes, not liking that I'd opposed him. Big Frank glared at me. I held his gaze. We got into a staring contest like a couple of elementary school kids. Finally, he chuckled and the tension left his shoulders when he realized I wasn't going to back down.

"You're a tough one, Steele. I always liked that about ya."

Glancing at my watch, I smiled my regret. "I really have to go, Mr. D."

"Yeah, me, too. Don't be such a stranger, hear? And listen, next time ya want to go to Element, just check in at the door. I'll put your name on the VIP list."

"Thanks very much, Mr. DiMarco. I appreciate that."

"Old friends watch each other's backs, right?" He winked at me then headed over to the Centrina executives.

Big Frank said something that set off a bray of loud, masculine laughter. As the boisterous group moved off to their meeting, Maria trailed behind them like a ghost.

Watching her, seeing the expression on her face, was like looking at a mirror to the past. I used to walk a dutiful two steps behind Bobby in the beginning, when I first started dating the UNLV Rebels power forward, one of the Big Men on Campus. By the end, I kept four steps behind his shadow, hoping to go unnoticed.

Since Bobby died, maybe because of the way he died, I walk behind no one. I can't. Because, if I do, it was all for nothing.

CHAPTER EIGHTEEN

Nothing Personal

STONE EXPERTLY WEAVED the Lexus between cars on the Strip, heading back to the Happy Traveler Hotel. His driving was controlled and precise, like everything else he did. Well, almost everything. In bed, the guy melted like butter if you nibbled a certain spot on his neck….

Dragging my mind back to the case, I told him what I'd learned about Caitlyn. I also mentioned that I'd run into Big Frank and relayed what he'd said about already having a guy to take care of Cavanaugh.

"He sounded like an extra in a bad mobster movie. So I guess that would make you the hired muscle." I pitched my voice dramatically low. "The out-of-town hit man who does the deed then vanishes into the night."

Stone didn't laugh.

But before I could pursue it, he asked, "How is it you know Frank DiMarco?"

"Maria and I went to high school together. We used to hang out at her house because she had a pool with a water slide and a huge crush on the twins next door." I smiled, remembering one particular hot summer night when Ash and Drew had sneaked over the wall to go skinny-dipping with us… Ah, yeah. Good times.

Big Frank had installed an upgraded security system the very next day, banned me from the house for a week and threatened Maria with convent school.

I looked over at Stone. "What about you? How do you know 'the Demon'?"

"I don't, actually. Only what Jamie was able to find out. Nothing personal."

"So, how'd you end up working for him?"

"A matter of chance."

His tone implied that luck had had nothing to do with it, but he didn't say anything else. Staring at him, I wondered what he was thinking and whether I'd ever know who this man really was. My instincts told me it wasn't likely.

"I'm a bit peckish. What do you fancy for dinner?"

"Um, it's still lunchtime."

"Right, American terminology. I forgot. I meant the mid-day meal. What are you in the mood for?"

I was definitely not in the mood to be frustrated by Stone's half answers or nonanswers. I swear I could not figure this guy out. He claimed to want a more intimate relationship, but then shut me out like a stranger on a bus. I deserved better. So, for now, "nothing personal" was going to apply to us, too.

"I need to get back to my office. I've got a ton of work waiting for me." Actually, I'd probably catch a nap on my sofa, but he didn't need to know that.

"You've still got to eat. I can stop somewhere for takeaway if you'd like."

"That's okay. I'm not even hungry."

At the next traffic light, he glanced over at me, studying my face. When comprehension seemed to dawn, his gaze became distant. We spent the rest of the drive in silence. But I guess he wasn't ready to admit defeat. As he pulled into Madame Verushka's parking lot, he kept his eyes to the front and his voice casual and tried again.

"Will you join me for supper tonight? I assume you'll be hungry by then."

"Oh, I'm sure I will be. But I already have plans with someone else." Namely, Chef Yeun who owned the Asian noodle shop near the agency.

Stone cleared his throat. "Perhaps afterward we can meet for drinks—"

"Sorry. I'll be busy for the rest of the night." That part at least was true. Yeah, I knew I was being bitchy but really didn't care. Let him wonder where *I* was and what *I* was doing for a change.

His expression became inscrutable, but his eyes frosted over with displeasure. "Anyone I need to know about?"

I just smiled, hoping I looked as smug as I felt, and enjoyed the hint of jealousy in his tone. Reaching for the door handle, I slid across the leather seat. "Thanks for the ride."

"Try not to enjoy yourself tonight."

A FEW HOURS LATER, I *was* enjoying myself.

In fact, I felt absolutely marvelous. Warm and naked and coated in orange ginger massage oil, I groaned with pleasure. Strong hands plied my bare flesh, stroking my body and releasing the tension I hadn't even realized was there. I moaned again as Lukas manipulated a particularly sweet spot.

"God, I reeeally needed this."

"What you need is a man," a familiar voice interjected.

I opened one eye and glared—if it's possible to glare with one eye—at my mother. She slipped off her robe and arranged herself on the table across from me.

"Could you maybe say hello before you start in on me?"

"*Piacere, cara mia.* Hello, Lukas."

He had suspended his ministrations, his fingers resting near the small towel draped over my butt. "I am a man, in case you do not notice."

You couldn't help but notice.

From his flowing hair and chiseled face to his bulging biceps and sculpted thighs, Lukas was six feet of finely engineered Germanic perfection. Joey's girlfriend, Santina, had had the business acumen to hire only attractive males to work here at Indulgences. Most of her clients were perpetually dieting, and beefcake had zero calories.

"Yes, you are, Lukas dear. You're a gorgeous man, but a married one, unfortunately."

Appeased, he went back to massaging my low back. I tried to relax again, more than happy to let him.

"As I was saying, *cara.* Regular sex is a vital part of a healthy lifestyle."

My head popped up from the table. "Can we not talk about this?"

"I can't go without for more than a few days."

"Eww."

Mom lay on her still-flat stomach in a strapless bra and tap pants. She turned to look at me while Josh, her hot blond masseur, caressed her shoulders. "What *eww?* You and your brothers didn't exactly come from the cannoli shop. And your father is still a very sexy man, let me tell you."

"Thank you so much for that mental image, Mom. Double eww."

Lukas lightly pushed my head back onto the pillow. "You tense up and ruin all of my work. No more talking, *ja?* I try again."

This is your fault, I mouthed at my mother.

She just laughed and closed her eyes. I did the same, trying to relocate the Zen state I'd been in before she'd entered the treatment room. After a few moments, the aromatherapy candles, soft instrumental music and Lukas's hands worked their magic.

I must have fallen asleep because, the next thing I knew, he was lightly shaking my shoulder. Damn. I could have used another half hour. With a contented sigh, I roused myself from the massage table, shrugged into my robe and walked back to the dressing area.

I'd just tucked in my camo T-shirt and zipped my jeans when my mother came in. As she opened her property unit— Santina didn't like to call them lockers—I leaned back on the overstuffed chair to wait. Mom took her cream silk blouse and matching slacks into one of the curtained dressing niches. We were the only clients tonight, so she had her choice.

"You'll never guess who I ran into at the club, at Nina and Robert Tatti's anniversary party."

"Nope, I never will."

She raised her voice as if the drape were a soundproof barrier. "Little Eddie Delvecchio, can you believe it? Well, he's not so little now—he made it to at least five foot eight— and still good-looking." She paused, and then spoke the dreaded words. "I mentioned you, of course, and he promised to give you a call about going out sometime."

Membership in Paisano's, *the* Italian-American social club, was cheaper and more efficient than any professional dating service you could name. However, I wasn't interested. Especially not in "Fingers" Delvecchio, so named because they'd always been either in his nose or up some girl's skirt.

"Is he the best you think I can do?"

"What? He's a nice Italian boy from a good family—"

"Mom."

She sighed. "So, maybe he's not exactly your type. I was only trying to help."

"Thanks, but I can find my own type."

"Then why haven't you?" Her voice was soft, concerned.

As she opened the curtain, lines of strain creased her forehead and bracketed her mouth. Her features had gone from fresh and dewy to showing every one of her sixty years. Her gentle gaze was full of sadness, love and sympathy. I looked away without answering.

We both knew why.

"I've had plenty of dates." I forced myself to laugh. "More than plenty."

"You mean, you've slept with a few men. That's not the same as being in a committed relationship."

The chair rocked a little when I shoved out of it, trying to sound angry instead of defensive. "It's the twenty-first century, for Christ's sake. I don't need a man to validate my life."

"How about to value it?" Mom crossed the distance between us and took both of my hands. Despite the strength of her grip, her fingers trembled. "How about needing someone to respect and appreciate you, baby? We all need that. I'm not asking you to get married tomorrow—just stop being afraid to fall in love again."

I flinched at the irony of her words and gently slipped my hands away. Had I loved Bobby? I'd thought so at the time. I never got beyond lust with the other guys I'd dated. And I didn't know how the hell I felt about Stone.

"Your father and I knew Bobby was trouble, but we felt it was best to trust you, to let you spread your wings and make your own mistakes." Her voice broke. "You have no idea how much I regret that decision, Stella. We never talk about that night—"

I withdrew emotionally at the same instant my feet took a step back and turned away. I didn't deserve her love or her trust. Not after what I'd allowed to happen.

"Why do you keep shutting me out of your life, *cara?* I'm your mother and I couldn't love you more. No matter what."

Shame crashed over to me, hot and piercing. My throat tightened with the sudden need to cry. I turned back to face her even though I didn't have the courage to speak. She loved me, yes, but her understanding and forgiveness would be out of the question if she knew….

Mom and I stood there looking at each other helplessly. With so much standing between us, she didn't know what to say and I had too much I couldn't say. Therefore the gulf of silence remained.

Santina peeked into the dressing room to tell us it was time for our next spa treatments. Her appearance broke the tension and offered a welcome diversion. I gazed at the woman who'd wanted a little girl so badly after having three boys, and yet had never once told me the tomboy she'd ended up with was a disappointment.

"I love you, too, Mom. I really do. I just need…more time."

She held open her arms in a silent gesture of truce. I couldn't deny her need to comfort, not when I'd withheld so many other things from her. After returning the hug with genuine affection, I determinedly shook off my dark mood. "So, let's go get pretty some more."

"You go ahead, honey. I have to put on my face first." It would be a while. Viviana Mezzanotte is a firm believer that beauty takes time.

"Don't bother just this once, Mom. You look great as you are." I gave in to a guilt-ridden impulse and kissed her.

She touched her fingers to her cheek and smiled over my rare gesture before following me into the salon.

On Wednesdays, Indulgences closes at six o'clock. However, Santina had generously offered a special favor to my mother. She lets us choose a limited number of treatments and only charges for the first two. Mom and I have standing seven o'clock appointments one night each month. Even though we've been doing this for a while, I still don't admit to liking these hedonistic girlie rituals.

But, the truth was, I loved having someone else deal with my hair. It really was a pleasure to just lie back and relax while Robbie shampooed, conditioned and detangled. Now, I was sitting in a padded chair with a glass of pinot grigio while he blow-dried it all. Mom sat in the next chair chatting with Santina, who was personally refreshing the ends of her pageboy cut.

My future sister-in-law is a stunning tribute to her business. Her bronze skin is flawless and her curly black hair shines with health. Santina had once been a successful model. Several framed magazine covers decorated the wall behind the reception desk.

"So, Tina, your birthday's coming up, isn't it. I don't suppose there's anything you've had your eye on?"

"Not very subtle, Steele." Her voice rang with the lightly musical accent of her native Kenya as she teased me. "You tell your brother he must think of his own gift."

My mother turned with a wide smile and almost spilled her wine. "An engagement ring, maybe? I think a princess cut diamond with—"

"It will happen if and when the time is right, Miss Vivi." Santina misted hairspray over Mom's head. "Neither John nor I are in a hurry."

She's the only one who called him that. My brother's name is Giovanni—John in Italian—but he'd gone by Joey his whole life. Until he met Tina—he'll be whoever she wants him to be, he loves her that much.

Mom blew the cloud of noxious fumes away from her face with a huff. "Well, I'm in a hurry for my son to make an honest woman of you. I want more grandchildren and it would be nice if you got married first."

Santina deftly evaded the part about having kids as she poked and fluffed strands of hair. "We do not need the symbols or ceremonies to know that we belong together. I have John's love and that is enough."

I lowered my eyelids to half-mast and swallowed the dregs of the wine to hide my visceral reaction.

They met when Joey stopped his patrol car to help Tina fix a flat tire. And although they both admit now to an instant attraction, it was Santina who asked for the first date. She is the most self-assured woman I know. She knows exactly who she is, what she wants out of life and isn't afraid to go after it.

Me? I've got more questions than answers and I try to avoid asking the questions in the first place.

After another hour, I'd had my fill of primping. I left the salon with an intricate French braid and a reddish-brown polish called Kiss My Brass on my toes. Carrying my boots, I padded to the car in disposable foam sandals. I drove home slowly with the windows down. There was a relatively cool breeze blowing and I had a warm glow from two glasses of wine.

It was after ten-thirty so traffic was light. Just me and the folks working graveyard at the casinos. I drove on autopilot while my mind was occupied with everything and nothing in particular. *Check on Kenny Asher again. Get the Harley back. Send the minimum payment to MasterCard. Trail Cavanaugh again tomorrow. Pick up toothpaste.*

Do something about Stone.

Thinking back to what Santina had said, I didn't necessarily need the symbols either. But I sure would have liked some of that certainty, that sense of belonging. Everyone I'd just spent the evening with was going home to someone—Santina to Joey, Mom to Papa. Meanwhile, I was going to an empty house.

I turned onto Skyland Drive and hit the remote door opener when I got close to my driveway. After putting Anna's Honda to bed, I went back out and shut the garage. I'd forgotten to check the mail. Sorting as I walked, I headed for the front door. Every wall in my house could be papered with all of the junk mail I get.

I fished my key from the backpack and turned the knob. It smelled weird in here. Something must have gone bad in the vegetable drawer. I shut the door behind me. Absently running a hand over my new French braid, I began to walk toward my office—

A tingle ran along my nerves. I held my breath, limbs frozen, as the instinctive part of my brain screamed at me. Caution raised the fine hairs on my neck. I listened hard, trying to make sense of my reaction. Then my eyes adjusted to the darkness.

Somebody had been here.

CHAPTER NINETEEN

A Woman's Castle

IT WAS LATE AT NIGHT.

I lived alone.

Some creep was stalking my house.

And now I'd been the target—not the victim, never the victim—of a break-in.

Thanks to my friend Scott's dealership, I own six handguns, all duly registered with the Clark County sheriff for concealed carry. Thanks to monthly training sessions on the firing range, I'm a good shot with any of the different weapons. But, now that I needed one, where were they? Locked in the damned wall safe of my office, that's where.

Aunt Gloria always used to say, *"If a P.I.'s gonna use a gun, she better be prepared to take a life or to lose one. The best weapon a woman has is her brain."* Maybe I could yank it through my ear and gross the burglar out so much that he'd leave.

I backpedaled as quietly as possible. Hyperventilating, I slowly reopened the front door. The beam of light from a streetlamp gave me enough illumination to find my cell phone. Forcing myself to exhale slowly, I felt better knowing that I could run out while screaming to 9-1-1 for help.

And with a semblance of control came a sense of bravery.

I stole deeper into the house, carefully placing each foam flip-flop as I moved over the tile floor. The only sound was the rush of blood thudding in my ears. I didn't sense any movement, nothing to indicate that someone was still here. I did, however, find one source of the cloyingly sweet odor.

A huge bouquet of what looked like five dozen roses filled a tall vase. It sat on a brand-new glass-topped table surrounded by six chairs. I actually blinked several times. The flowers and Art Deco-style dining set were still there. So were the geometric curtains hanging in the bay window and the matching rug on the floor.

What the hell was going on? This was beyond weird. Feeling like I'd somehow entered the Twilight Zone, I took a chance and flipped the switch. Light flooded the room from a new chandelier and revealed the other reason for the funny smell. The walls had been painted a warm butter-yellow.

In the living room, my laminate bookcases were gone. My television was now installed in an entertainment center with built-in cabinets and open shelving on either side. A sofa and two love seats had replaced my comfy armchair. Everything was in shades of yellow, pink and orange, from the striped couches to the plaid throw pillows and paisley drapes.

What kind of stalker redecorates your house?

I took a deep breath. Then another one.

My knees felt a little shaky but I didn't want to sit on anything. Those forensic guys can find all kinds of bits and pieces as long as you don't tamper with the evidence. After closing the front door, I made my way back to the kitchen. Leaning my elbows on the island counter, I dropped my face into my palms and rubbed my eyes.

Someone had been in my house. Someone had touched my stuff, removed my possessions. Oddly enough, though, this had a different vibe than the phone calls or the peeping creep. I didn't feel the same kind of menace. I'd definitely never dreamed about anything like this.

Still, I should call somebody. The police, definitely, to report the crime. My friends, probably, to ask for a place to stay. And my family, maybe, though I hated to worry them. Especially when it looked like all that was taken was—

Oh, hell.

I jumped off the bar stool and ran down the hallway to my office. Sometimes I bring case files home and of course my personal papers are in the file cabinet. After checking around, I relaxed a little. It didn't look as if anything was missing. Judging by the layer of dust, nothing in here had been disturbed at all.

Down the hall, though, the guestroom was redone in that country farmhouse style, including a yellow duck quilt. Yech. Then it hit me. If my demented interior designer had been in here… Recalling the comment about my panties, I dashed across to the master bedroom with genuine dread.

Bracing for the worst, I turned on the light. There was a new mahogany dresser, a companion lingerie chest and a vanity table. Emerald green curtains hung from a wrought-iron rod. My pictures now hung on the freshly painted teal accent wall. It looked like a page out of the catalog I'd left on the patio.

Everything had been replaced…except for my bed. There was a plain white envelope lying on top. I picked it up between my thumb and index finger, holding it by one corner. After tucking my cell phone into my jeans, I carefully extracted the heavy linen card stock and read the neat script.

I've kept my promise. If you'd like the bed that goes along with your new set, you shall have to invite me in.

Squeezing my eyes shut, I crushed the note in my fist. The release of tension was so sudden that I slumped onto the corner of the bed. It wasn't him. It wasn't last night's prowler. This wasn't a violent threat, but rather one to my peace of mind. I sat there, trembling, as a kind of relief washed over me.

I hated admitting, even to myself, that I'd been scared. That I still was. My body had no such trouble. My heart pounded; my hands shook with the aftereffects of an adrenaline overload. I'd been prepared to fight or to flee. I was not, however, ready to face the illusion of my invincibility.

Then again, I hadn't lost control of my environment. It had been taken from me. My rights, my choice, my free will—

none of those had mattered. It was like *I* didn't matter. Relief gave way to outrage and I yanked my phone out of my pocket. I didn't even give him a chance to speak.

"You arrogant Scotch bastard!"

"Evening, Stella, love."

I felt the veins bulging in my neck as I yelled into the phone. "Are you out of your damned mind?"

"Well, I may admit to being crazy about you—"

"How did you do this?" I stood up and started to pace the floor. "How did you get into my house?"

Stone sounded annoyed when he answered. "Very easily, I'm afraid. You really ought to consider better locks."

"I will. Along with an alarm system, motion detectors, floodlights and vicious man-eating guard dogs. Whatever it takes to keep people out of here." My legs propelled me across the room.

"Aren't you overreacting just a bit?"

"No, dammit, I'm not! If you could get in, so could—" I snapped my mouth shut and fired his note at the wall.

His tone changed instantly to concern. "Who could get in? Has there been some sort of trouble in the neighborhood?"

"Not that I've heard." That was true, at least.

"Something's upset you, however. I noticed earlier."

Pausing by the bathroom, I rubbed at a knotted muscle in my neck. Lukas would not be happy that I'd tensed up again so soon. It had been a hellacious twenty-four hours. But what didn't kill me made me stronger, right? "I can handle it myself."

"I'm quite certain you can, love. But you don't have to."

The offer of support, of protection, was so clear that it made me ache. I blinked against the sting of tears. Did wanting to take him up on it make me weak? Did it make me dependent, the one thing I refused to be? I wasn't sure. I wasn't sure about anything right now.

"Um, thanks…"

"Mmm. I presume you're thanking me for the décor, as opposed to accepting my help. Heaven forbid. You'd rather bite my hand than hold it."

That snapped me out of my uncharacteristically weepy mood. He's right. I'm no damsel, despite my distress. "My living room is pink. I don't do pink."

"All right. If there's anything else you don't care for, it's a simple matter of ringing the decorator."

"I hate the ottomans. I would have picked real coffee tables. And what lunatic mixes stripes, plaid and paisley? It's awful."

"You've got your fighting spirit back, I see." His voice dripped sarcasm.

Yeah, I did. I started pacing again. I felt stronger, having something to focus on, something that I could control and change. "I'm not crazy about the Deco stuff in the dining room. And the guest room looks like Martha Stewart threw up in there."

"Oh, bloody hell, woman! At least the place no longer resembles a month-by-month rental flat. It's obvious you couldn't be bothered, so I had it done."

That stopped me again. It was the one thing I'd avoided thinking about. "Why?"

He chuffed impatiently. "Why what?"

I rested my hip on the edge of the dresser. "Why did you break into my house, take my stuff without permission and attempt to impose your own mark on the place?"

"I was being nice, damn you. You seemed distraught earlier. I knew you'd refuse my compassion, so I'd thought to surprise you with a small gift."

He considered half a houseful of expensive furnishings a small gift? Christmas and birthdays with him must be unreal. I wouldn't know. He probably wouldn't even be here by then…. But I still didn't get the gesture and said so. "This is pretty extravagant, considering we barely know each other."

"We might, if you'd stop avoiding me."

"I'm avoiding another…disappointment." I straightened, looking at the bed I slept in alone. "We might have had the hots for each other, and spent an awesome night together, but it was a mistake to think it could go any further."

He sighed. "You're the 'glass almost empty' sort, aren't you?"

"No, I'm the 'see the glass for what it is, not what I want it to be' sort."

"Stella, love, I believe the mistake would be in not giving our continued attraction a chance."

"That just proves my point. We don't see things the same way at all. We've got little in common. We're nothing alike." I went over to check that the window was locked. I'd forgotten to put the screen back in. "This isn't going to work, Stone."

"Then get to know me. Let me know you. Because I think you'll find that we are indeed alike. And, more to the point, we're a pair."

"A pair of what?" I muttered, checking my office window.

Stone chuckled. "Ah, there's my Stella."

"I'm not yours."

"The lady doth protest too much." When I grunted at him, Stone inferred what I didn't want to say. "Admit it, go on. You're absolutely mad for me. Otherwise I wouldn't have this effect on you."

"I'm mad *at* you. That's not the same thing." Even I could hear that my tone lacked conviction. Stifling a yawn, I blamed it on exhaustion. I was emotionally and physically wiped out.

"You're tired, love. Off to bed with you." His words were soft, both comforting and kind.

For a brief second, I was so tempted to ask for that damned bed. And everything that came with it. But I wasn't ready to let go yet, wasn't ready to lose any more of myself. Instead I snapped at him, agitated and defensive. And aching inside.

"Don't tell me what to do, Stone."

"I'll stay on the line whilst you lock all the doors."

I reached for the dining room window. The kitchen one had been fine. "Don't tell me—"

"Stop being so bloody obstinate or I'm coming over."

"All right, all right. I'm checking."

He made a frustrated sound. "This is a first, you know. Women don't usually consider my company a threat."

I snorted. "You're no threat to me, Stone. I've just had enough of you for one week."

His voice lowered to a soft rumble. "I doubt I could ever get enough of you."

I rolled my eyes, smiling as I walked toward the French doors. That's when I noticed the new patio set. The wooden lounge chairs and side tables were a vast improvement over the plastic stuff I'd had before. I really hated to admit how much I liked them.

"Actually, Cameron, you're too much."

He must have picked up on my wistfulness because his tone turned seductive, stirring hot memories and fresh lust. "I remember being a perfect fit."

But it wasn't desire that suddenly made my stomach plunge. When I reached the first door, I realized it was unlatched. The second one was not only unlocked, but slightly ajar. Had it been like that all day? Or had it been opened while I was in the bedroom? I looked around wildly, my heart slamming against my ribs.

"Stella? Are you there?"

"The door."

"Stella, what's wrong?"

My voice cracked as I hissed into the phone. "The patio doors aren't locked. I know I—"

"Oh. Sorry, that's my fault. The couches were too large to fit the front door so we had to bring them round the back. We must have overlooked bolting them again."

The tears I'd been repressing since last night finally fell. I slammed the second door shut and yanked both locks into place. "Damn you, Stone! Damn you for scaring me like this!"

"That was never my intention, you know that." He went quiet for a few seconds, waiting. Finally he cleared his throat. "Are you going to tell me what's really going on?"

"No. It's nothing. Some stupid phone calls."

"They can't be nothing to have frightened you like this." His voice hardened determinedly. "I'll just get my keys and be there in ten minutes."

My pulse jumped at the thought. I'm human. I wasn't crazy about the idea of being alone right now. But I also didn't want this man to keep trying to run my life. I hadn't forgotten yesterday's kiss. Tonight I doubted my ability to resist him.

"Don't, okay? I really don't want to see you right now." Feeling angry and nervous and resentful, I scrubbed the tears from my face and went to make sure the door into the garage was locked. "I'm fine, Stone. I'll be fine."

He drew a sharp breath, growling softly on the exhale. "You are by far the most stubborn, most irksome woman I have ever come across."

I walked down the hall normally. "That's not my problem. Self-reliance is what keeps me alive."

"It's also what's kept you alone."

My vision went red as I sucked in a breath. I couldn't freakin' believe he'd just said that! "I don't need to hear this shit from the guy that walked out on me."

"No, you don't." He sighed again. "How about this, then? I'll remain on the phone with you until you fall asleep. That way I can at least pretend you let me help."

He wasn't pressuring me directly, but I still heard the entreaty. He was asking me to let him in, something I hadn't done with any man for five years. I surprised both of us by grabbing onto his offer like a lifeline.

"Okay, Stone. Pretend I said thank-you."

Yeah, I was furious with him. But I really didn't want to be by myself. He was better than lying alone in the dark, imagining shadows in the silence. Or calling my mother. Besides, if I didn't agree, he'd probably drive over anyway and he'd already proven he could get into the house.

"I'll pretend that you're already naked, as well."

"I'm hanging up. Call me back on the land line in five minutes."

After double-checking the locks I turned out all of the lights. Except the one in the foyer. And the one over the stove. Nerves still humming, I walked to the back of the house. In my bedroom I took the cordless off its charger. I had shucked off my jeans and T-shirt by the time the phone rang.

"Now are you naked?"

"Yep, and I'm about to get very wet."

"You try a man, Stella, you really do."

"Try to entertain yourself while I take a shower."

I laid the phone on the bathroom vanity, provoking him with the sound of running water while I brushed my teeth. I picked it up once and caught the end of a groan. Served him right.

About fifteen minutes later, I shut off the spray. I would normally stand under a hot shower until it runs cold. Tonight, though, I just wanted to wipe away the tension and get into bed. I tossed my shower cap into the second sink and dried off before grabbing the phone again.

"Still with me?"

"No. I'm in a fantasy world that involves a good deal of peach-scented body wash."

"You went snooping again, didn't you? Just for that I'm not bothering with underwear."

His exaggerated moan made me grin as I pulled on clean panties and a tank top. Getting under the covers, I snuggled into my pillow with the phone against my ear. Just hearing him breathe on the other end made me feel safer. I hated that.

"Talk to me."

"What shall I tell you?"

"There's only one thing that interests me." I yawned and closed my eyes.

He made a soft noise, like he'd shifted positions trying to get comfortable. "I was born in Leith. That's the port access to Edinburgh. It's famous for being the seat of the monarchy during Mary Queen of Scots' short reign. My parents had a council house in Canongate, a rougher area near dockside."

"Canongate." I murmured the name. "That's your company."

"Aye. You can take the boy out of Scotland…"

I hummed in amusement. "What was it like growing up?"

"Hardscrabble for the most part. Dad worked laying brick and my mum did secretarial. Me, I ran errands for the shop-keeps in the High Street to earn a spare pence. Even so, we never seemed to have much but each other."

I made a sound, softly encouraging him to keep talking.

"Mum always joked that my dad couldn't doubt she'd married him for love. He never laughed, though, since her posh folks disowned her when they ran off. The MacManus side still wouldn't speak to her even after I came along."

He kept talking, finally sharing something of himself with me, though it was all ancient history. I tried not to, but I was falling under his spell again. It had to be that voice, all softly accented vowels and rolling *R*'s, lulling me to sleep.

My last thought was a passing wish that Cameron were lying beside me, holding me to keep the nightmares away.

CHAPTER TWENTY

Someone to Watch Over Me

SHE WAS TALKING in her sleep.

Cameron listened to the soft murmur of her voice and felt an ache in his chest. Gazing out the wall of windows in his living room, he imagined her across the distance from his condominium to her house. The sweetness of her face and the way her lips parted in slumber, the feel of her curled against his side…

"I wish I were there too, Stella, love."

His mum could never sleep unless his father was right there next to her. He smiled, remembering. That'd been at the heart of the biggest row his parents ever had. Dad had taken on a lot of overtime and suddenly wasn't home much. Mum was put out, but his father only said it was something he had to do.

"When I was about six, almost seven, Dad had been working into the night for over a month, and by then my mum was fit to be tied. Family time was more important than a bit of extra wage. Dad agreed with her, but still kept working all hours. Things were quite tense for a while. I walked on eggshells rather than test Mum's temper.

"Then on her birthday it all came clear. Dad was so proud to give her this tiny gold filigree cross. She was Jean MacManus, you see, daughter of landed gentry, while Colin Stone was working-class and nothing more. Dad wanted to give her everything she'd have had if not for marrying him, but the necklace was the best he could do."

Cameron would never forget the look on his mother's face.

She'd cradled the gift in her hand, tears streaming down her cheeks, and laid into his father but good. She didn't need expensive jewelry when she had his love. If he ever pulled a stunt like that again she'd make him more than sorry. Then she'd kissed him so soundly that Cameron had fled the room in childish embarrassment.

"Mum wore that cross every day, never took it off for anything, until the day she died."

Stella sighed but said nothing. He listened to her rhythmic breathing for a few moments, glad she'd finally fallen asleep. Then he quietly wished her a peaceful night and hung up. He didn't know who had frightened her, but he knew how to give her a measure of confidence.

He got up, stretching his legs, and then rang Jamie's number. As always, his assistant sounded fully awake despite the hour on the East Coast. She seemed to sleep as little as he did. After explaining what he wanted, he gave specific instructions on how it was to be handled.

"I need this in place by morning. Can you do it?"

"Hey, I learned from the best."

"Thanks, Jamie."

Cameron rested his forearm against the glass and looked out over the neon night. Even from twenty-five floors above, the energy and carnival atmosphere were tangible. The Panorama Towers stood directly behind Las Vegas Boulevard. From any of his windows, he could see the Bellagio's choreographed fountains, an instant reminder of his one night with Stella.

Stroking the pad of his thumb over the whorls and loops of the gold cross, he waited for the sun to rise.

CHAPTER TWENTY-ONE

Bumps in the Road

THE PLACE WAS GONNA look like a goddamned bunker.

He was in position on top of the community center, watching the army of Guardian Security techs swarming her house.

At least he'd had a look at that blistering body when she'd opened the door in her underwear. Even the techno-geeks had gotten stiff, he could tell.

Man, this had to cost. They were installing all kinds of stuff in the yard—looked like lights and motion sensors—and wiring every point of entry, even the damned garage window. These guys weren't playing around. They were probably even going to put underwater cameras in the pool.

Cursing under his breath, he lowered the binoculars.

He'd just have to find another way to get to her.

CHAPTER TWENTY-TWO

Shiny, Awkward Strings

"I DON'T LIKE being in debt, Stone. I really don't like being indebted to *you*. And I hate having no idea how much I owe you."

I'd slept like the dead last night, less anxious and dream-free. I didn't even remember hanging up the phone or turning out the bedside lamp. My memory ended with Stone's voice and began with the sound of somebody leaning on my door-bell at o'dark-thirty this morning.

I am not a morning person.

Especially when faced with a crew of twenty guys who wanted to put holes in my walls and dig up my yard.

It took two minutes to confirm that they didn't have the wrong address. It took two more minutes to put on clothes. And then another fifteen plus a pot of coffee to establish that the premium security measures Guardian's technicians wanted to install had already been paid for in full.

Three guesses who'd footed the bill. The first two counted even less than my continued objections.

"Stella, love, I've already assured you—more than once—that there is no debt. I consider the alarms and such to be part of your present."

"How the hell can you afford this anyway?"

"I'm quite rich and I'm rather wealthy."

My stomach fluttered as panic danced over my nerves. "Presents are little things like chocolates or DVDs or kitchen appliances. Stuff this expensive comes with colorful, shiny, awkward strings that I refuse to get tangled—"

"Having tied the knot, I'd say our lives are already entangled, wouldn't you? Besides, I refuse to not worry about you. You'll simply have to set aside your commitment phobia and accept that I've taken on responsibility for your safety."

He'd say. He refused. He'd taken, Where the hell was I in the decision-making process? Just because I'd been drunk and impulsive enough to repeat some vows didn't mean—I didn't want to think about this right now. I had a more immediate issue.

"*I* am responsible for my safety. I don't need all of these gadgets and gizmos. I can't afford them, so *you'll* have to tell the Guardian guys to go home."

"Sorry, love. Not only can I more than afford this, but I have a biological right to protect those I care about. The 'Guardian guys' as you call them have a job to do. Let them."

I yelled in frustration, scaring the hell out of the techies sipping espresso in my Art Deco dining room. Then I banged the phone on the counter a few times. Because it wasn't just Stone's imperious attitude making me mad, it was my own reaction. I was actually impressed and flattered by all of the trouble he'd gone to.

Dammit.

I lifted the phone and gritted my teeth, making an effort to modulate my voice. "Thanks. Really."

"Dear lord, did you just express your gratitude without the world coming to a screeching end?"

"Okay, okay. Thank you very much for the alarms and the sensors and everything. I like the vicious man-eating attack dogs." Losing my battle with a smile, I patted the fuzzy head of the nearest German shepherd. He stared at me with bright plastic eyes while his buddy lolled his pink fabric tongue. "I still hate most of the furniture, though."

"So you've said. I'll take care of it. And, Stella?"

"What?"

"Just because you don't owe me anything doesn't mean this won't cost you."

The smile dropped off my face as my defenses came up. "Oh, yeah? It figures. I knew there had to be strings attached. How much, Stone? How much are you going to hold me to?"

"Everything you have. No matter how long it takes." His voice was warm, as smooth and rich as butter cream, and I knew instantly that he wasn't talking about money.

I turned my back so the techies couldn't see my face. Exactly what kind of biological rights was he going to claim? Was I willing to trade my body for a nice patio set and new curtains? I hated to think I could be had that cheaply. But then maybe the furnishings had nothing to do with it. My question came out as a rough whisper.

"What do you want?"

"Don't sound so worried. All I'm asking, for now, is that you spend time with me."

SPENDING TIME with Stone turned out to be a lot harder than it seemed. By the time the Guardians had established a perimeter and battened down the hatches, I was late for the office. Jon gave me no end of grief, for that and for my atypical mood.

"What is wrong with you?"

"Nothing." I dropped my backpack onto the reception desk.

"There must be. Something's missing from your face."

I wrinkled my brow. "What the hell are you talking about?"

"Ah, there it is." He nodded sagely. "I almost didn't recognize you without the scowl."

"Oh, shut up. We have work to do."

Jon grinned and handed me several message slips. "Start with these. All but one are from Mrs. Cavanaugh."

I flipped through them. Maria had called twice yesterday after I'd left, and three times this morning, demanding a status report. "Geez, she just hired me two days ago."

"Cherie Michelac hired you over a month ago. Hers is the last message."

I knew a reprieve when I saw one. "I'll call her back first. Would you get me a cappuccino?"

Jon stared at me. "You're asking for coffee? *You* are *asking* for coffee?"

"Oh, for crying out loud. Yes, would you please get me a freakin' cappuccino?"

"This is so not like you, Steele." He crossed his arms, studying me. "And I can only think of one out-of-the-ordinary explanation. Does the divine creature who came by on Tuesday get credit for your sunny new disposition?"

I tried scowling again, uncomfortable with the answer. "Maybe."

Jon didn't say anything else as I headed back to my office, but for some reason he didn't look happy. I didn't have time to dwell on it, however. I had reports to write, bills to send out, and background checks to finish. But first, I had clients to appease. After quickly updating Cherie, I dialed Maria's number.

"What in the world were you doing at the Palazzo yesterday? I assume you weren't looking for me since you never returned my calls."

I took the punch and rolled with it. "I apologize, Maria. I left the agency early last night. I needed to follow up on some information."

"For my case? It's about time. What have you found out?"

I ignored that one, too. "I was just at the casino checking out a lead. As soon as I have something concrete, I'll tell you, I promise."

Okay, I know what you might think. But you'd be wrong. Even though I'd assumed a lot about Cavanaugh's happy travels, his encounter with Caitlyn might still have been a one-time thing. And while I don't condone cheating, I also don't want to help break up a marriage without more proof.

"You don't know what I'm going through, Steele. You have no idea what's going through my mind." Maria's voice sounded thick, as though she were tearing up. "I just need to know for sure. The wondering is worse than the knowledge."

That made me think about Stone, about the two and a half months he'd been gone. I still didn't know where he'd been or what had kept him away. He claimed he was back for good. If that were true, then I should now be able to unearth some information about him. Mumbling some platitudes to Maria, I got off the phone.

I wandered up front on the pretext of getting some water. Jon had the Kingman file spread out on his desk. However, a glance at his computer screen showed his attention was on Savannah and Brick. Good. That meant he wouldn't come into my office for a while.

I booted up my computer and made a halfhearted attempt at a simple Internet search. I didn't know Stone's full name and so wasn't surprised when I only came up with a kid from New Zealand and a porn actor. Next I tried a couple of online phone directories, but the numbers on his business card were obviously unlisted.

After that, I stopped playing around. I logged into the AutoTrax subscription database and started a search of the Lexus's license plate. Thirty seconds later I had a name, address and phone number…for that executive office suite on Rainbow Boulevard. Determined to get past the corporate barrier, I typed in the URL for the Clark County Tax Assessor.

The site allows you to search for real property records by the owner's name. This time I got lucky. Canongate Consultants owned a condo on Dean Martin Drive. Holy shit. The place was a two-bed, two-bath valued at $1,839,000. I clicked the link to see who'd signed the deed. No luck there, either, though. The signatory was Jamie Barrett of Canongate, Inc. in New York.

I seemed to be going around the same circle, so just for kicks I looked for Stone's name on the Bureau of Prisons Web site. He wasn't out on probation or parole as far as I could tell.

With a grunt of frustration, I shut down my computer. I had to rush to an orthopedic specialist appointment. I wanted to get video of a work comp claimant limping into the office with his cane. It would play nicely in court when I showed the footage of him in a pick-up basketball game right afterward.

From there I drove to North Vegas. Kenny Asher was still making himself scarce, but I had a nice chat with Mrs. Sharp while she hauled bags of shredded tree bark around her garden. "The yard looks a lot better than the last time I was here. Did Kenny do that?"

"Heavens, no. Poor Beth was out here cutting the grass while the children tried to pull out the weeds." She smiled, but her glance at the neighboring property was still critical. "They didn't always get the root, you see, so the weeds will be back."

"Where was Kenny?"

"Careful dear. You don't want to overfertilize." She moved my arm holding the hose to the next rosebush. "Mr. Asher was in the house, of course. As usual. I did see him carrying one of those large liquor store boxes, but couldn't locate the card you'd given me."

It was too much to hope that she'd gotten a picture. But Kenny had to run out of beer some time. After all the flower-beds and window boxes had been mulched, I gave Mrs. Sharp another one of my business cards and left her to finish watering her roses.

The next few hours back at the agency were spent creating and shuffling paperwork. By the time I'd finished, I was almost late for my other job. The bar was unusually busy for a Thursday. Mom had expertly herded a rowdy birthday crowd into the bar so they could keep celebrating without disrupting the other diners.

Lucky me.

The birthday boy was popular. Every friend he'd made since second grade seemed to be here. My shift was mostly a blur of raucous laughter as I refilled glasses and wore a path between the tables and the bar. Stone came in around ten, but we barely had a chance to talk.

"And here I'd thought to catch you during a free moment."

I shook my head and laughed, pouring a margarita with one hand and scooping ice cubes with the other. "No such thing tonight. You want a McEwan's?"

His left eyebrow arched in surprise. "You're keeping my ale on hand now, are you?"

"Yeah, well, I ordered a case a while back. Just to see if anybody would drink it." I shrugged and shook up another apple martini. "What? It's no big deal. It's just beer."

"As you say." A slow grin spread across his face.

"Do you want it or not?"

"Aye, I'll have a bottle. Since you just happen to have it in stock."

I shoved a frosted glass at him and went to deliver martinis. Stone sat and nursed his beer for a good half hour. Still, with the bar short-staffed and jumping, there wasn't time for him to do more than let me know that Gray had been on his best behavior all day.

"We'll give it another go tomorrow. Have you got Cavanaugh's schedule?"

"Yeah, Maria told me he's on day shift—4:00 a.m. until noon. As long as that doesn't change, I can take him after court. I'm on the witness list, but the attorney thinks the case will settle."

"Right, then. I'll follow after the girl and see what else she's up to."

It was disconcerting how easily we'd fallen into a working partnership. I didn't want to think about what that meant personally. But I sure as hell wasn't acquiescing because of his gifts. It just made sense to split the surveillance, that's all.

The birthday boy looked like he was in for the long haul, so Stone drank the last of his ale and stood up. "Shall I stop back after closing and escort you to your vehicle?"

"Nah, don't bother. It's going to take me a while to clean up after the party animals, then I've got to help Dad and Rafe with the weekly inventory. One of them will walk me out."

"Ring me when you get home."

I avoided his gaze, instead watching the frozen tequila swirling in the blender. "Listen, I appreciated what you did last night, okay? But let's not make a habit of it."

He reached over to tilt my chin. "Eventually you'll have to make a decision, Stella. Because what we are to each other isn't going away and neither am I."

With that, he strode out the door. Plastering on a smile for the customers, I went back to work. But inside I seethed. I wasn't about to spend every free moment repaying his gift. I had my own life and I liked it that way. He'd be smart not to hold his breath waiting for my call.

Besides, by the time I pulled up to my house at three-twenty-five the next morning, I just wanted to crash. Stumbling off the Harley rubbing my eyes, I tripped one of the sensors. I was instantly blinded by floodlights bright enough that planes could land in my yard.

I cursed the spots dancing in my vision and tried to remember the code for the garage. Was it 7621 or 7261? To hell with it. I was tired and the bike could stay in the driveway tonight. I walked up the path to the front door and flipped my keys to the one for the new dead bolt.

Too late, I remembered that I had to turn the smaller key for the alarm before opening the door. An ominous mechanical beeping filled the foyer. I spun for the keypad on the wall but still couldn't remember the code. 7162? 7126? Dammit! As the beeps crescendoed into a wail, the security system didn't make me feel protected so much as imprisoned.

As soon as I got this thing shut off, I was going to call Stone after all. Call him a lot of nasty names, that is.

CHAPTER TWENTY-THREE

Expect the Unexpected

UNLIKE SOME P.I.s, I actually enjoy getting dressed up.

The best cases were the ones where I could go all out with disguises. I have a collection of hats, wigs, eyeglasses and vocal imitations. I once talked to a guy in a bar over the course of an hour without him ever realizing the brunette, the blonde and the redhead he'd been hitting on were the same woman.

This morning, though, I just had to dress for court. I'd put on a light blue summer suit, a cream-colored blouse and camel pumps. Mom had bought the clothes for me on one of our rare shopping excursions. I'd commented on the outfit and, thrilled by my interest in anything feminine, Mom took it right off the mannequin.

I'd styled my hair in a chignon and put on enough makeup to look professional. In my briefcase were both the original video-tapes, and one that showed highlights of interest. I had extra copies of all of my reports in Kim Westgaard's case. An envelope held enlarged photos of the claimant. I was totally prepared.

To sit on a hard wooden bench in a stuffy hallway for two and a half hours.

After waiting the whole morning for *Denton v. Westgaard Hardware* to be called, opposing council had suddenly agreed to the settlement. I'd still bill for my time. I was walking out of the Regional Justice Center with the insurance adjuster when someone caught my arm.

"Steele? I knew you were here this morning, but I almost didn't recognize you."

I attempted a warm smile, but couldn't look the man in the eye. Instead, I made introductions. "Maryellen Moser, this is Doug Holbrook."

"Hi. How are you?" Maryellen's face had the look most people get when they meet Mr. Holbrook, sort of flattered and awed at the same time.

He's tall and lanky with a shock of white hair, very formal posture and old-fashioned manners. His quiet confidence and brilliant mind made you feel safe putting your life into his big, gentle hands. It was those traits that had persuaded my parents to hire him.

G. Douglas Holbrook was an elder statesman, a grandfather figure, a keeper of confidences.

He shook Maryellen's hand in greeting, and then dismissed her in the same breath. "It was a pleasure to meet you, Ms. Moser. If I could impose on you, though, I need to speak to Steele for just a moment. I'm sure you understand."

Once we were alone, I clutched my briefcase and shifted from one foot to the other. "How did you know I was here?"

"That young man at your office told me. Unfortunately, he wasn't sure which courtroom you'd be in, so now I don't have much time."

"Okay, what did you need to—?"

"I'm due to appear before Judge Aguilera's bench in five minutes. Stop by my office on Monday."

"Um, sure, but what is this about?"

His penetrating gaze seemed to both pass judgment and invite confession. "Your brother called me yesterday."

"What?" Vince never contacted anyone. He didn't even answer my letters. "What did he say?"

"I wish I'd found you sooner, but it will have to keep until next week." He glanced at his watch. "I'm sorry, I have to go. Judge Aguilera hates when people show up late to his courtroom."

"Wait, Mr. Holbrook—"

"Call my office about Monday, Steele." With a brief wave, he jogged back into the courthouse.

Watching him vanish inside, I felt like my protective shield was disappearing along with him. In that last letter I'd asked Vince to keep silently paying the price for my relationship with Bobby. Instead of responding to me, he'd called his lawyer.

Maybe I'd finally asked for one too many pieces of my brother's soul.

Frustrated, worried and helpless to do anything until after the weekend, I started walking toward the parking lot. There was no need to get upset until I was sure there was something to be upset about. And if I repeated that enough times, I might even believe it.

I'd borrowed another one of Anna's cars, another Honda, and so headed for the nearest drive-through window. Once the Guardians had confirmed my identity and shut off the alarm last night, I'd gotten a whole four hours of sleep and missed breakfast before rushing to the courthouse.

I ordered something that I could eat with one hand then called Jon for any messages. I only cared about the one that still made my gut clench. Mr. Holbrook's message said *something came up*. That must be a standard male catch phrase, seeing how Stone had once used it, too. I'd be glad never to hear it again.

Turning into the nearest parking space, I shut off the engine. The few bites of burrito supremo I'd eaten were threatening to resurface. Something had come up? What the hell did that mean? If anything had happened out at Indian Springs, I would have heard about it.

At least I thought so….

My thumb fumbled over the buttons as I dialed Douglas Holbrook's office and made an appointment for ten o'clock Monday morning.

Drumming my fingers on the steering wheel, I tried to figure out what to do next.

The logical answer would be to call Joey or Mom. But neither of them knew I was still in contact with Mr. Holbrook.

Or why.

Cursing, I stuffed the rest of my lunch into the carry-out bag. I'd lost my appetite. In the meantime, I had other work to do. Mentally shoving my fears aside, I called Maria at work to find out where her husband might be.

"Hi, it's Steele. I just—"

"Mrs. Bagdasarian. How are you?"

I smirked, instantly remembering the code name from high school. We'd used the "fictional friend's mother inviting us to stay over" whenever we wanted to go out late. "You're not alone. Got it. I know Gray's shift is supposed to end at noon. Any idea where he might be?"

"Yes, I'm sure I have that with me. When do you need it?"

I glanced at my watch. "It'll take me about fifteen minutes to get to the Palazzo. Does he use the employee parking lot?"

"Of course, that will be fine. I'm sorry to cut you off, but my husband has a doctor's appointment and I need to talk to him before he leaves."

A doctor's appointment. How original. "Okay, see if you can stall him long enough for me to find his car in the garage."

"Thank you, Mrs. Bagdasarian."

"Talk to you later, Maria."

Half an hour later, I was trailing Cavanaugh's Mercedes south on Paradise Road. I'd taken off my suit jacket and rolled up the sleeves of my blouse. I'd also exchanged the high heels for a pair of running shoes. If I had to get out of the car, I'd look like an office worker on her lunch hour.

My next call was to Stone's cell phone. "What's Caitlyn up to?"

"Hello, Stella. I'm quite well, thanks. So good of you to ask. And you?"

"Hi. Fine. What's going on?"

"All business today, eh?" When I didn't respond, he went on. "I spent a thoroughly uneventful morning outside of her apartment building. She didn't emerge until just past eleven. That's when things finally got interesting."

"Really? Where did she go?"

"To a bank branch near the Nellis Air Force Base. There weren't many people about, so I pretended to make phone calls and then withdraw cash from the ATM. I watched through the glass while Caitlyn went into the safe-deposit vault."

At the next light, I followed Gray when he made a left turn. "Great, you've found the money they stole. Big Frank will be relieved."

"Not quite. Caitlyn was inside for barely five minutes before storming out again. She fairly ran from the bank, looking furious enough to kill. I'd say it's a safe bet that whatever she expected to find was gone."

Up ahead, the Mercedes signaled another turn. "I guess there's no honor among thieves after all. Where is she now?"

"Another cheap hotel, presumably waiting for Cavanaugh. This one is the Vista Buena Inn on—"

"Sierra Vista Drive. Gray's right in front of me." I glanced around the parking lot. "I see the red Mustang. Where are you?"

"Look for a silver Maserati near the Welcome sign."

My brows shot up. "I thought you drove a Lexus."

"I do. However, today's Friday."

"Oh, well sure. That explains everything." Nonplussed though I was, I didn't ask for details at first. Then I just couldn't help myself. "You have day-of-the-week cars. Exactly how *quite rich and rather wealthy* are you?"

He chuckled softly. "I inherited a minor peerage when my uncle died. Suffice it to say I can afford to indulge my liking for luxury vehicles."

I left it at that since I was driving a different car, too. One that I needed to hurry up and park. By the time I grabbed the camera out of my backpack, Caitlyn was already stalking toward the Mercedes. I rolled my window down just as she started yelling.

"Where the hell is it?"

Cavanaugh opened his door and stepped out, one hand raised in a placating gesture. He looked around, speaking softly. Because of the distance I couldn't catch what he said, but Caitlyn's reply was loud and clear.

"Don't tell me to calm down! I want an answer. What did you do with it all?"

I snapped several pictures of Gray placing his hands on her shoulders, of his oh-so-sincere expression. From this angle it appeared to be a tender moment instead of a confrontational one. When Caitlyn shook him off, he turned her by the arm and pointed toward the hotel.

He said something that made her look around also, as if just realizing they were exposed. Finally she shrugged and nodded her head. Gray walked toward the registration office. She glared after him, visibly angry, one hand pressed to her stomach like she was going to be sick.

I captured the look on her face but lowered the camera when, instead of waiting for Cavanaugh, she went back to the Mustang. Something about her defiantly anxious expression triggered a hunch. Going with my gut, I made a snap decision. I hit the redial button on my cell phone.

"Hey, Stone, you take Gray. I'm going after Caitlyn."

"Why the change of plans?"

I started my engine and put the Honda into first gear, but waited for Caitlyn to pull out. "Call it women's intuition. I think Cavanaugh just told her where he moved the money and she's about to counter his double cross."

"What makes you—"

"Later. She's leaving."

I stayed a few cars behind Caitlyn for the next half hour. She seemed to be driving around aimlessly, only stopping once for soda at a Circle K. I followed her around the Boulevard Mall, down Maryland Parkway, across Flamingo Road. She finally turned off near Desert Springs Hospital.

Caitlyn drove into the parking lot of a row of medical offices. When she got out of the Mustang, she stood beside the car staring at the ground. Then she walked toward the end of the building and went into the last door. The sign out front read Desert Rose Women's Clinic.

My instinct that something was wrong had been right. But my hunch that the case would soon be resolved was wrong. In fact, I'd say the Cavanaugh situation had just gotten even more complicated.

CHAPTER TWENTY-FOUR

The Sound of Silence

I WAITED OUTSIDE the clinic for forty minutes, hot, thirsty and bored out of my mind.

At one point I walked in, pretending to be a new patient, just so I could use the bathroom. I didn't see Caitlyn. She must have been in the exam room already. However, her name had been written several lines above mine on the sign-in sheet. She was scheduled to see Dr. Perez-Allard, one of the obstetricians.

I guess that was all the proof I needed. Cavanaugh had definitely cheated on Maria more than once.

Another hour passed, then I followed Caitlyn to the pharmacy, a dry cleaners, the grocery store and finally to her apartment building. I couldn't be sure that a strange car would go unnoticed, so I settled in with my binoculars back at the grocery store across the highway.

Caitlyn might get a sudden urge to run out and count Big Frank's stolen loot.

She didn't. She spent the rest of the afternoon inside. I wondered what she was doing, how she felt. Was she calling her friends and family with joyous news, or lying in bed crying her eyes out? I wondered if she'd told Gray yet and how he'd reacted to his impending fatherhood.

Then again, it wasn't my concern. My job was to take the pictures, not to speculate on their effect.

Hearing the first notes of Sinatra, I reached for my cell phone. "Midnight."

"It's me, Stella. Where are you?"

"Camped across the road from Caitlyn's apartment. You?"

"I'm at the Sunset Ridge casino over to Henderson, watching Cavanaugh lose heavily at blackjack."

"Really. How heavily?"

"Well, he's already lost his shirt and his trousers aren't far behind. The bloody fool is knocking back gin and tonics alone at a hundred-dollar-minimum table."

I groaned in mock pain. Even the most novice gambler knows not to go up against the dealer. The only thing dumber than that was to chase your bets, thinking the cards will get better soon. "How long has he been there?"

"Since leaving that hotel. He was quite put out when he saw that Caitlyn had gone. He made several calls on his mobile, but I take it she didn't answer. Where did she hie off to?"

Without questioning why I should protect her, I said, "She just ran some errands before going home. Hang on. I think I see her now."

I raised the binoculars and adjusted the focus across the rush-hour traffic. It was Caitlyn, dressed in her Palazzo uniform, coming down the front steps. I slid a glance at the dashboard clock, noting the time. She got into the Mustang and started out of the parking lot. I didn't bother to follow.

"She's going to work. I doubt she's going to lead us anywhere else, so I'm calling it a night. What about you?"

"I'll watch Cavanaugh for a bit longer, then I have other business to attend."

I waited for him to elaborate. I waited for him to ask what I had planned. I waited for him to suggest dinner, or drinks or down and dirty sex. But he didn't say anything else. The pause stretched on until I started to feel stupid.

"Well, I guess I'll talk to you later."

"Have a good night, Stella."

He hung up, leaving me to toss my phone into the passenger seat with unnecessary force. What the hell was that about? Was he playing head games or maybe trying to get back at me? God, that man irritated me. In the four days he'd been back in my life, I'd felt constantly annoyed and unsure of myself. In a word? Confused.

I wasn't sure about getting involved in a serious relationship with Stone. I wasn't even sure about having a casual relationship. And it's not like I could have seen him tonight anyway, since I had to work the bar. But, dammit, a girl liked to be asked at least.

The agency was on my way to the second job. Jon wouldn't be back in until Monday, so I stopped by long enough to clear my desk for the weekend. I opened up and flipped on the lights. Given recent events, I relocked the door behind me. As I passed the reception desk I saw that Jon had left me two message slips.

Sasha Merrit, one of the waitresses at the restaurant, wanted me to check her daughter's latest boyfriend for any criminal records. Jill Showalter had called as well. I rolled my eyes. She wanted me to get proof that her neighbor's garden statue was an alien king who wanted to make Jill his love slave.

Starving, I walked down the hallway to the kitchen. Jon had turned off the espresso machine so I had to settle for a Coke out of the fridge. Opening the freezer, I picked out one of the entrees left over from Papa's restaurant. After shoving it into the microwave, I headed back to my office. The first thing I did was to check the windows. Then I turned on the lights.

While my computer booted up, I dug the digital camera out of my backpack and started downloading the photos from its memory card. I pulled the Cavanaugh stuff out of my in-basket. Embezzlement, gambling, missing loot, possible pregnancy. This case had it all and probably a lot more.

But I'd only been hired to get evidence of Gray's cheating and I'd done that. It was time to close the file on this one.

I gulped down little bits of heaven disguised as lasagna while writing up my first and final report. Gauging the time, and assuming Cavanaugh was still making donations to the Sunrise Ridge blackjack fund, I called Maria at her home. The housekeeper answered and then put me on hold.

Maria came to the phone a few minutes later. "Hi, Steele. Are you looking for Gray again?"

Her speech sounded blurry, not quite inebriated but not sober either. "Are you okay?"

"I get migraines, so I took something for my headache. What can I do for you?"

"Do you have some time Monday afternoon? I'd like to meet and go over the case with you."

She dragged in a long, slow breath. "You found something, didn't you?"

I winced as she started to cry softly. I normally don't give bad news over the phone, but there was no use in lying to her. "I'm sorry, Maria. I know how hard this must be."

"I didn't want to believe—this can't be—oh God, I can't believe this is happening to me!" She was openly sobbing now.

Squirming in my chair, I tried to get off the line. "Listen, maybe you should go and, I don't know, lay down or something. We can talk about this on Mon—"

"Tomorrow."

"Excuse me?"

"I said, tomorrow. You have to meet me tomorrow. I can't wait until Monday."

I rubbed the back of my neck and held on to a sigh. On the one hand, I'd get this over with sooner. On the other hand, Monday would allow her time to calm down. In the end, though, she didn't give me a choice. I agreed to meet her at Trattoria Bertolini for lunch at eleven-thirty.

Thirty minutes later, after printing off several shots of Gray and Caitlyn in the least offensive embraces, as well as a copy of my report, I stuffed it all into my backpack. Then I stripped off what was left of my suit, went to the credenza drawer where I keep extra clothes and changed for my other job.

I loosened my hair—I'd had it in the chignon all day—and pulled on a clean T-shirt. This one read, B.I.T.C.H. means Babe In Total Control of Herself. The phone rang as I was leaving. I picked it up at Jon's desk, thinking Maria was calling back.

"Midnight Investigation Services."

No one answered.

Silence curled and twisted along the phone line, wrapping me in its menace. I held my breath as my heart tap-danced on my ribs. Listening hard, wondering if he would say anything, I shivered as anxiety skittered along my nerves. The quiet continued.

I gripped the receiver tightly and closed my eyes. Seeking strength, I concentrated on logic. My fear was what he wanted. He wanted me off-balance and demoralized. He wanted me weak. I opened my eyes again and stared out of the front window before drawing a shallow breath.

"Fuck. You."

I slammed down the phone, clinging to my anger. I refused to be intimidated. I told myself that several times as I left the agency. Once I got to the bar, I'd be surrounded by bright lights and people for the next six hours. But after that…

After that I'd have to go home alone.

CHAPTER TWENTY-FIVE

Just Another Job

"So, YOU AND Steele, huh? I had no idea when I hired ya that she was your, uh, what, girlfriend, partner, what?"

"She's mine. Let's leave it at that." Cameron took another sip of the single-malt Glenfiddich in his glass. The fiery trail of scotch melted some of the ice crystals forming in his veins. He set the glass aside.

Frank DiMarco chuckled knowingly. "Yeah, that's how I felt about my Gina, God rest her soul. I knew the minute I laid eyes on her she'd be my one and only." His voice turned hard. "Too bad that asshole my daughter had to go and marry don't feel the same way about Maria."

Cameron smiled tightly. "Marriage isn't for everyone."

He tipped his head back and watched cigar smoke spiral toward the already cloudy ceiling. Though DiMarco was puffing away on his, Cameron simply gave the tip an occasional rap to keep ash from falling to the carpet. They sat in what might appear a companionable silence. But he sensed what was coming.

"You're gonna be able to get my money back, right?"

"I'd thought the girl was the key to locating it. However, it seems that Cavanaugh has pulled a fast one. I don't think we'll get much from her."

DiMarco smacked his glass down on the tabletop. "I'm just supposed to overlook four hundred large? Just go on actin' like nothin's wrong?"

Cameron slowly turned his head to look him in the eye. "I always finish what I start. Always."

"Good. 'Cause I definitely want this shit finished."

"Finished how?"

DiMarco looked away, his expression making it clear that he wouldn't—or couldn't—say what he meant. "My son-in-law needs to be taught a lesson. You make sure it's one he don't never forget."

Cameron fisted then flexed his hand, watching the smoke. Memories drifted to the ceiling along with it. One of these days he ought to find himself a hobby. There must be something he was good at besides violence….

Resigned to never collecting stamps or building ship models, he got up and walked out. He had a job to do.

CHAPTER TWENTY-SIX

In the Heat of the Night

HOT, DRY AIR smacked me in the face as soon as I opened the back door. At two-thirty in the morning, the sky over Vegas looked like an old bruise, murky purple with a yellowish tinge. It looked exactly how I felt. It'd been a long, eventful, emotional week and I was glad it was over. Almost.

I still had to actually leave the bar.

Standing in the doorway, I stared out at the night. And the nearly empty parking lot. My cousin Tom, the other bartender, had already left for a date. Papa had taken Mom home as soon as the restaurant closed, and Rafe left not long after them. So now I was by myself, faltering over that first step. And feeling like an idiot the longer I stood here.

I'm not exactly one of Charlie's Angels, but I can hold my own when I have to. I grew up with three rough-and-tumble big brothers. I'd taken on a guy twice my weight and somehow lived to tell about it. But, once I left this building, it was so very *night* out there….

Suddenly I heard Aunt Gloria's voice in my head. *Fear is a damned useless emotion. If you want to get anywhere in life, all you need is a healthy respect for the stuff that might kill you.*

Squaring my shoulders, I pulled the door shut, set the locks and marched out into the darkness. Actually it wasn't even that dark. In fact, there was a streetlight down the block, and another one near the silver Maserati parked next to my borrowed Honda… I halted midstride, finally recognizing Stone's latest ride.

He was leaning on the hood and waiting. For me.

The artificial light gave him a golden aura, highlighting his dark-blond hair and emphasizing his muscular build. He looked good—strong and solid. In fact, right now, he was the best thing I'd ever seen. It took considerable willpower not to run to him.

Instead, I reined myself back, like I wasn't at all surprised or glad to see him. I slung my backpack over one shoulder and put a little saunter into my stride. When I reached him, I casually rested my hip against the Honda's fender, matching his stance.

He glanced at the lettering on my chest. "Nice shirt."

"What are you doing here, Stone?"

"What do you think, Stella?"

The streetlight cast shadows below the planes of his face, making it hard for me to read his expression. "Is this your way of asking?"

"No. I'm telling."

Normally, that would have gotten a rise out of me. But not tonight. Tonight I was too tired and lonely and, yes, dammit, scared. "Fine. I'll see you at home."

Only when he cocked his head and gave me a quizzical look did I realize what I'd said. "You know what I meant."

"Aye, I did. But I doubt either of us is in the mood to argue right now. Shall we?"

I nodded once and got into my car.

Ten or so minutes later I pulled up to my house. After activating the magic decoder ring that now opens the sacred portal, I eased into the garage. Stone parked the Maserati and got out. I'd half expected Stone to flash his headlights and keep driving. The other half of me fidgeted with my key ring like a teenager on a first date.

"Thanks for seeing me home."

"I'll see you to the door, as well. Those were quite colorful expletives you used last night."

I avoided his gaze, anticipating what I'd see there, not sure I wanted to expose the vulnerability in mine. Somehow I remembered the correct sequence and managed to open the front door. I tossed my backpack inside but didn't flip on the light. Hesitating on the threshold, I spoke over my shoulder.

"Um, do you want to come in for a drink or something?"

"Or something."

The low rumble of his voice held both a challenge and a sensual promise. It was a promise I knew from experience he could fulfill. I stared down at my hands, twisting the keys between my fingers. "I don't know if I want to let you in."

He understood that I wasn't talking about the house. "We're already working together as partners. Over the past few days we've shared information, surveillance duties and one hell of a kiss. Is it really so great a leap to sharing more?"

I finally looked into his eyes. Despite the dim, I could see that his gaze still had a touch of frost. However, I also sensed it had nothing to do with me. Could it be he wanted to be alone tonight even less than I did? Still I hesitated, caught between my growing need and the unknown.

God, there was so much unknown. We were both prisoners to the secrets we kept.

"You're no coward, Stella, so stop running from me."

"You're the one who ran." For once there was no real heat in my retort, just a question.

Something akin to regret flashed across his expression, quickly stilled. "Aye, I did. But I came back."

"Why?"

He frowned and looked away from me. "You know why."

"Tell me anyway." I reached out to him then, touching my fingertips to his face.

"For you, love." His voice was merely a whisper this time, his tone a caress that almost disguised his uncertainty. "I came back for you. And for this."

Easing me closer, he enfolded me in his arms and guided my lips to his. He kissed me once, twice, with a sweetness so unexpected it damn near brought tears to my eyes. I clutched the back of his head, slanting my mouth over his again and again with brutal sexuality. I didn't need an emotional ambush on top of everything else.

Cameron managed to get under my skin anyway. He simply stroked my hair with gentle caresses and passively accepted whatever I dished out. That told me more than I wanted to deal with now about his intentions and our future. I tried holding myself back. But even as lust surged through my body, against my better judgment, my heart sighed in welcome.

Just like the first time, I was going to leap without looking.

Breaking the kiss, I eased away and turned to go into the house. As I walked along the hall toward the master bedroom, I didn't hear the front door close. But I didn't have to look to know that he followed me. The crazy sparks igniting the air were all the indication I needed.

In my room, I lit the aromatic candles the decorator had left. The soft glow and the combined scents of patchouli and vanilla set the mood. But instead of undressing, I sat on the bed to wait. That's when I saw him in my peripheral vision, resting his forearm on the frame, his big body filling the doorway.

"What are you doing all the way over there?"

"Ask me." His pale gaze pierced the distance between us.

Tilting my head coyly, I smiled at him. "Did you have a particular question in mind, or can I just make one up?"

"There's been no one since you."

It was a courtesy, a safety issue, and yet the significance of his words thrilled me. I answered haltingly, truly hating to acknowledge his impact on my life. "Not for me, either."

Sexual heat fairly shimmered off him and his answering smile was slow and seductive.

"So how come you're still so far away?"

"I told you I'd not go near your bed again without an invite. So ask me, Stella. Because I'd hate to break a promise."

"I desire and humbly request the pleasure of your company this night." I quoted from one of Jon's manuscripts in a mocking Scottish accent, then slipped into a low curtsy. Not very regal when done in motorcycle boots and a B.I.T.C.H. T-shirt.

He laughed softly and finally came into the room. Watching me watch him, he started unbuttoning his shirt. One thing about Stone that had deeply attracted me from the first was his comfort in his clothes and in his skin. A moment later, he stood before me in nothing but that magnificent skin, unselfconsciously letting me look my fill.

The flickering candlelight threw his body into sharp relief, accentuating well-honed muscles and long limbs. The breath caught in my lungs as I admired him. My blood thickened and throbbed like the hard-on jutting proudly from between his thighs. He was absolutely beautiful and all mine tonight.

I quickly shed my own clothes and returned the favor. His eyes burned as they swept over me, all traces of ice long since melted away. My heart wrenched and a shiver of longing danced over my bare skin. He was looking at me, through me and into me. Yes. My answer to everything at this moment was yes.

I held out my hand and he moved to stand in front of me. When he stroked my cheek, I closed my eyes against the stunning effect of his touch. His nearness affected me on too many levels, leaving me both comforted and confused.

Covering his hand with mine, I turned it over to kiss his fingers. When I heard the faint hiss of his breath, my eyes flew open. Gingerly angling his hand toward the light, I saw that the knuckles were swollen and bruised. I immediately recognized the look of them. Either he'd been at the gym boxing without gloves or he'd been in one hell of a fight.

"What did you do?" The line of his normally soft mouth thinned in response. "Stone? What happened?"

His expression became a mask and I knew that he wouldn't answer. With a heavy sigh, I started to pull our hands apart and take a step back. He refused to release my fingers. I refused to look at him and cursed the goddamned silence that kept us apart despite how close we stood. I tried again.

"No." His rich baritone and complex tone gave the word more weight than a simple command. "Stella, no."

Force I could have dealt with. Charm I could have ignored. But the raw emotion I heard in his voice couldn't be easily dismissed. Not when it so clearly echoed my own feelings. In sorrow and anger, insecurity and need, I did what women have done throughout the ages.

I turned back and gave myself to my man.

Our bodies fused, his arms going around my waist, my hands raking through his hair. His mouth covered mine hungrily. This kiss was hard and demanding and utterly basic. In return mine was hot and eager and punishing. Our kisses bordering on violence, we fell onto the bed in a tangle of urgent desire.

His hand stroked my ass while I nipped at the erogenous spot on the side of his neck. His body shuddered with pleasure and he groaned aloud. Lifting me, he suckled my breast, teasing my nipple with his tongue. I braced one hand against the wall, reveling in the sweet tugging sensation that traveled all the way to the apex of my thighs.

After my other breast received the same attention, I moved in for another kiss. A *looong* one. Then, I slid down, settled my head on his thigh and took him into my mouth. His fingers tangled in the strands of my hair while I licked and fondled him to the point of pain.

He was breathing in harsh rasps when he finally cradled my head, compelling me to look up. "Stella."

"I want you, too, Cameron." I cat-crept back up his body, making sure our skin never lost contact.

I threw one leg over him to straddle his hips, but he grabbed me around the waist and rolled me underneath him. Cuffing my wrists, he drew my arms over my head and parted my legs with his knee. His mouth came down on mine in a fiercely erotic kiss as he penetrated and impaled me.

Gravity doubled in the pit of my belly, eliciting a moan that bubbled out of my throat. The sex was wild, reckless and rough. Scorching tension coiled inside me, making me ache for release. But at the same time it felt so damned good to have him thrusting into me, over and over again.

My whole being trembled, desperate for the orgasm building like a storm inside me. I dug my nails into his back and arched my hips, silently begging for more. Then not so silently when he slipped his hand between us and found the button that ignited my afterburners. Writhing in mindless ecstasy, I cried out as waves of pleasure ripped though me.

My climax seemed to turn him on even more. He was moaning low in his throat as he drove himself into my body. I reached down to cup the cheeks of his ass and urge him deeper. When my teeth scraped that sensitive spot on his neck, he finally went over the edge. With a growl that sounded like equal parts torture and triumph, he plunged into me one last time and came.

Time seemed to slow along with my pulse. We lay together, the mingled sound of our labored breathing filling the room, the sheen of sweat fusing our skin, until his weight became uncomfortable. I poked him in the ribs so he'd get off me. And he did—right onto my hair.

"Ow!"

"Sorry, love. You've such pretty hair, it would be a shame to rip it off your head." He raised up on his forearm and brushed the length of it out of the way.

Cameron rolled onto his back and I curled up against his side, resting my head on my elbow. His arms were crossed over his chest, drawing my attention. I traced the outline of the tattoo on his triceps. "What does this winged dagger mean?"

"It's a flaming sword of retribution, actually. The British Special Air Service insignia."

"Is that what those bruises were about, retribution?" I stroked a finger just behind his knuckles.

He lowered his eyes and was quiet for so long I thought that he'd again refuse to answer. But after a moment he spoke in a clipped voice. "Those were from an errand."

I stared at him for a moment but he still wouldn't look at me. With an impatient sigh, I jerked away from him and sat on the edge of the bed. Hands pressing into the mattress, I hunched my shoulders and talked to the wall. "This isn't going to work, Stone."

"Perhaps not, in the end."

I glanced over, frowning. "Then why even—?"

"Because of the intangibles, Stella." I felt him shift position, heard the conviction in his voice. "Tell me all we did was fuck just now and I won't believe you. Tell me you feel nothing when we're together and I'll call you ten kinds of a liar."

"There's a lot more involved than just sex. The problem isn't what's obvious—it's what's hidden."

"Are you ready to confess then?" I whipped around to stare at him, a cold knot in my gut. "Want to tell me all of your dark and sordid secrets? Are you certain you want to know mine?"

Apprehension scampered along my nerves as we studied each other. Searching his eyes, now glacier blue and distant, I wondered if the black marks on my soul could be seen. I broke eye contact first, twisted away and kept quiet.

"Is that a no, love? Then don't ask me what you can't answer."

I shivered, telling myself it was because of the air-conditioning on my damp skin. Hanging my head, I drew in a deep breath. Like a circle in a spiral, we'd come back to where we'd begun—unsure of why we'd gotten together and unwilling to let go. "What are we supposed to do about this... About us?"

He reached over for my hand, gripping it firmly in his own. "We live in the moment, sort it out as we go along. It's all we can do."

"Is it enough?"

"For now. Until it isn't anymore."

When he tugged my fingers, I leaned over to kiss him lightly. Then I got up and went into the bathroom to clean up. He went in after me, blowing out the candles as he reentered the room. I waited for him under the covers. He settled in and wrapped his strong arms around me. With only the slightest hesitation, I slid my arm across his flat belly.

"Cameron?"

"Aye, love?"

"I want my new bed."

He made a soft sound of amusement and I knew that he smiled in the darkness. "I'll see that you get it."

CHAPTER TWENTY-SEVEN

More Than Words

THE FIRST TIME I awoke, the sun had just begun to rise. Cameron was already up. Mmmmm.

My body started vibrating under his hands before I was completely conscious. Every nerve ending tingled with awareness. I kept my eyes closed, focused internally on the sensations. His fingers glided over my flesh, slow and impatient at the same time. My breath was ragged, my thighs damp with desire when I finally looked at him.

He was even more gorgeous in the early light, softer somehow. And yet I'd never seen anyone so intensely focused. Being the object of that attention was an exhilarating sensation. His mouth widened into a sensual smile as he lowered his head to kiss me. I sighed against his lips. That was all the encouragement he needed. Settling his hips between my legs, he levered his weight onto his elbows and kissed me deeper.

I stroked my hands over the smooth, rigid muscles of his back as he slid into me. He set a gentle, drawn-out rhythm, so different from last night's erotic assault. I nibbled a pattern on his shoulder; he nuzzled his face in my hair. He tucked his hands beneath my ass, pleasuring me with long, deep thrusts. The exquisitely fluid friction continued, accelerated, until the tension burst with our orgasms.

Gathering me into his arms, he rolled us over so that I lay on his chest. We hadn't spoken while we made love; we didn't now, either. Somehow it all felt very…right. But I was too tired and sated to think about the implications of this un-expected intimacy. The steady beat of his heart lulled me back to sleep.

The next time I woke up, it was to a cool, empty bed. For a couple of disoriented seconds, I wondered if that last bout of sex had been a dream. Then the tender aches I felt when I rolled over assured me that Stone had really been here. But he wasn't here now. So I started looking around for a piece of paper.

Call me cynical, go ahead.

He hadn't left a note this time and, once again, he'd ne-glected to say goodbye. Nothing. Not a word. A heavy sense of loss weighed on my chest, crushing the breath out of me. I flung my forearms over my eyes, struggling to crawl out from under my churning emotions. As always, I clung fast to anger. Otherwise I might sink into the hurt and drown.

Just because we'd felt something, experienced some kind of connection, that didn't mean it would last. And just because we'd made love sure as hell didn't mean I was going to fall in love. How stupid would that be? Well, no way was I going to waste tears or another thought on him. Scrubbing a hand over my face, I looked over at the bedside clock.

Oh, shit!

I scrambled off the bed, tripping when my leg got caught in the tangled sheet. Shit, shit, shit. Running into the bath-room, I wrenched the tub valve to full and pulled on a shower cap—no time to wash my hair. I was supposed to meet Maria in less than thirty-five minutes.

Faster than I'd thought possible, I was dressed in jeans, boots and a button-down shirt with my hair in a simple ponytail. I'd brushed my teeth and smeared on some moistur-izer, but hadn't bothered with makeup. Stomping down the hall, trying to remember where I'd left my backpack, I pulled up short in the foyer and blinked in surprised confusion.

Stone was barefoot and shirtless and casually sitting at the breakfast bar reading the *Journal*. I stared at him.

"Morning, love." He got up to hand me a cardboard cup

from the local Starbucks. "Sorry it's gone a bit cold. I can fly a small plane, but couldn't figure out your coffeemaker."

"Um, thanks." Shaken by my sudden flash of relief, I automatically accepted the cup. "I, uh, have to go. I'm meeting a client…"

He smiled, understanding but amused. "Well, that lets us avoid the morning-after awkwardness, eh?"

I nodded, unsure under the circumstances how to get rid of him. He looked damned comfortable in my kitchen. I was sort of okay with him being there. It was freaking me out.

"I've made arrangements for the bed. It should be delivered within the next hour, along with new furniture for the living and guest rooms. Once it's all in, I'll lock up behind me."

"Thanks. Thanks a lot." I nodded some more while I tried to think of what to say. And what to feel.

His smile flattened out as he held my gaze. "You thought I'd gone again."

"It doesn't matter to me." I shrugged, the very picture of nonchalance. "I don't care."

His expression went utterly still, but the blue of his eyes intensified, the glaciers thawing. "What if I wanted you to?"

A dozen clichés crowded on my tongue: "Only time will tell," "Actions speak louder than words," "The proof is in the pudding." How dumb is that last one? So I didn't say any of them out loud. I wanted his body, not his heart. What did I care whether he came or went? It's not like we were—

I felt a funny little flutter in my stomach and my throat was suddenly tight. Averting my gaze, I turned to look for my pack. It was right where I'd dropped it by the front door. Hefting it onto my shoulder, I walked past him to the garage entry. "Don't forget to lock the French doors this time."

"YOU ARE LATE."

Trattoria Bertolini was all but empty this early, so few heads turned at Maria's greeting. The words sounded especially sharp in this upscale rustic atmosphere where one would expect only the soft clinks of fine china and the whisper of new money.

The setting was somebody's overdone idea of what an authentic Tuscan *ristorante* should look like. Maria had dressed the part. She wore a simple peasant blouse—made of silk—and a long black skirt—also silk—with a wide red belt. Her hair fell loosely on her shoulders, her makeup was minimal, but her gaze was far from simple as she tracked my approach.

I barely resisted the impulse to check my watch as I sat down. I thought I'd made damned good time, considering I'd breezed past the maitre d' only six minutes behind schedule.

"Our appointment was for eleven-thirty. Not even eleven-thirty-six. Eleven-thirty." The harsh rebuke sounded odd given Maria's breathy little-girl voice.

When our waiter materialized at my side, I didn't hesitate to order a drink despite the fact that it wasn't even noon. Based on her welcome, I anticipated a long and difficult meeting. "Vodka—one of the top-shelf brands—on the rocks and orange juice."

"A screwdriver, yes, ma'am." He nodded obsequiously.

"No, I want the vodka shot and a separate glass of orange juice. Thanks." As he left, I leaned forward in my chair and gave Maria what I hoped sounded like my most sincere apology. "I'm sorry for the wait, I really am. I was unavoidably delayed with another matter."

For a second, it didn't look like she'd let it go. But, since I had something she wanted, Maria backed off.

"It's all right." Her smile said otherwise and she made quite the production of looking at *her* watch. "I realize I'm not your only client."

The waiter came back with my drink while another server placed salads in front of us both. I stared at mine.

"Um, I didn't—"

"Oh, I hope you don't mind, Steele. I took the liberty of ordering the meal." Maria dismissed the waiter with a wave.

I did mind. But, since she was paying, I was shutting up. "This is great. Thanks." I disposed of the vodka.

Maria lifted a satchel onto her lap. It was made of the kind of buttery Italian calf leather that I'd need a bank loan for and I tried not to drool. Her hand trembled as she took out a small gold tin with an enameled inlay top. She discreetly tapped out two small white capsules. I glanced at the tiny blue logo when a third rolled off her palm and onto the tablecloth.

She scooped it back into the pillbox. Figuring she had another headache, I paid studious attention to my salad, giving her the illusion of privacy. Once she'd chased the pills with a mouthful of sparkling water, I tried to think of some small talk.

"So, a Vegas institution has come to an end."

Maria tipped her head. "What are you talking about?"

"I read in the *Journal* that the marriage license office won't be staying open twenty-four hours on weekends anymore."

"Sin City stops making couples respectable?" She smirked. "That's ironic. So, no more Britney Spears-type 2:00 a.m. weddings followed by 4:00 p.m. annulments, huh?"

"No. I guess not." I toyed with my juice.

"But then, the whole fairy-tale ceremony is no guarantee, is it?" Maria forked a slice of cucumber. "Tell me what you found out."

I watched her expression solidify as she braced herself to hear what she already knew. Damn, my job sucks sometimes. "I'm sorry."

"I could have been wrong. I mean, you could be wrong." She pushed her salad away.

Instead of answering, I reached for the file folder in my backpack. I had to slide it across the table because she wouldn't take it from me. Maria stared at the folder like it might rear up and bite her. Then she finally picked it up and opened the cover. She avoided the envelope I'd marked, *May 4 and 5 Cavanaugh Surveillance,* removing the typed report instead. She read it slowly, seemingly analyzing each word.

I perused the pattern of the chopped eggs scattered over the wilted spinach leaves on my plate and waited.

After a few minutes, she grunted and slapped the report on the table. Her eyes were damp, her face flushed. Maria focused on something beyond my shoulder and spoke in a bleak whisper. "I don't understand what you wrote."

I blinked a few times. Her husband was playing hide the cannoli with a girl two-thirds his age. What's not to understand? My confusion obviously showed because she pressed her lips tightly together and the color deepened in her cheeks.

"I—I can't—" She cleared her throat. "I can't read that report. Well, I can. But it's difficult and I'm too upset to get through it."

"Um…" I was still confused. Aunt Gloria had taught me to write concise, factual reports with no ambiguities that might bite an investigator on the ass in a courtroom. "I'm not sure—"

"I'm dyslexic, okay?" She hissed it defensively.

My brows rose before I controlled my reaction. But that did explain a lot. I thought back to the many times kids had laughed while Maria struggled to read aloud in English, to how often I'd gotten frustrated trying to tutor her. I, like everyone else, had just assumed she wasn't very bright.

"I'm sorry. I had no idea."

"Neither did I, not until I wanted to take a class at the community college." Bitterness seeped from her voice.

I tried to diffuse it. "Hey, but look at you now, a successful casino executive."

"Sure, nepotism at its finest. I'm the only executive whose father doesn't trust her to do any work." Maria raised her glass, muttering, "That's going to change," before she took a sip of water.

She didn't elaborate—maybe she was taking a job in another casino—and I didn't push. "Okay, well, anyway, I can tell you what I wrote—"

"Or…" Maria sighed audibly. "I can just look at the pictures."

"You don't have to."

Did I mention my job sucks? And so did my salad—too much vinegar in the dressing—but I had nothing else to do but eat while Maria slipped the photos out of the envelope. Anything to avoid watching the betrayal and hurt steal across her face. But when I glanced at her, some of the tension had melted from her posture.

"These don't prove anything." Her expression brightened as she examined the photograph, looking for clues to the problems in her marriage, searching for answers in the other woman instead of within herself. "They're just talking—okay, he kissed her in this one…. Did you hear anything they said?"

The missing money wasn't technically part of my assignment, so I didn't mention it. "No, not really, but—"

"So it doesn't mean they're having—that they *were* having, you know, an affair."

"Maria…"

"And even if they were, look at these." She held up the pictures I'd taken yesterday at the Vista Buena Inn. "It's obviously over. Look at the anger on the girl's face. Look at the regret on my husband's. *Look!*"

Despite the vehemence in her tone, I saw denial in her eyes. There was nobody to blame for this but me. I'd censored the photos, protecting Maria as a friend, instead of being honest with her as a client. I spoke quietly, hating to hurt her, doing my job. "I'm looking, Maria, but I also saw them—"

"No." She tossed the pictures on the table. "It was a mistake. My husband loves me and I—we can work this out. Maybe find a marriage counselor."

I smiled, encouragingly I hoped. "Sure you can. Things will work out." Until he does it again. "I hate to ask this, I really do." I lowered my voice. "Did you find anything… unusual…while going through Gray's things?"

Maria gave me a tired smile. "How unusual? I already saw his collection of porn magazines and Matchbox cars."

"Um, any large amounts of cash?" I shifted uncomfortably.

"There were some questionable transactions at the casino, so your dad hired somebody to look into it."

She stared at me like I was speaking a foreign language. I wasn't sure she understood what I was accusing her husband of until I saw the flinty edge in her gaze. It vanished as quickly as it appeared but she still didn't answer me.

Agitated, Maria grabbed her satchel, inhaled sharply and stood up. "Thanks for your help, Steele. Really. But I won't need your services anymore."

As she turned to leave, I stood up as well. "Wait. What about—"

"Keep it. The reports, the money. Keep it." And with that she was gone.

PLEASANTLY FULL from the veal piccatta and spinach gnocchi in mushroom cream sauce I'd ordered after Maria left, I was back home by two. I had to swerve the bike to avoid the back end of the furniture truck pulling out of my driveway. Oh, goody. What did the Psycho Decorating Fairy bring me this time? Leaving the Harley in front of the garage, I dragged myself inside and turned toward the living room…

I suddenly missed empty. Empty rooms weren't so bad.

The new entertainment center was still there—Stone had been smart enough not to mess with my film collection again. But the orange plaids and pink paisleys had been exchanged for red, yellow and black stripes. The new theme appeared to be Rural Mexican Village.

There were serapes on the floor acting as area rugs, a wrought-iron sofa with overstuffed woven cushions and deer antler lamps on the end tables. Groupings of terra-cotta pots posed on every available surface. Fake wooden beams had been secured to my ceiling and a red clay fascia turned my fireplace into a kiva.

"Oh, you're home!" An eager woman with more makeup on her face than weight on her body rushed over to me. "I had *so* hoped to finish before you got back." She clapped her claws together, making the dozen bracelets on her arm clatter. "I'm Zoe and I'm *so* privileged to be your interior artist! What do you think?"

"Jesus" was the first thing that came to mind as I stared at the four primitive oil paintings of the Madonna vandalizing my wall. "I'm...speechless."

Zoe clapped her hands again, apparently thrilled by her own decorative genius. "Isn't it something? I'm just *so* happy with how it all came together. It's the perfect people room."

Luckily I don't know any perfect people. Otherwise, I'd have to invite them over now that I had furniture. Then I'd have to throw parties and shit and who knew where that would lead? "Yeah, it's something all right. Uh, is Stone still here?"

"I believe he's in the guest room. Just *wait* until you see the vision I've created in there!"

I could wait, I really could.

As I moved down the hall, I could hear the rumble of Stone's voice. It sounded like he was on the phone in my room, but I wanted to check out this "vision" first. I stood in the entry and just stared. The room was done in a nautical blue and white sailboat motif no guest of mine would ever see. Then Stone raised his voice.

"I bloody well know what I agreed to do for you." He paused, apparently listening. "It never is." Another pause was followed by a sigh. "Just have the wire transfer in order, won't you?"

I couldn't stand this guest room for another second; that living room was a nightmare; and the "interior artist" needed to go back to her padded cell. I crossed the hall to give him hell, reaching the doorway just as Stone spoke again.

"Don't worry. It will look like an accident."

CHAPTER TWENTY-EIGHT

Barely Able to Breathe

EVEN HIS TEETH HURT.

That was from clenching his jaw, though. The guy who'd hammered the crap out of him hadn't touched his face.

Gray Cavanaugh winced as he hung up the phone. He'd had to call out from work, something he'd only done twice before in his life. But no way could he go to the Palazzo pissing blood and barely able to breathe. He lay back down on the sofa where he'd tried to sleep last night.

He didn't bother to close his eyes.

Every time he did, all he could see was that ice cold, merciless gaze. The beating had been almost surgical in its precision, blow after vicious blow ramming into his ribs and kidneys… The guy never spoke a single word, but Gray suspected that his father-in-law had sent him.

He reached for the gin on the floor. Mrs. Amalfi, the housekeeper, had gotten tired of bringing him G&Ts and left the bottle. After adding another shot to the watery tonic in his glass, he took a deep swallow. But the sharp burn of the booze couldn't numb the anxiety knifing through his gut.

He was in deep shit.

Caitlyn had ignored all of his calls after she'd bailed on him at the hotel. He'd caught up with the ungrateful little bitch at her apartment when she got home from work. He'd already given her ten grand, helped get her the job at the Palazzo and spent every free minute banging her brains out.

But now she wanted more. A lot more. He'd knocked her up and she had the sonogram picture to prove it. Once upon a time he'd wanted kids, but since Maria couldn't... That was then. The real problem now was either he did the right thing by her and the baby, or Caitlyn would talk—first to Big Frank and then to Maria.

He figured DiMarco might have discovered the missing cash, but the worst he could expect was probably another ass-kicking. Frank just wanted his money back. But if Caitlyn told Maria, his whining ball-breaker of a wife would run right to Daddy. And if Frank found out about the affair, then life as Gray knew it would be over.

He finished off his drink. It was time to get the hell out of town.

CHAPTER TWENTY-NINE

A Piece of My Heart

STONE GLANCED AT ME from the corner of his eye, went still, then casually ended the call. "Contact the others and I'll get the details en route."

I cocked my head to one side as he turned to me, wondering whose face I was really seeing. "What was that about?"

"A surprise for my good mate, Brian. He's getting married."

"Yeah? When?" This was the first time he'd mentioned anyone in his life besides Jamie. I figured it was a step forward in our relationship.

Except he didn't meet my eyes.

"Soon, it would seem."

I watched him rub his thumb uneasily across his cell phone. He was already gone in every way but the physical. I started spackling cement into the cracks of the wall around my heart.

"So I was right this morning about you leaving. I just got the timing wrong."

"It's a last-minute sort of thing." His hearty tone didn't match his lack of expression.

I glanced at the brand-new, we're-supposed-to-share-it bed, then back at Stone. I saw a stranger who wore a shroud of static-charged patience, a visitor anxious to be on his way. However I wasn't about to put a revolving hinge on my front door or on my heart.

"We have a decision to make—"

"And we will." He looked at me then, a reassuring smile

curving his lips. His eyes remained distant, though, as he crossed to me. "It's just for a day or two."

Weak-willed moron that I am, I allowed him to hold me. I even leaned my head on his shoulder while he stroked a hand down my back. And I waited for him to invite me along. I waited for him to take our relationship beyond the casework and the bedroom. Who goes to a wedding without a date, right? Only he didn't say a word.

His silence sliced at me, adding another wound that would scar over rather than heal. I wrenched away. "Is this going to be a regular occurrence, you disappearing into the night?"

"It's still midday and I haven't left yet."

I ignored his lame attempt at humor. "Don't be a freakin' smart-ass, okay? Just answer my question. Because you're lying to me. You're not going to any bachelor party or wedding."

His jaw clenched to match the set of his shoulders. Yet oddly I thought I saw grief in the back of his eyes. "I didn't lie. Exactly. I simply stated two facts and allowed you to infer a connection."

"Dammit, Stone! You told me not to ask if I'm not willing to answer. But I have no idea which topics are off-limits."

"I hope that eventually almost nothing will be taboo between us." He took my hand. I hated the comfort I got from the gesture and from his implication. "But my job will always be off-limits. There will be times when I'll have to travel on short notice. And I won't be able to tell you where or why. Those are the terms I agreed to because of what I do."

I still had no clue what *that* was and now he was telling me I never would. I had some movie-related ideas, like maybe he worked for MI6 or the CIA. But no matter, our relationship had just taken two steps back. At least this time I was awake when it ended. I released his hand.

"I didn't agree to those terms, Stone. So if you're leaving, you'd better go."

A spark of rebellion lit his gaze. "I should return in a matter of days. Tell me you'll be here."

"I'll be here." He started to smile, until I added, "But the locks will be changed."

He did smile then. "Do you honestly think that will keep me from you?"

"HANG ON." Nikki tapped my arm as we turned the corner from the Palazzo's lobby past one of the casinos. "I want to get a couple of drinks before we have to stand in line for an hour."

My friends had come to pick me up for girls' night. I hadn't let them in the house. No point in letting them see Zoe's handiwork when the Salvation Army was coming to remove it from my sight. And, okay, I hadn't wanted to answer a whole lot of questions about where it all came from.

Anyway, we drove up the Strip in the Mercedes-Benz that Anna was "test driving" for the night. She'd slipped a twenty—and Nikki's phone number—to the valet to ensure it was in pristine condition when we returned. I couldn't speak for Anna's condition when Nikki found out what she'd done.

"It won't be that bad tonight, right, Steele?" Anna was looking on the bright side as always.

The last time we'd come to Element, we'd waited forever with the rest of the plebian masses only to be turned away because the club was "at capacity." See, there was no way to know whether you were wasting your time. The only access upstairs was by a single escalator and then a darkened tunnel. Or so I'd heard.

Nothing draws a crowd like the illusion of exclusivity.

"You never know, Anna. The bouncers might mistake us for celebrities." Since Big Frank probably hadn't had a chance to put my name on the list, I didn't tell my friends we might not have to wait.

We looked fantastic, considering we might not be going anywhere. We were dressed like the three stages of one hell of a good time. Anna looked sweetly sexy in an off-the-shoulder blouse and comfortable jeans. Her bright red curls spiraled down her back. I had on a pair of low-rise jeans and, believe it or not, something other than a rude T-shirt. Tonight I was wearing a black V-neck tank top and strappy sandals.

Nikki's tousled hair looked like she'd rolled out of a magazine ad and into bed. Her filmy camisole and skinny jeans showed off her curves to perfection but I was waiting for her to sprain an ankle in those sky-high stilettos.

"Lindsey Hilton was here the other night stealing back one of her shipping heir boy toys." Nikki's job as a casino host who catered to high rollers allowed her to tap into the absolute latest gossip. "Now everybody in town has decided this is *the* hot spot."

We turned another corner and Nikki came to a screeching halt—literally since her stiletto grazed the marble floor. The serpentine line of people weaving through the velvet cordons was twice as long as last time. She crossed her arms and looked around for a cocktail server.

"*Ay, mierda, chicas.* I told you we should have snagged some drinks first."

I knew she'd be a grumpy pain in the ass until she got an apple martini in her so I accepted the short straw. "You two save my place and I'll make the bar run. Anna, what are you drinking?"

She tilted her head and looked off into the distance. I guess she was consulting the spirit guides or something. Past experience had taught me not to interrupt the conversation. She finally looked back at me and smiled. "I'll have a fuzzy navel tonight."

"Hey, girl, keep your personal hygiene to yourself."

She laughed, just like she always did when she chose that drink and I made that joke. That's the difference between friends and lovers—consistency. I wasted a microsecond of thought wondering where Stone was, what he was doing.

Okay. That was a full second.

When I stepped out of line, there were already fifteen people behind us. I'd started for the nearest lounge—the drinks served on the casino floors were watered down—when one of the bouncers approached me. "Miss Stella?"

I stopped, taken aback that one, he knew my name and two, by the name he'd used. "Uh, yes?"

"I'm Bruno." He sure was. Dark-skinned, heavily muscled and the size of a small truck. "Would you come with me, please?"

Cocking an eyebrow, I also copped an attitude. "Is there a *problem,* Bruno?"

He looked confused and then instantly apologetic. "No, miss, not at all. In fact, we've been instructed to take very good care of you. Mr. D's orders."

As it turned out, Big Frank had not only put my name on the welcome mat but he'd also unfurled the red carpet. I pulled an astonished Nikki and a beatific Anna out of the line to follow Bruno. He led us past another, tank-sized bouncer to a hidden entryway with its own elevator to the upper level of the club.

In a word? Posh.

From here I could look down on the three bars, the black tiled dance floor and the 94-foot waterfall bordered by glass cylinders of flame. The club below had mirrored walls but up here, a block of windows offered views of the Strip, making the lights and excitement of Sin City part of the decor. Bruno escorted us past some of the private VIP booths.

Nikki and I controlled ourselves enough not to peer inside looking for movie stars. Anna flat-out gawked, squealing when she saw "Matt and Lance!"

Bruno stopped at a reserved table in one of the smaller booths and introduced us to our personal hunky cocktail server. "Ladies, enjoy your evening. Anything you want, tell Nigel and it's yours, compliments of Mr. DiMarco."

Oh, geez. That was totally the wrong thing to say to Nikki. Part of her job was to fetch, carry and kiss up to rich gamblers who sometimes made outrageous demands. So when the opportunity arose… She was firing off requests before we'd even settled into the red velvet settees.

"Nigel, honey, could you start us off with an ice cold bottle of Piper-Heidsieck cuvée Brut champagne and some seafood appetizers? Thank you!"

"Coming right up, miss."

Anna gave Nikki a reproving look. "That's the start *and* the finish, right? Heidsieck is, like, eighty dollars a bottle."

"Actually the bottle service in most clubs is closer to three hundred with the markup." Nikki flipped her hair over her shoulder and smiled at a too-pretty guy walking by our table. "Just relax and enjoy, babe."

"So, what's with the star treatment anyway, Steele?" Anna asked. "I thought you were joking with the celebrity comment."

Nikki turned to me and wiggled her eyebrows suggestively. "Yeah, *chica*. What *are* you doing for, with or to Mr. DiMarco?"

"Um, ew. It's not like that, Nik." I paused as Nigel set three champagne flutes on the table. Once he'd poured and gotten our approval, he left to get our food. "Actually I think this is a bribe. But Anna's right. I don't want to run up a huge tab and have him think I took his 'suggestion' to back off of a case."

Anna snorted—she's the only person I know who looks cute doing that. "You never back off from anything. Not even when you should. You are stubborn that way. I think it's because in one of your past lives you were an Amazon warrior princess—"

Nikki rolled her eyes and interrupted. "So you're working on a case that involves Demon DiMarco? Are you nuts? Take his suggestion."

"No, he's not involved. Not directly. And, technically the case is closed but I still don't want him to think he can order me around." Just then Nigel came back with a tray the size of an SUV hubcap covered in tiny dishes of crab, shrimp, lobster and scallops. Okay, I guess I am bribable. I chose a mini crab cake and picked up my champagne. *"Saluté!"*

Over the next half hour we polished off the Heidsieck and all the canapés. Nikki ordered a second bottle before we hit the dance floor to work off the calories. Another thing about hard-to-get-into, expensive-to-stay-in nightclubs? They attract very beautiful girls and absolutely smokin' hot guys. While Anna shyly flirted with her dance partner, Nikki was all but having sex with the gorgeous blonde she'd chosen.

Me, I was more dancing next to than with Roberto. I thought I recognized him from an underwear ad. He had inky hair that fell artfully over one eye, a deep dimple in his cheek and a practiced smile. His dance moves left little doubt about his bed skills.

Not that I was looking to hook up tonight. I didn't need any more complications. But there was no reason not to enjoy the attention Roberto was intent on bestowing upon me. That would be rude. And besides, I didn't have to wonder about *his* intentions. I didn't have to care what *he* thought or felt.

But a song later, I'd had enough. I was about to extricate myself from Roberto when from out of the crowd a large hand dropped onto his shoulder. Both of our gazes followed it along the muscular arm and up to Stone's fixed expression. I should have been surprised. I should not have been pleased.

I rarely do what I should.

Stone didn't say a word. He didn't even spare my dance partner a glance. He just kept those intense blue eyes on me until Roberto ducked under his hand and rechanneled his lust to a double D redhead nearby. Stone's grin could only be described as smugly possessive.

"Why don't you just club me over the head and drag me back to your cave by my hair?" Not that I wanted Roberto back, but it was the principle of the thing.

"Don't tempt me, Stella, love."

I crossed my arms and glared at him. "Try it. See what happens to you."

"Or, better still, I'll put a ring on your finger."

That sound? It was my heart screeching to a stunned halt and slamming into my ribs. I stood there gaping, at a complete loss for words. I didn't want a ring—did I? No, I wasn't ready for one. And, despite our odd circumstance, I couldn't believe that he was, either.

But guys don't joke about that kind of thing.

I ducked the threat completely. "What the hell are you doing here anyway? Shouldn't you be on a plane with Brian or something?"

"I was able to arrange for a last-minute replacement." We were standing close in order to talk over the music. That's how I heard the uncomfortable tone in his voice.

"Is that going to be a problem?"

"Yes." He didn't elaborate. He didn't have to.

Something shifted inside me, like everything had gently settled into place. It had been so long since I'd felt happiness I barely recognized it. "I'm sorry. And, um, thank you."

Cameron cupped my neck and kissed me in reply. God, this man knew how to express himself without speaking. My soul heard everything his body said and rejoiced. Several breathless moments later, I turned toward the stairs, figuring he'd want to leave the dance floor. But he surprised me again.

"I like this song."

Wow. I'd thought Roberto had moves.

Cameron kept the beat with each sway of his hips, each thrust of his pelvis. His dancing was easy and confident, sensual rather than sexual. He was hardly the most skilled guy on the floor, but something about him still caught the eye of several women around us. But his eyes never left me.

I leaned toward him. "You're good at this."

"None of my mates would set foot on a dance floor, but I discovered early on it got me girls."

He was damned close to getting this girl. I didn't know what was sexier—Cameron or the way he made me feel. When he twirled me around, intimately pressing his body against mine, the temperature inside the club soared. The soft friction of his shirt on my bare back was nothing compared to the rasp of his lips on the curve of my neck.

As the music turned sultry, sort of pulsing and broody, our motions were oddly in sync. When I swayed, swiveled or rocked, he followed. Then he slid a hand to my waist and took the lead. I let him. We continued to dance close and it was like the world fell away, leaving only the two of us.

I didn't like the next song, though, so with a little regret I took him upstairs to the booth. My friends were already there, killing the second bottle of Heidsieck while they waited for me to return. I stood awkwardly beside our table. Cameron's hand on my hip didn't make the decision to sit down or say good-night easier.

Anna gaped, apparently stunned to see me with a guy for the first time in forever. Nikki just looked pissed that I'd betrayed the sanctity of girls' night. *You leave with the women you came with.* No matter how unexpectedly sweet the guy is.

"Um, hey, look who I ran into. This is Cameron Stone."

"Oh, that's the name of that guy you—" Anna broke off when Nikki kicked her under the table and took away her glass. "But he's her special Valentine!"

Cameron glanced at me, but I stayed focused on the girls, gesturing in turn. "These are my best friends, Nikki Lopez and Anna Grant."

"Pleasure to meet you both at last." He shook hands without letting go of me, which made Anna's eyes go as wide as her grin.

"Sooo… Cameron. Cameron, Cameron." She tried to look stern but failed comically. "Are you going to stick around for breakfast this time?"

"Anna!" Nikki and I protested together.

She shrugged at me, arms crooked and palms upturned. "What? I *told* you he'd call. Didn't I tell you he'd call?" She turned to Nikki. "Can we have more champagne? I love the bubbles."

"I think you've had enough, don't you?"

"Love. Bubbles. Hey, that rhymes!"

"No, it doesn't. You've definitely had enough, *chica.*" Nikki grabbed the empty bottle before Anna could check for fumes. She looked at me. "I've already taken her keys. Are you ready to go or…?"

Cameron spoke up. "I'll see to Stella."

"Woohoo!" Anna giggled and clapped her hands.

Nikki gave me a look. "You will call me tomorrow, *mija.*"

"I will. Be safe getting home."

"You be safe once you get home!" Anna winked broadly.

As Nikki helped her toward the elevator, Cameron regarded me with a challenge. "So you told your friends about that night. Did you also tell them I'm your husband?"

"Not only no, but hell no."

What was I supposed to say? Hey, girls, not only did I get drunk and have sex with a guy who followed me to the bar, but I eloped with him the same night!

How could I admit that I'd been so far gone I didn't remember vowing to love, honor and cherish a complete stranger until I found the marriage certificate two days later? Should I have confessed that I couldn't get an annulment because I had no idea where to locate the groom?

Like I said before, I only look stupid.

Cameron might be my husband due to a legal technicality, but did I want it to be a reality? I'd never pictured myself married, let alone to a guy I knew next to nothing about.

He seemed to hold back a sigh. "I'd like us to try and make this work, Stella, love. So when will you let your friends and family know about us?"

I didn't miss a beat. "When I think our marriage has a snowball's chance in hell of lasting."

CHAPTER THIRTY

The Ties That Bind

"SO, YOU'LL NEVER believe who ran off and got married!"

I flinched at Aunt Carmella's announcement, damned near nicking the tip of my finger with a crab shell.

It was Sunday. That meant I was in the kitchen with all the other Mezzanotte women. It's more like two kitchens since years ago my mother had the space renovated to incorporate the dining room. Now she had twice the countertops, an extra sink, a second fridge and a double wall oven.

Still only one dishwasher, though. Go figure.

The old living room is now the dining room so that she can seat everybody. Not easy, but always entertaining. Especially since one of my three aunts is forever not talking to another of my three aunts. Meanwhile the family room is where the men congregate to watch TV or play cards and talk about their wives. My father and brother, the chefs, don't cook at home.

Sunday dinners—for which food started hitting the tables at 11:00 a.m.—were big, boisterous weekly affairs. The door was always open, so my parents' home in Spring Valley overflowed with family of all ages, sizes and volumes. The kitchen was probably the loudest room, what with my mother, aunts, sisters-in-law and cousins all talking at once.

Aunt Victoria was making minestrone soup as Rafe's wife Laura fried more calamari. My cousin Giada chopped mushrooms for the crostini, Santina prepared the antipasti trays, and Mom was stuffing a pork loin while I shelled seafood for the *frutti di mare*. The steamy air was fragrant with the scent of tomatoes, basil and oregano and the spice of gossip.

Aunt Carmella had finally captured the room's attention by telling us about Lia Grosso's elopement. "She broke her mother's heart, let me tell you. Broke it!"

"Oh, come on, Ma," Giada protested. "Miss Bianca will get over it. The wedding was getting out of hand anyway. Who needs ten bridesmaids?" Next to me she muttered under her breath, "I hated the dress she picked out for us."

I hummed in absent response, jaw clenched as I thought about my own mother's eventual hurt and disappointment.

"You know, Steele, that," Giada nodded at the pile of raw seafood, "would go a lot faster if you used a paring knife."

"I'm in no hurry." I hate the feel of small, sharp blades.

"I'm surprised, I really am." Aunt Julia didn't look up, her hands flying over the marble board as she shaped *orecchiette* pasta. "Lia's such a good girl, not the type to be impetuous."

Carmella ignored her since it was their week not to talk. "Her poor mother has been planning this wedding since the day Lia was born. All for nothing!"

"Bianca is in such a state. What is she going to do with those foiled invitations or the dress her husband paid all that money for?" Aunt Vic clucked her tongue.

No one had been invited to my ceremony. I'd worn jeans and a haze of alcohol. My husband—a man I'd known less than twelve hours—had paid for the marriage license. As for the wedding itself? I vaguely remembered the drive-through window at The Little White Chapel on the north end of the Strip….

Carmella was still on a roll. "The worst part has to be the embarrassment. I mean, what does Bianca say to people? How can she look her friends and family in the eye?"

Mom spoke up as she made her way to the oven with the pork. "I just don't understand why Lia sneaked off, like marriage is something shameful. The least the girl could do is explain herself."

I carefully stayed out of the conversation. It would have been too hard to talk around the lump in my throat. Hoping nobody noticed me, I kept ripping the heads off the shrimp.

But the Mom Radar must have kicked in because she nudged me with a laugh. "I don't have to worry about this, do I, *cara?* I stopped planning your wedding after your Bridal Belle Barbie left Ken to go on missions with your brother's G.I. Joe."

I offered a genuine grin in response. Ironic, huh? I'd spent last night with Combat Cameron, alternating great sex with some good laughs. There were still unspoken barriers to overcome. But I preferred his battle-scarred mystery and challenge to the clean-cut All-American boy who'd ruined my life.

"Rafe and I thought about eloping." Laura's tone was so tongue-in-cheek I didn't know whether to believe her.

Mom definitely didn't. "You did not! Did you?"

Santina winked at me, then addressed Mom with a straight face. "John and I have considered this, as well."

"No!"

That was my niece and nephew screaming in unison, not my mother. It was also my cue to exit stage left. When Laura turned to check on her kids, I held out a hand to stop her. "It's okay. No, I'll go. I've got him."

As casually as possible, I bolted out of the kitchen. Paul came rushing toward me on chubby toddler legs, arms wide spread and big fat tears leaking from his brown eyes. I caught him around the waist and swung him into my embrace.

"What's the matter, sweet boy?"

"Legwa won't pway." He pouted dramatically then laid his head on my shoulder. "Wanna pway wif shiny fings."

I glanced into the dining room where Allegra was curled into one of the chairs, her nose buried in a book. I noted that the tablecloth hung longer on this side. If I interpreted the situation correctly, she'd stopped Paul from yanking the water glasses and cutlery off the table. What a meanie.

"Ah, well, that is a problem, little guy. We're gonna need that stuff for later. How about a hug to make it better?"

"Huuug," Paul sighed in his adorable voice. He wrapped a soft arm around my head, engulfing me in the scent of Johnson's Baby Shampoo and Cheerios. I closed my eyes for a second to capture the moment in my memory.

Yeah, so I love kids. Just because I don't want my own anytime soon doesn't mean I can't enjoy them. Especially my niece, the coolest ten-year-old on the planet. Allegra glanced up from the pages with a deadpan expression, then returned to her latest Nancy Drew mystery.

"He's chewing on your hair, Anti-Steele." She calls me that because I'm such a pushover when I babysit them.

"It needs to be washed anyway." But I reached up to free the hunk of strands from Paulie's lips just the same.

"*Stella!* I want to talk to you. Right now!" Joey's bellow entered the front door two seconds before he did.

Allegra kept reading. "Sounds like you're in trouble."

"Good observation skills, girl detective. I could use you down at the agency."

She grinned at me, showing the spaces where her eyeteeth still hadn't come in. "I'm so there, just as soon as I get my criminology degree."

Allegra is the only member of the family who thinks my job *rocks out loud*. We took a self-defense class together this past winter. No bully will ever bother her; trust me. She's already decided she wants to be a P.I. like me. Rafe is less than thrilled, to put it mildly.

"Hey, Allie. Why don't you take Paulie…somewhere?"

Despite Joey's lame attempt at a smile, she picked up on the obvious tension in his tone. Allegra dutifully set her book aside and came to get the baby. She's a really great big sister. That didn't stop her from trying to get something out of it though.

"I'm available after school on Tuesday or Wednesday, Uncle Joey. That would be a great time for you to take me out in your patrol car, don't you think?"

He kept glaring at me as he responded. "No, I don't think."

She tipped her head coyly, an alternate reward at the ready. "Then maybe you could show me how to collect crime scene evidence."

"Sure, Allie, sure. Just," he waved his hand toward the yard, "give us a couple of minutes, will you?"

"Thank you, Uncle Joey," she singsonged as she left the room.

"She was awfully polite, *don't you think,* considering how rude you were to her?"

My spine stiffened along with my attitude before I even heard what his problem was. Then he took a couple strides across the floor until he was in my face. That was unlike him—he damned well knew better. My stomach fluttered a little. Joey is usually so even-tempered.

"What the hell is wrong with you, Steele—"

"I have no idea what you're—"

"—upsetting Vince like that?"

I snapped my mouth shut and stepped back from the fire in Joey's eyes.

"What were you thinking? Never mind, you *weren't* thinking. Otherwise you would have told me—the brother who can actually help—that some guy's after you. You would have told *me* about the phone calls instead of Vince, who is going fucking crazy worrying about you."

He kept his voice down so the family wouldn't hear, but I couldn't avoid a single acid-tinged word. A chill prickle of shame raced over my skin. I couldn't meet Joey's gaze. Obviously this was the Sunday for all of my sins to be dragged into the light. I just wished I knew how to possibly atone for any small part of them.

Instead all I could do was mumble. "I didn't mean to upset him, Joey. I just needed his advice."

He crossed his arms and glared at me. "What kind of advice could he give you from prison?"

Although Vince steadfastly refused to let me see him, in five years Joey had never missed visiting hours at the Indian Springs Correctional Center. Mom used to go in the begin-

ning, until Vince asked her to stop. Rafe calls, I think. Poor
Papa has spent the past five years in a vacuum of silent denial.

"That's between me and Vince, okay?"

"No, Steele, it's not okay. I'm the cop. I'm the one you
come to when some guy is prank calling your house."

I scrubbed a hand over my face. "I'm handling it, Joe."

He looked ready to smack me. I wasn't sure I'd stop him.
"I'll start cruising by your place at night. In the meantime you
should think about getting an alarm—"

"I did. Guardian put in a whole security system."

Joey's brows shot up. "Oh, yeah? How did you afford an
outfit like that?"

"I, uh, took out a loan." Repayment still to be determined,
but no doubt requiring access of my soul.

"I'm going to patrol anyway—"

"You really don't have to." Stuffing my hands into my
pockets, I finally glanced at him.

Yeah, that was the expression I'd expected. Full-blown
Alpha male on the warpath. Like the other men in my life,
Joey didn't think much of my independence.

"You're my baby sister and it's my responsibility to protect
you. Yeah, I know, Vince's, too. But he's already done everything he could for you."

I didn't hear what Joey said after that. The low blow had
rendered me temporarily deaf to everything except the sound
of blood rushing to my cheeks and a subconscious awareness
of footsteps approaching the foyer.

Five years. A mere fraction of the life sentence Vince was
serving. Two hundred sixty weeks that I've been imprisoned
by my guilt. One thousand eight hundred twenty-five days that
I've lived on my own terms and not always thought of him.
Forty-three thousand eight hundred hours that my oldest
brother had to sacrifice for defending me…

"Look, Steele. You don't know what it's like out there.
Vince never wanted you to know. But, as tough as he is, he's
got to be on his guard at all times. If he's distracted and lets

his defenses down…" Joey paused, like he was searching for the right words.

In the brief silence, every nightmare, every movie I'd ever seen about prison life weighed like rocks on my imagination. The facts were uglier than fiction. If Vince got beat up or stabbed or even killed, it would be my fault. Just like it was my fault he was incarcerated at all.

Joey sighed. "You won't recognize him. There's a—a shield, I guess, this invisible armor around him. Like the one you try to put on. But in his case it's become a part of him. He's harder, colder—"

I heard a sharp intake of breath and turned to the doorway.

"Giovanni, you're here. Good, good. We need you for the card game. Stella, go and help your mother, yes?"

Papa acted like he'd just happened by. But from his poignant expression, I realized his were the footsteps I'd heard before. He never talked about his firstborn, his Vincente. I didn't think he could cope with the mix of love, anger, pride and disappointment. But he'd listened.

"Sure, Pop. I'll be right there," Joey replied. "Make sure Cousin Rick doesn't palm any of the aces."

Papa nodded once and started to leave the room. Abruptly, he came back to wrap one arm around each of us and kiss our cheeks in turn. Then he walked away without a word. He loved us and he worried; he felt powerless to keep us safe, but he trusted us to make our own way. His kiss said all that and more.

On top of everything happening today, his kiss was enough to make carefully repressed tears sting the back of my eyes.

Joey caught my attention. "By the way, Vince said to give you a message."

"What's that?" I blinked several times, clearing my vision.

"Mick Haining."

I frowned. "Who? I mean, is that the message?"

Joey stared at me intently. "That's the message. So you want to tell me why you're asking about Vince's old cell mate?"

The proverbial cartoon lightbulb lit up over my head. Who

else would my brother have to talk to? I felt an odd sense of relief. My telephone whisperer had a name. As any Native American will tell you, knowing the true name of your enemy is powerful medicine.

I offered Joey a little smile. "Oh, it was just something that came up in one of our letters."

He watched my face. It was a waste of time. I'm much better at poker than he'll ever be.

"Uh-huh. Well, if it's important enough for Vince to pass the name through me, then it's worth me checking into."

As he left the dining room, I stared at his back, equally grateful for and frustrated by his concern and determination to ride to my rescue. Between Cameron and Joey, the ties that bind were likely to strangle me.

CHAPTER THIRTY-ONE

In Your Eyes

KNOWING STELLA HAD spent the entire day with her family, Cameron had expected her to go home. Instead she'd turned up on his doorstep. He moved aside to let her into the condo, careful not to touch her. The hostility radiating from her did not exactly invite it.

"So, this is what 'rich and wealthy' looks like."

"I'll have a set of keys and an entry card made for you. That way you won't have to knock."

"I'd knock anyway. Wouldn't want to interrupt a top-secret bachelor party." She jolted past him then stopped as if unsure of where to go.

This place was undoubtedly a world away from where she'd been. He imagined she smelled of sunlight and fresh baked bread, crayons and a grandmother's perfume; aromas he associated with family gatherings. The condo was odorless. He'd long since cleared away his soda can and microwave dinner packet.

He walked toward her but kept his distance, studying her pallor and the bleak look in her eyes. "Is your family all right, then?"

Her smile was bittersweet. "Yeah. They're great. Better than I deserve."

"Has there been another of your 'it's nothing' calls?"

"No, no. That's not it."

She began to pace. Her long strides carried her from the

marble tile to the plush carpet and back again. The floor-to-ceiling view of the Strip was the focal point of the flat, therefore the furnishings were neutral in color and design. By contrast Stella resembled a caged wolf, primal and wary and poised to strike if cornered.

She halted in midstride, turning so fast that her hair swung about her face. Dark brows knit, she drew a deep, agitated breath. "Do you ever wonder why people can't see you, the *real* you, for what you are?"

It was an odd question. But having mastered the art and skill of subterfuge, he felt well qualified to answer her candidly. "People see what they want to, love. They see what makes them comfortable, what fits into a neat category of past experience. As for those who are closest, they tend to see only the best in you."

A bit of the tension gradually seeped from her posture. However the burden of whatever was troubling her remained.

"Care to tell me what's happened?"

"No." She shot a glance in his direction then amended her answer. "Not…now."

He cocked his head, acquiescing. "Would you care to know what I see?"

"No." She continued pacing. He simply waited. Finally she looked at him directly, hands on her hips. "Okay, what?"

"Trust."

She laughed harshly. "What makes you think I trust you?"

"You're here."

Cameron opened his arms. After several reluctant seconds had ticked by, Stella walked into them.

CHAPTER THIRTY-TWO

What's Done is Done

AT TEN O'CLOCK on Monday morning, I stood poised on the threshold between the fantasy I'd been clinging to, and whatever harsh reality Doug Holbrook was about to hit me with.

His secretary, Carol, had escorted me through the firm, past the little cubicles full of interns and paralegals, to an enormous corner office with a balcony. If you hadn't known that Mr. Holbrook was one of the best attorneys in the state, his office would have convinced you.

"Steele. Come on in. Thanks, Carol."

My stomach twisted with anxiety as the door swung shut. I'd slept barely two hours last night despite Cameron's efforts to soothe me. He'd simply held me when, to my utter mortification, I'd awakened screaming. He didn't ask. Even if he had, I couldn't have shared those nightmares with him.

It had been bad enough living through them.

Mr. Holbrook indicated one of the armchairs. Then he surprised me by distancing himself behind the expanse of his antique escritoire. He rested his forearms on the desk surface, making him look more like a judge than a grandfather today. Not the most reassuring body language.

His smile was perfunctory as he tried to make small talk. "How are your parents doing, Steele? I've been meaning to treat myself to your father's *saltimbocca* again soon."

"They're fine."

He nodded. "I hope you had a nice weekend."

"My weekend sucked, thanks. Let's cut to the chase."

I'm never this rude to him, I swear. But I was on a razor's edge of tension. I'd waited long enough to find out why Vince had called him last week.

"All right, I'll get straight to the point. Your brother has instructed me to have no more contact with you."

"What?"

Mr. Holbrook took on a professorial tone. "*He's* my client, Steele. Even though you've been coming here all this time, I ultimately represent him."

"Yeah, I know that—"

"Do you?"

I reined in my temper with difficulty. "Of course. That's why I've asked you to keep trying." And took a home equity loan to pay his hourly rate.

"Despite that, Vincent has always made it crystal clear that he is not going to appeal his conviction. Yesterday he fired me as his attorney."

I leaned forward and frowned. "No, he can't do that. We have to—"

"He can and he has, Steele. He asked me to tell you that 'what's done is done and cannot be undone.'"

"He quoted freakin' Shakespeare at me?" My voice rose to an incredulous squeak.

Mr. Holbrook shrugged, ignoring my language. "Those were his exact words."

I sat back and pressed my hands to my lips, shaking my head. I'd known, of course. The subconscious part of my mind had been telling me all night that a dream was about to die. This particular dream was more like an illusion, but I still didn't want to let go of it.

"Okay, well, find another way. There has to be some other way."

"You know the answer, Steele."

I reluctantly held his stare. His piercing gaze conveyed understanding and compassion. And complete resolve. I looked down at the clenched fists in my lap. His voice was gentle when he broke the silence.

"It's over, my dear. I know how you must feel. But as much as you might wish things were different, your brother does not."

"What—" I cleared my throat. "What now?"

He pushed back from his desk and stood up. "You accept what happened and live with it. Vince killed a man to protect you. He pleaded guilty and he intends to serve out his sentence."

I slowly got to my feet. Mr. Holbrook took my hand, patting the back of it. I know he saw everything I felt. My grief, my anger, my guilt.

"If you need…anything…in future, you have my number."

"HEY, LADY. Spare some change?"

I heard the question as if from underwater and made a swatting motion to send him on his way.

I'd left Mr. Holbrook's office and now stood outside of the building entrance in a daze. Where the hell did I park? And more importantly, what was I driving today? My mind was empty and I couldn't focus. But I couldn't stay here. I had no reason to come here again.

Suddenly I felt a tug that snapped me back to the moment. The guy trying to panhandle me was also trying to grab my backpack. He looked clean-cut and was decently dressed. But his bloodshot eyes were darting back and forth like a metronome, the pupils constricted by more than bright morning sun.

I recognized the look. Another All-American boy gone bad.

"Give it to me!"

"Sure thing, asshole." Shifting my weight, I brought my knee up and aimed for his groin.

He twisted just in time and smacked me in the face, still gripping the strap. I allowed him to slide it off my shoulder just so I could get a better hold of the pack itself, but I refused to let go. Two people hurried past as we fought.

"Just—gimme the money—bitch."

"You don't—know me—well enough—to call me that."

I stopped grappling, surprising him. Then I pulled as hard as I could and closed the distance between us. When he stumbled, I rammed the heel of my hand into his nose. His eyes welled up and he let go of my pack to clutch his face. But I wasn't finished. Rage so intense that it scared me erupted in my gut.

He'd picked the wrong woman on the wrong day.

I shot my right fist into his diaphragm then sucker punched him with my left. He doubled over, struggling to breathe, and fell to the ground. By now a few people had gathered not to help but to watch. Only their aghast and fascinated faces stopped me from thoroughly beating the shit out of my mugger.

I stepped away from him and picked up my backpack. "He tried to rob me."

One woman tremulously held out her cell phone. "Do you want me to call the police?"

I shook my head. "He didn't get anything."

"Except an ass-kicking," somebody muttered.

"Yeah, call the cops! Call them." The mugger had finally gotten his second wind. "I just wanted a few bucks to feed my kids. My three sick kids. And my mother. She's, uh…old." He glared at me from the sidewalk. "You saw her. You all saw what she did to me. Call 9-1-1! I want her arrested."

Wiping a hand across my nose, I realized I was bleeding. I looked down at the guy. I don't know what he saw in my expression but it shut him up.

"You want the cops?" Reaching into one of the outer pockets, I fished Joey's card from my backpack. "Here's the number for the Southeast Area Command. Ask for my brother."

With that I walked away, still not sure where I'd parked.

BY THE TIME I dragged myself into the agency about twenty minutes later, even the little bell over the door pissed me off.

My mugger was probably going to sue me, I'd backed into one of the poles leaving the parking garage and Jon wasn't at his post. And how's this for irony? One of the bills in the pile on the reception desk was from Holbrook, Behle & Knowles, Attorneys at Law.

"Hey, Steele." Alerted by the chime, Jon briefly stuck his head out from the kitchen doorway. I grabbed the mail and message slips as he started yelling from the other room. "I haven't made much progress on locating the 'crumbs' of Cookie's assets."

I really didn't care right now, but he kept talking.

"Barry called to say the widow is getting impatient—the funeral was this past weekend. I was surprised they'd waited so long, but I guess it takes a while to arrange burial at sea."

Okay, that got my attention. "We live in the desert."

"Gee, you noticed." I imagined him rolling his eyes. "For your information, Alexander James Kingman was an honorably discharged U.S. Navy veteran. So sometime on Saturday, they conveyed him off of a vessel deployed from San Diego. I did some research. You can't just toss the casket in the harbor—you actually have to go out to deep water and—"

Jon had turned around in time to see me walk past the doorway. I kept walking. He chased after me a few seconds later with a wet paper towel.

"What happened to your face *this* time?"

I snatched the towel from him when he tried to wipe my cheek. "The other guy looks worse."

He sighed and lifted a hand. "Are you okay? Do you need—"

"I need you to leave me alone for a while." I closed my office door on his worried expression.

After dropping my backpack on the floor, I went to the far wall to look at the painting that hung there. My fingertips traced the slight ripples in the paper where Vince had layered the watercolor paint. The shades of burgundy, brown and gold represented the La Madre Spring trail in Red Rock Canyon, one of our favorite places to hike.

The contrasts in my oldest brother's personality had always

intrigued me. After getting suspended from school for fighting, Vince would spend hours in his room composing love songs on his guitar. He'd patiently play board games with me, then be escorted home by the cops for random acts of vandalism with his friends. Those same contrasts had landed him in prison.

I went over to the sofa and flopped onto the cushions, draping my arm over my eyes. My hand was a little sore from earlier. I hadn't always been this tough, hadn't always been able to defend myself. That's what my three big brothers were for. But eventually the overprotected-princess thing had gotten old.

So in my freshman year at UNLV, I'd moved in with my boyfriend Bobby Mattingly. He was smart, good-looking and well-mannered. But he was also a junior, an older man with his own small apartment just off campus. My parents had not approved. At all. But at eighteen I was technically an adult and determined to show them I could make it on my own.

Determination is a mere step away from pride. And pride goeth before the fall.

When Bobby started losing his temper and lashing out irrationally, I'd been too proud to tell my family. Then one night— *that* night—I'd finally realized I was in over my head. I'd found a big stash of drugs in the bedroom closet. Bobby would have been suspended from basketball for using, but dealing would have gotten him kicked off the team and expelled from school.

Upset and scared, I'd done what I always did when I got myself in a jam. I'd called my big brother to bail me out of it. Typically, Vince didn't reprimand or lecture. He just told me to pack my bags because he was taking me back to Mom and Papa. Vince would help me; he'd make everything all right.

I'd flown around the apartment, haphazardly tossing my stuff into any container I could find. I remember hoping Bobby would go straight to the party some guys were having next door, giving me a chance to get away. But he came back and caught me trying to wipe my fingerprints off the kilo. He also saw my suitcase and the boxes.

Drifting on the tide of troubled memories, I remembered trying to placate him. But he'd been high; he'd been angry. He'd been dangerous.

"You're not going to ruin me!"

The first punch had come out of nowhere, quickly followed by too many others. My screams blended into the wail of electric guitars from the party then tapered to harsh gasps. He'd cracked one of my ribs this time…

I squeezed my eyes tighter shut, trying not to see the past.

He'd let me crawl to the bedroom, like a cat toying with its prey. Pain stabbed my side while I prayed for the strength to hold my weight against the door. Bobby hit the other side like a boom of thunder.

"I'll kill you, bitch. I will kill you."

And I believed him. I believed the look in his eyes. It was callous, calculating, terrifying on the face of a man who claimed to love me.

When I'd drawn a painful breath to try and yell for help he'd strangled my effort and squeezed tighter until my vision narrowed to a black tunnel…

I rolled onto my side, my arms clenched over my long-healed ribs, unable to stop the flashbacks.

Bobby had dragged me out to the living room, demanding I unpack. When I'd clutched at the frame of the kitchen pass-through, my fingers had brushed over the butcher block.

Turning, I'd made a slashing motion at Bobby, who jumped back and released me, only to realize the blade was upside down.

He'd just laughed. "What are you going to do with that?"

Tears slipped from under my lids as I relived the fear and humiliation all over again.

Bobby whipped his hand out and slapped me. Off guard, I staggered and he grasped my neck again. His thumb pressed my throat, cutting off my air again.

Just then the front door burst open and Bobby turned his head when Vince shouted my name and charged in.

Wiping the tears away with the heels of my hands, I sat up. The next moments had sped by in a blur of violence. I'd gone into shock at that point, watching in detached horror as Bobby's knees buckled and he fell to the floor with the steak knife in his abdomen.

His stunned and accusing stare haunts me to this day.

"I'll take care of this. Trust me, okay? No one ever has to know." Vince had rushed my suitcase and boxes down to my car then handed me the drug packet and his house key.

"Listen to me, Steele. Listen! You go to my place and stay there. Ditch the drugs—if they're found here the cops'll think you were involved."

I'd kept glancing at Bobby. The lips that I'd kissed so many times twisted into a white-lipped sneer. *"You bitch. I am so gonna make you pay for this."*

Vince had gripped my shoulders, shaking me slightly until I'd looked at him. *"When the cops or our parents show up, tell them you came to me for help after he beat you up, say you left him. Then don't say anything else, to anyone, ever."*

"But, Vince—"

He'd gently shoved me toward the door. *"Promise me. Say it."*

I'd uttered the promise and then I'd gone willingly, relieved that Vince would defend me against the school bully and cover for me with Mom and Papa like he had for all eighteen of my years. It was stupid. Childish, cowardly. Selfish. And the easy way out.

I don't know what I'd thought Vince would do. I guess I hadn't been thinking much at all as I threw the drugs in a trash Dumpster and drove numbly to my brother's house. But I'd never expected Bobby to die from his injury. I sure as hell hadn't expected Vince to voluntarily plead guilty to manslaughter at his arraignment.

Shouting that it wasn't his fault, I'd been escorted from the courtroom for disrupting the proceedings. I broke my promise and talked to Mr. Holbrook. That's when I'd found out about the second stab wound. The autopsy was inconclusive as to which was the cause of death.   .

The only time I'd seen Vince after that, he'd pressed his hand against the glass and tried to smile for me. *"I can do the time—you can't. Better me than you, little star. Never you. So keep your promise."*

To this day I wonder what would have happened if I'd had the guts to leave Bobby on my own, instead of begging Vince to come and rescue me again.

That was the one nightmare I never seemed to wake from.

CHAPTER THIRTY-THREE

Manic Monday

"I DON'T KNOW, Gray. We're not supposed to drink on the job…."

He gave the cocktail server his most charming smile. "My shift is almost over, Shelly. By the time you bring it to me, I'll be off the clock. Besides, I married the boss's daughter. What's he gonna do? Fire me?"

She laughed uncertainly at his mocking tone, but dutifully went to get him a double gin-and-tonic.

He ran a hand through his hair and his fingers came away damp. Damn, was it hot in here, or was it just him? He'd been sweating like crazy since he got in. He had everything carefully planned, but there was still so much that could go wrong….

He half listened while one of the pit bosses relayed a request for credit. The guy at the nearest blackjack table had kept getting eights and splitting them until his bankroll ran dry. Gray surprised them both by approving the risky spot loan. What did he care about handing out the Palazzo's cash? If the guy wasn't good for it, Gray wouldn't be around to worry about collecting the debt.

He rubbed at his temple. This headache was kicking his ass. It had started over the weekend with Maria crying and whining about marriage counseling. He'd taken two aspirin every four or five hours all day yesterday but the pain had to be stress-related. It got worse when Caitlyn showed up this morning.

She'd tried to seduce him first, coming on all soft and sexy.

Then she'd lost her temper and demanded to know where the money was—she wanted her share now. He'd played her, assuring Caitlyn he loved her and promising she'd get what was coming to her. She'd bought his act and fussed over him. She'd even given him a couple of pills when he'd complained about his headache.

The medication hadn't done a damned thing for him, though, when his dear old father-in-law showed up. Pushing Gray into his own office, Big Frank spent the next ten minutes threatening him, demanding he pay back every cent he'd stolen. As he'd opened the door to leave, Frank had growled that making him—or his family—unhappy would be unhealthy. Extremely unhealthy.

"Here you go, Gray."

"Thanks, babe." He winked at Shelly then took a *healthy* swallow of his G&T in front of her, the pit bosses, the gamblers and the security cameras in the ceiling.

He didn't give a shit about corporate policy. He'd be on his way to long gone within the hour.

GRAY SHOOK HIS HEAD and tightened his grip on the steering wheel. Probably shouldn't have had that double G&T on an empty stomach. The alcohol in his system was making him dizzy. His vision was blurring a little, too. He ought to pull over or grab something to eat, but he didn't want to stop until he got where he was going….

A short honk startled him and he yanked the wheel. He'd begun to drift into the next lane. Man, what was wrong with him, spacing out like that? He shook his head again, trying to clear the light-headedness. Definitely needed some food to counteract the booze. But this stretch of Boulder Highway went through a residential section of Henderson…

Gray jerked awake again. He cranked down the car's air-conditioning with a shaking hand; sweat was chilling his skin. He'd find a place to make a fast stop in Boulder City. The next exit was only a few miles down the road. But then he had to keep going. He had four hundred thousand reasons to keep going….

He heard the deep blare of a truck horn as if from a distance, but he was too tired to keep his eyes open….

CHAPTER THIRTY-FOUR

Tell No Tales

"HE'S DEAD."

I knew that. Bobby had been dead for five years. So I couldn't understand why the voice was restating the obvious. And shaking my shoulder. I blinked a few times as Cameron rattled my teeth again. "Stop it."

"Are you listening now, then? He's dead."

"Yeah, *okay*." I frowned a little, wondering if my dreams had been too vocal.

He squatted down next to the sofa so we were at eye level. As he tilted his head, his expression was equal parts amusement and annoyance. "You've no idea what I'm talking about."

"None." I sat up and swung my boots to the floor. Raising my arms, I stretched, trying to undo the knots in my upper back. Being a red-blooded male, his gaze went right to my breasts. I leaned forward long enough to give him a quick thanks-for-the-compliment-but-not-now kiss.

"So, you want to tell me again now that I'm paying attention?"

"Cavanaugh. He's snuffed it."

I heard the words but it took a few seconds to process them. What? Was he sure? What happened? Then faint tendrils of memory tickled my brain. "How do you know?"

Stone winced as he stood up, rubbing his leg above the right knee. "DiMarco's getting impatient, wants his money back now if not sooner. So I was following a few lengths behind Cavanaugh when he went under the side of a lorry trailer. Made a nasty mess of the Mercedes, I can tell you."

"He just suddenly ran into a truck."

His eyes narrowed at my tone. "No. He'd been driving a bit erratically, hedging into the right lane and jerking back. Then his car began to drift into the oncoming traffic. The other driver attempted to swerve but Cavanaugh went right under. Poor bastard probably died on impact."

"Is that what the cops said?" I got to my feet, wanting to deal with this standing upright.

"There were other witnesses. I chose not to complicate the matter with a lot of unnecessary explaining."

Crossing my arms, I studied him. I'd never played cards with Stone but I had a feeling his poker face was even better than mine. "So. It looked like an accident. You do good work."

He quirked an eyebrow in quickly veiled surprise. "Aye, but not this time."

"You just happened to choose this day and that time to follow Cavanaugh. How convenient."

Stone crossed his arms over his chest as well. "Not at all, Stella. I've a job to do and I was doing it."

My pulse beat a little faster as I watched his face. "Big Frank told me he'd 'hired a guy to take care of' Cavanaugh."

"That he did."

"*Did* tell me or *did* hire you?"

He didn't answer. Stone just stood there, glaring at me while the temperature in the room dropped several degrees.

I couldn't believe what I was asking, but I had to know. "Did you have anything to do with Gray's *accident?*"

"No, nothing."

I shot a pointed glance at his healed knuckles. "I find that hard to believe, Stone."

His gaze iced over and my veins followed suit. I'd never seen him look that distant, that lethal, before. Physically I held my ground, but verbally I backpedaled as fast as I could. "I'm sorry. I shouldn't have accused you of being a killer."

"I have been a killer, Stella, love, and so I'm not offended. It takes one to know one after all." He returned the sharp look I'd given him.

Shaken by his implication, I could only stutter. He didn't know about Bobby. Did he? "Wha— What are you—?"

"However, your naming me a liar is the real insult."

I could call him a murderer but not imply he was lying?

The utter ridiculousness of that loosened my tongue. "Okay, get the hell off your high horse. There's no way for me to know when or if you're telling the truth. We've known each other, what, a total of a week?"

"And in that week, I've already told you more about myself than anyone in the world knows, save two other people." His words were clipped, his voice as harsh as his features. "I've kept things from you, yes, omitted certain aspects of my life and my work. However, I've never outright lied to you, and—"

"Cameron—"

He cut me off, his body language closed and ominous. "You have my word that I never will. *If* my word is good enough for you."

I held his gaze, not sure what to say. I felt embarrassed and guilty but also resentful, pressured. He kept asking for something I just didn't know if I could give. He'd already told me that if I let him into my life, he wouldn't settle for anything less than everything.

On the other hand, though, he'd done so much for me in a short time. From sharing case information to the furniture to his quiet support, he couldn't have made it any clearer that he wanted a future. And the more time I spent with him, the more I thought I might want one, too.

"Your word is fine."

"Well, thank you so very much for that." Sarcasm dripped from each syllable. He started to move away, his face animated, then he turned and gestured angrily. "Dammit, Stella! What must I do to prove myself? Is the benefit of a doubt honestly so much to ask for?"

"No, but—"

He stepped closer, his eyes a darker shade of blue now. "If we're to be partners, sleeping together or working together, you'll have to be willing to meet me halfway. If you would—"

"If *you'd* shut up for a minute, I could finish what I started to say." Once he quieted, I inhaled sharply. "Being partners means trusting each other, I know that. But trust doesn't come easy to me. All I'm asking for is time. And, for what it's worth, I won't lie to you, either."

His gaze thawed a little as he uncrossed his arms and scraped a hand through his hair. "You try a man, you truly do. It's only when you're about that I lose composure."

Sensing his mood had lightened, I teased him. "That was you losing your cool? Wow. I'd hate to see you really angry."

"Aye, you would."

His expression and attitude were considerably warmer now. He leaned down to accept the make-up kiss I offered, then took me into his arms for something deeper, more meaningful. I still felt rushed. But I had to admit I was really loving these soul kisses of his.

"Hm, I don't know about this partnership thing, Stone. We might not get much work done." The feel and taste of his mouth had left me breathless.

He dropped his arms abruptly. "Then let's go, shall we?"

Confused by the sudden shift, I shook my head. "Go where?"

"The Palazzo. We've still got work to do and not much time. I want a look at Cavanaugh's things before his office is cleared out and they're turned over to the widow."

Leaning back against my desk, I rested my hands on the edge. "Maria fired me, remember? And now that Cavanaugh's dead, the case is closed."

"Not my part of it. DiMarco's money is still missing and Caitlyn's still a key to finding it."

I thought about the expression on Caitlyn's face the first time I'd seen her with Cavanaugh. And the way she'd looked right before she'd left Gray at the motel. What would she do now that he was gone? She'd be scared and lost, most likely. She'd try to find the cash.

"Yeah, and I may have an edge to push her over. Are you ready to go, *partner?*"

"*HUNH.* I didn't figure on it happening that way."

Big Frank had adopted a sober expression after Cameron sprang the news on him. The police apparently hadn't notified the family yet. He folded his hands on the desktop and nodded gravely, reminding me vaguely of Doug Holbrook. Very vaguely. Frank had a light in his eyes that couldn't possibly be grief or even slight unhappiness.

"I'm certain this comes as a bit of a shock."

I scoffed at Cameron's understatement. "Yeah, you look all torn up, Mr. D."

He gave a dry chuckle. "You and me, Steele, we don't bullshit around. So I know you'll forgive me if I ain't one for crocodile tears. I'm glad the no-good son of a bitch is outta my little girl's life."

"Just out of curiosity, who was the guy?"

"What guy're you talkin' about?"

"Stella…"

I'd have had to be blind to miss the look Stone sent me. But I stayed focused on Big Frank, arching an eyebrow as I quoted him. "The one you got to take care of Cavanaugh, so he wouldn't be a problem anymore."

He liked to joke that he ran a family-owned business, but never specified whether he meant family or The Family. See, thanks to TV and movies, if you're Italian-American, everybody assumes you're *made* or *connected* or whatever the hell you call it. However, the DiMarco holdings had always gotten a clean pass from the IRS, the FBI and the Nevada Gaming Control Board.

Mr. DiMarco was no mobster. I just think he likes the illusion of 1950s Vegas, when a gangster named Moe Dalitz and another Frank named Sinatra had been the kings of the desert. But, that being said, I'm pretty sure he'd broken a number of legs in his time.

"You think I took him out?" He laughed at me, one of his deep belly rumbles. "The guy I hired is a forensic accountant, not a hit man. Name's Riesel. Besides, before I'd put a hit on Cavanaugh, I would've got my money back first."

Cameron spoke up. "There's still a chance of finding it. We'd like to take a look 'round Cavanaugh's office."

"Yeah, sure. Let Jessica, his secretary, know I said it was okay." He looked at Stone then smiled at me. "I think this is great, you two workin' together and all. Had I known, though, I would've saved Maria payin' your bill on top of what this character is chargin' me."

I smiled at him. "Are you willing to spend a little more?"

Big Frank gave Cameron an exaggerated glare. "Women. All they're interested in is a man's wallet."

"I'm talking about a 'finder's fee,' Mr. D. A young, single mother might be desperate enough to make a deal."

He looked confused. "And who might that be?"

"Stella thinks Cavanaugh's girl could be pregnant. If she is, she might be persuaded to help locate your missing funds."

A dark cloud swept over Big Frank's features, extinguishing the usual twinkle in his eyes. "You sure about this, Steele?"

"Not positive, no." I shrugged. "But I followed her to a doctor's appointment. An obstetrician."

He turned away, closing his eyes as he ground out some ugly swear words under his breath. After a moment, he rubbed a large hand over his face and shook his head. "You're wrong. I am sorry Cavanaugh's dead. Otherwise, I coulda killed him myself."

JESSICA FOOTE was a crier.

I've never understood women who snivel at any drop of a hat and they make me uncomfortable. All of that naked emotion. Ugh. I shoved my hands into my back pockets, impatient, while Cameron skillfully extracted information.

"I—I just can't believe it, you know? Gray was always so

alive." She wiped her leaking eyes with a ball of wadded tissue. "He was such a great boss. So attentive and quick with a compliment, you know? He was a real pleasure to work so closely with."

That brought a fresh onslaught of tears. Judging by the bright scarlet color of her eyes, she'd been blubbering for a while now. Given her overblown reaction, Caitlyn must not have been Gray's first affair. And gossip has no equal like a woman scorned.

Cameron spoke in a placating tone. "We're interested in anything that might have upset Cavanaugh before he left this afternoon."

Jessica rambled on about the people who'd had contact with Cavanaugh today and cried some more. Her stuffy nose made it hard to get what she was saying. Cameron made sympathetic noises but I zoned out, wondering how to get past her into the office. Then Caitlyn's name caught my attention.

"What a be-yotch. I can't believe he picked her over—I mean, what could he possibly see in *her,* you know? She's nowhere near as pretty as—" Jessica clutched the tissue ball in a tight fist. "The way she was screaming at him this morning…"

"Really?" Cameron asked. "What about?"

She sniffled, her eyes suddenly wary. "Oh, I wouldn't know, you know? I wasn't eavesdropping."

"Of course not. But perhaps you could take a guess?" He offered a smile of encouragement.

I might as well have been a potted plant for all the attention Jessica was paying me. So I took a few subtle steps back until I had a clear shot at the doorway. I could hear if I wanted to and still get started looking for…whatever I found.

"Well, Caitlyn has this ugly, high-pitched, whining voice, you know? She said if Gray didn't keep his promise, she was gonna make him sorry. He must have said something to calm her down, though, coz then it got quiet and she looked really happy when she walked out."

"Thank you, Jessica. That's quite helpful."

"Well, Mr. DiMarco said to tell you whatever you wanted to know, you know?"

I smirked at the eagerness in her voice. It was obvious she hoped Cameron wanted to know her bra size and telephone number.

Cavanaugh's office was basically a box with simulated sunlight bulbs and utilitarian catalog-order furniture. The carpet was industrial grade since the public would never see it. There were no personal items save one: a large, framed wedding photo of Gray and Maria. However, it was turned to face the door, not the occupant.

After a cursory search of Cavanaugh's filing cabinet—it was almost empty except for a bunch of forms and some personnel files—I moved over to the desk, where I assumed the interesting stuff would be found. I pawed through his in-box, rifled the papers on the desktop then opened the top left drawer. Nothing but pens, note pads and paper clips.

Cameron came in just then, alone. "I've sent poor Jessica off to get more tissues and a coffee."

"Poor Jessica, huh?"

He affected a sympathetic tone. "Apparently the argument with Caitlyn wasn't the only one she 'really didn't hear.' Most were fairly minor or work related. However, DiMarco left a bit of an impression since he threatened to tear off and reposition Jessica's favorite part of Gray's anatomy."

Snickering, I closed the drawer. "Big Frank must issue threats so often that it slipped his mind and he forgot to tell us."

Inside the wide center drawer, I found a California road map and a handful of brochures for Mexican resort hotels. I might have thought Cavanaugh was planning a vacation. Except that I also found employment applications written in Spanish. I remembered Maria's comment the day we'd had lunch as I handed them to Cameron.

"Look at these. Maria complained about her job and then said something about it changing soon. Maybe this was what she meant."

"Or perhaps this was what Cavanaugh used to calm Caitlyn down."

The right-hand drawer was locked. I looked back in the middle drawer, where most people would keep the key, but didn't see one. "I guess Gray carries it around with him."

"Allow me." Cameron set the brochures and map down, then reached into his back pocket. He picked the lock in under three seconds.

"Impressive." I bowed my head slightly. I'd never been able to do that in less than ten. Inside the last drawer was a box of condoms, a bundle of twenty-dollar bills, a small address book and a stack of documents. "Who keeps two thousand bucks in cash in their desk?"

"How do you know the amount?" He picked up the paperwork.

I thumbed the edge of the stack, mentally calculating how much was missing. "Bartending is mostly a cash business. These are brand-new bills, still in the original bank wrapper, and all U.S. currency comes in bundles of one hundred. Looks like Gray spent about five hundred of this."

"Perhaps that's what he used to gamble with the day I followed him to the casino in Henderson."

I reached for the little black book while Cameron looked over the papers. Even without a thorough study, it was obvious that all the names were female. Cavanaugh had marked tiny symbols next to some of them. Performance scores no doubt. Maria's symbols had been crossed out. What a freakin' lowlife.

"It would seem blackjack wasn't the only gamble Cavanaugh took. Have a look at this."

Cameron handed me one of the documents. It was a whole life insurance policy with three money order receipts stapled to the front, showing the premium had been paid starting in March. I flipped several pages then stopped and whistled. "I don't think Gray was worth a million myself."

"Keep skimming until you come to the designation of beneficiary page."

My eyebrows shot up when I found it. In the event of his death, the insurance company would cut a check for one million dollars to Caitlyn Folger.

CHAPTER THIRTY-FIVE

Corners of the Mind

WE NEVER DID catch up with Caitlyn.

She was supposed to be at the front desk until six, but she'd left work due to a sudden illness. Morning sickness? Or something else? Cameron drove us to her apartment—in a silver Jaguar since it was Monday—but there'd been no answer. Jamie promised to try to find out what she could. Caitlyn might have relatives living nearby.

Since Mezzanotte's was closed and neither of us had any other pressing cases, we spent the night at home—I mean, at my house.

Despite our marital status, it was only our second date. Cameron helped me make dinner. That is, he watched while I did all of the cooking. Then we sat on the floor in the living room since I'd gotten rid of all the furniture and we watched a movie. That is, I tried to watch the first ten minutes while he seduced me.

"You know, love, this would be much more comfortable if you'd kept at least one of the settees." He supported his weight with one hand on the hard floor while the other hand swept my hair aside.

A little pang of guilt tapped my conscience as he nuzzled the sensitive skin on my neck. That furniture hadn't been cheap and I shouldn't have let my temper control me. "The material was too scratchy. We wouldn't have been comfortable anyway."

"Mm. As you say. But perhaps there's still something to be done? Those clothes look awfully constricting."

I gave an exaggerated glance down at the oversized Academy T-shirt I'd taken from Joey and the cargo shorts I'd thrown on after work. "Oh, yeah, these are pretty snug. I guess I should take it all off, huh?"

His hands were already at my waist before I'd finished my sentence. Afterward, sweaty and out of breath, one of us suggested cooling off in the pool. But the water was like a bath, slick and sensuous against bare skin, and one thing led to the only thing we had in mind…

I didn't sleep again that night. The first and best reason was Cameron. He's an imaginative and surprisingly tender lover. We couldn't see or taste or touch enough.

But the other reason was Maria. I hadn't called her. I wasn't sure if I was supposed to know about Gray. The social or professional etiquette wasn't clear to me. She'd hired me to learn the bad things about him but, now that he was gone, she probably wanted to focus on the good.

I did, however, call my brother the next morning. We met at my friend Scott Lavin's gun dealership, The Moral Imperative. After we'd had our weapons checked at the front desk and donned protective 'eyes and ears,' we moved back to the target range. Joey knows I'll probably never use any of my guns. But once a month he makes sure I know *how* to use them.

"So, did you find out anything for me?" I had to shout for Joey to hear me over the echoing report of my shots. Of the dozen rounds I'd fired, all of them had made it into the target's body area, just about half in the center mass.

"There's nothing to find out, not yet. The car was towed to the impound lot for the TSB guys to look it over and the coroner's report won't be in for a week at the earliest."

I waited while he emptied his clip into the paper silhouette. "Why is it going to take that long?"

"It's not like a routine traffic accident is a priority." Joey shrugged as he reloaded his Glock with a fresh magazine.

Raising my Beretta, I took careful aim and squeezed out six more shots. "Are you sure it was routine?"

He gave me an impatient look. "I'm not sure of anything—it's not my case. This falls under the Transportation Safety Bureau. But, from what Howard told me, there were plenty of people who saw Cavanaugh knocking back booze right before he left. Unless the next of kin asks for it, I doubt there's any reason for an autopsy."

I lowered my weapon, keeping it pointed at the floor, then set it on the shelf to reload. My thoughts jumbled around my head as I shook cartridges into my hand. It's not like I had that much experience with death, let alone with murder. So who was I to question what the police didn't? But I couldn't shake the gut-level instinct that something was wrong.

"I just think it's awfully convenient, you know? Big Frank gets rid of a thieving employee, Maria doesn't have to split her marital assets and Caitlyn gets a huge payout. Everybody wins."

"Except Cavanaugh. I doubt dying was convenient for him."

Okay, maybe my imagination and general lack of trust were getting the best of me. "Yeah, you're right. Accidents happen all the time. If Gray was stupid enough to drink heavily and drive, well…"

"My guess is the guy was getting a jump start on his trip." At my quizzical look, Joey shrugged. "Howard told me they found a flight bag packed with clean underwear and hundred-dollar bills."

My brain started spinning off scenarios. Cameron hadn't mentioned that Gray stopped anywhere, so the bag had to have been in the trunk of the Mercedes already. Could he have stashed the money at his house? If so, how could I find out?

Joey and I fired off two boxes of ammo each before calling it a morning. After I'd checked that all of my cartridges were spent and stored my gun back in its case, we left the range. Inside the building, we'd just returned the safety glasses and earplugs when Joey went into Big Brother Mode.

"So, Steele. Now that you're not holding a weapon, you

want to tell me whose Jag that was I saw parked in your driveway at six o'clock this morning?"

Avoiding his gaze, I sidestepped the question. "What were you doing at my house at 6:00 a.m.?"

"I was heading for the park to run and thought I'd swing by to check on you. Now answer the damned question."

"No. My private life is none of your business—"

Joey gripped my arm and forced me to look at him. "Yeah, it is. Or didn't it occur to you that this guy might be your caller?"

I shook my head. "It's not him."

He frowned, his light-brown eyes filled with concern. "How the hell can you be so sure?"

"The calls started before I met him."

Joey scowled. "Maybe you met him *because* of the calls—"

"It's not Cameron." He started to open his mouth again but I covered it with my palm. "How many people do I trust? Almost none. So *you'll* have to trust me on this."

He wasn't happy about it, but he gave me a perfunctory kiss on the cheek before going his separate way. Joey had to get to work and I was driving out to see Maria. After an hour of non-stop shooting, my arms were a little shaky and a bruise was developing on the heel of my thumb.

When I reached the security checkpoint at the Canyon Gate Estates, I pulled off my helmet. Balancing the Harley, I smiled brightly for Officer Lancer. "Good morning!"

He gave me the same baleful stare from beneath his dark brows. "You're operating a different vehicle today." I blinked a few times. "I never forget a face, young lady, especially one that's supposed to be pretty."

"Um, thanks?"

"Bruise looks better." He nodded toward my face.

I unwrinkled my forehead. "Oh. That."

"Guess you're going to the Cavanaughs' again. Shame about the mister."

"Yes, it is."

He jotted down my bike tag on his clipboard. "If you can't

find a parking space in the driveway, make sure you don't block the neighbors in."

"Sure thing." It sounded like Maria's friends and family had rallied around in her time of need.

However, when I rounded the curve to the house, what I saw was three good-sized Salvation Army trucks. They seemed to be getting a lot of donations this week. A half-dozen burly guys carried boxes and furniture to the trucks while the other half walked back into the house.

The Harley was small enough to slip into a spot near the garage. I got off and hung my helmet on the handlebar before heading for the front door. One of the movers must not have seen me and I didn't have much space to maneuver around the nearest truck bumper. We both landed on our butts, the contents of the box he'd held scattered around us.

"Sorry about that, lady."

"No problem. Let me give you a hand." I'd reached to pick up some of the clothes before it registered that they were all men's.

Gray hadn't been cold for twenty-four hours yet and she was getting rid of his stuff? I shoved several pair of jeans, khakis and some polo shirts into the box. Then one of the T-shirts the mover grabbed caught my attention. It was a concert souvenir from the *Spirits Dancing* tour. Being a Santana fan, I recognized the distinctive album cover.

Gray must have been the long-haired guy in the photo booth strip with Maria.

I walked up to the front door but didn't bother to knock since it was wide open. The two-story foyer looked like the entrance to an upscale hotel chain. Lots of marble, brass and crystal. There was even a semicircular marble-topped table that resembled a concierge desk, complete with an overflowing floral arrangement and a telephone.

Two Salvation Army guys came down the sweeping staircase and waddled past me balancing a king-size mattress between them. Standing out of the path of deconstruction wasn't easy. The concierge desk ended up being the safest place to wait until I could figure out where to find Maria. Luckily for me, the housekeeper found me first.

"Stella?"

I turned at the sound of my name. "Mrs. Amalfi! I didn't recognize your voice when I called here on Friday. Why didn't you say anything?"

"Well, you sounded rushed so I didn't want to bother you…"

"You look great, Mrs. Amalfi. You haven't changed a bit."

Mom must be right about sixty being the new forty. Mrs. Amalfi had worked for the family back when Maria and I were school friends. When Mrs. DiMarco died, she'd dedicated herself to caring for Maria, so I shouldn't have been that surprised to see her here.

"There's a lot more silver than gold these days." She touched her once-blond curls, a tiny smile lifting her mouth. "Anyway, Stella, I'm so glad you've come. Maria is in *such* a state. It'll be good for her to have a friend right now."

I didn't know how much of a friend I was. Except for this case, we hadn't seen each other in years, hadn't kept in touch. But if Maria needed someone right now, I'd do my best. "I can't imagine how difficult this must be for her."

"She's not herself right now. A lot of people have called but not bothered to come over, whereas you simply came, just like when you were girls." Mrs. Amalfi reached out to briefly touch my hand. "I'm sure Maria appreciates that."

I watched the Salvation Army movers carry more furniture down the stairs before Mrs. Amalfi led me through to the living room at the back of the house. I took a second to admire the view. The thirty-foot wall of sliders overlooked a huge kidney-shaped pool and the golf course and the mountains beyond.

Inside, the room didn't look too shabby, either. The vaulted ceiling soared to the second floor, bracketed on three sides by polished wood balconies. The walls were painted a soft creamy white, reflecting the bright sunlight and contrasting with the bold primary colored accents on the neutral furnishings.

"Maria, dear, look who's come to see you."

She didn't answer. So with a nudge from Mrs. Amalfi, I went over to where Maria sat hunched on the overstuffed leather couch. I braced myself to deal with her grief, noting the dark gray business suit she wore with panty hose and heels. She rocked back and forth, clutching a pad and pen in her hands. I guessed it was a list of arrangements to be made.

"Maria?"

She looked up at me with a quizzical expression, her red-rimmed eyes unfocused. Then her face cleared and she smiled vaguely in welcome. "Steele. What are you doing here?"

"I came to see if you were all right, see if you needed anything."

"That's very nice of you but I'm fine." She looked down at her lap, repeating the words softly like a mantra. "I'm fine. I'm just fine."

I dropped my backpack and sat down, awkwardly patting her shoulder. My grandmother had passed back when I was five and I hadn't been welcome at Bobby's funeral. So my experience was limited. I tried to recall what to do in this situation; how my mother and aunts had handled bereavement visits when Gloria died. Only one thing came to mind.

"Are you hungry? Have you eaten anything?"

Maria glanced at her watch. "Not yet. Half an hour."

She didn't explain, so I assumed she had a luncheon or something and wondered why she hadn't cancelled. No one would object under the circumstances.

"So, um, how are you holding up?" It was a stupid question, just one of the many platitudes one pulls out for occasions when one has no concept of how badly the other person is hurting.

"Last night was difficult, of course. The house was emptier, the bed colder… I slept in one of the guest rooms." Her gaze flickered, taking on that steely edge, before she closed them for a second. "When I finally slept. Too many memories…"

"I'm sorry, Maria." I did the patting thing again. "I should go, let you get some rest."

"Maybe later. Right now there's too much to do. The funeral is scheduled for Friday morning at ten then, the repast will be immediately afterward. Robinson's will do the catering, of course. They're the best for large parties. People are always so famished after watching the body go into the ground, aren't they?"

Not sure what to say to that, I groped for a reply. I was saved the trouble when Mrs. Amalfi called out. "Maria? Is all of the exercise equipment going?"

"No, Sarah. The treadmill and stairclimber are mine."

"*Which* treadmill? There are three of them in the gym room."

Maria tossed the pad aside and stood up. "Excuse me, Steele. I'll be right back."

Well, this was awkward. I was more than ready to go. But I didn't know if drive-by condolences were good enough, or if I was supposed to stay and try to help somehow. Figuring I could make phone calls, I picked up the notepad to see how many people needed to be notified of the arrangements.

The list was divided into two short columns. The first row of names was under the heading *executive board members;* the second was *major shareholders.* Below them were abrupt notes written in a scrawl unlike Maria's usual careful script: *Majority vote? Daddy out? Tax liability?*

I placed the pad back where I'd found it. Big Frank must not have been able to keep the embezzlement quiet after all. But in terms of money, four hundred grand in a Vegas casino was like quarters in a bingo hall. Not nearly enough to fire Frank as Chairman. Unless…the cash Gray stole wasn't the only theft.

Shaking my head, I got to my feet. When Maria wanted my help, she'd ask for it. Wondering if Cameron knew anything about the Palazzo's finances and whether he'd found Caitlyn yet, I walked back toward the foyer and almost ran into Maria coming the other way.

"I'm sorry to leave you, but I've got to go."

"Here, take this." She pushed a small box into my arms,

causing the contents to rattle. Inside were four liquor bottles, one gin, a vodka and two whiskeys. "Those were the only unopened ones."

"Thanks, but—"

She waved her hand. "Take them, please. I won't drink it so there's no point to having them around."

Peering deeper into the box I saw that the liquor was all top brand. I started to suggest she keep them for guests or for parties, but she seemed determined. I figured I'd hold on to the vodka and give the rest away or something.

"Thanks, Maria."

"No, thank you, Steele. I appreciate your stopping by."

Mrs. Amalfi cleared her throat. "I think these gentlemen have it all, unless you've thought of something else?"

Maria rubbed her temple and frowned. "Yes, I changed my mind about his den. Same as before, empty any papers you find into a box and then everything in that room can go, too."

"Not the paintings and—"

"Yes, Sarah, all of that stuff."

"Very well." Mrs. Amalfi gave a quiet sigh before leading the movers back up the stairs.

My thoughts must have shown on my face because Maria avoided my gaze when she spoke. "It's too hard, Steele. There are just too many memories…."

I thought she was rushing things and figured she'd regret this impulse purging later. But it wasn't my place to comment. So all I could do was offer another platitude. "I'm really sorry for your loss."

"I really don't believe this. I just can't." Her little girl voice, already soft, faded to a whisper. Then she turned and walked back into the living room.

As I left, I tried to figure out how I was going to transport all of this booze. I'd just realized I only had room in my backpack for one bottle. Glancing over my shoulder to see if anyone was watching, I pulled out the vodka then stuck the box in one of the Salvation Army trucks.

The guys were still hauling stuff out of the house.

Not only was Gray gone, but within the hour it would be like he'd never been there at all.

CHAPTER THIRTY-SIX

Treasures of the Deep

"HEY, STEELE. You're just in time to hear my news."

Jon was beyond relieved to see his boss walk into the agency. If he had to ooh over one more department-store photo of Barry Dreyer's weird-looking kids…

"Hi, Barry. How are you?"

"I'm good, Stella, I'm good. I was just showing Jon here the latest pictures of the twins. You should see—"

"Sure, maybe later?" Steele cut Barry off with an eye roll only Jon could see. "Why don't we go back to my office so Jon can spill his surprise before he hurts himself."

"Funny. Ha ha."

Jon was pretty impressed with what he'd discovered, though. It had been like solving a jigsaw puzzle with missing pieces. He grabbed the file and followed them down the hall. The Kingman assets hadn't been easy to locate, but he'd followed the electronic trail until suddenly all was revealed. He felt like a computer geek version of Indiana Jones.

Once Barry and Steele were seated, Jon rubbed his hands together in anticipation. "So, I have good news and bad news."

"You found Cookie's money. That's the good news, right?" Barry asked.

"But the other news is apparently bad for Bunny." Steele's natural cynicism showed in her tone.

Jon wriggled his eyebrows. "Yep. The five hundred thousand in their joint bank account is all she's going to get."

Barry's expression made it clear he didn't look forward to telling little Miss Gold Digger to stop shopping for beachfront condos in Maui. "Other than the small bequests in the will to his two kids and some cousins, *everything else* was left to 'his beloved wife and faithful companion.' So what is everything else and where is it?"

"Patience, if you please. Like any good story this one needs to be told properly."

"Let's let Jon have his moment." Stecle propped her boots on the coffee table and settled into the couch, so Barry reluctantly leaned back in the guest chair and waited.

Jon consulted several sheets of paper in the Kingman file, but it was mostly for show. He wanted to impress Steele with the details of his treasure hunt. Maybe now she'd see him as more than a secretary, more of a partner and, eventually, as a friend.

"I haven't been able to get hold of Cookie's medical records yet, so there's no way of knowing exactly when he was diagnosed with the pancreatic cancer. But he's been busy for the past nine months. Cookie sold his vacation home in Palm Springs and his interest in the bakery chain to his kids." He paused for effect. "For a thousand dollars apiece."

"But," Barry sputtered. "That house was worth over a million and the business—I have no idea what that was worth!"

Jon spread his hands and shrugged before continuing. "He took out a second mortgage on his Vegas residence amounting to all the equity in the house."

Barry shook his head. "Another two million dollars."

"He sold the ten luxury sports cars to a classic car dealership and then leased them back on a monthly basis. And as for his coin collection he sold that outright."

"All of that came to $5,694,209."

Barry sighed. "So, what did he do with that much money?"

"I can't wait for the punchline of this joke." Steele grinned mischievously.

Jon smiled, too. "He put it in the bank."

"All of it?" Barry asked hopefully.

"All of it," he confirmed. "Specifically a local bank in San Diego under the name James A. King."

"Here it comes." Steele smirked.

Jon tossed the file on the edge of the desk and crossed his arms, enjoying the revelation. "Once I discovered the second name, I pulled another set of credit reports. At the bottom were inquiries from Sotheby's auction house and an upscale San Diego jeweler, J.E. Ramirez Gems."

"Oh, no," Barry sighed.

"Oh, yes. A phone call to Ramirez confirmed they accepted shipments from Sotheby's London and Zurich auction houses. 'James King' bought twenty antique watches at special auction, including a 1952 perpetual calendar chronograph Patek Phillipe for $1,773,206. A world-record sale for a wristwatch sold at Sotheby's, by the way."

Steele laughed out loud. "What's the one thing money can't usually buy, the one thing a dying man would want most? Time."

Jon grinned, openly admiring Cookie's sense of humor. "The bank records also showed counter debits in the form of cashier's checks made out to Forsyth & Sons Funeral Home for preparation and disposition and a specially ordered casket."

"In other words...?" Barry asked grudgingly, since he'd already guessed the answer.

"In exact words," Jon corrected. "He took it all with him."

CHAPTER THIRTY-SEVEN

Until the End

GRAY CAVANAUGH MUST have been quite popular at the Palazzo.

Either that, or his employees and co-workers had simply wanted excused time off from work. Cameron found it hard to believe all of these people had been friends. Especially since the turnout looked to be mostly DiMarco's contemporaries, as opposed to Maria's peers.

He glanced about at the mourners gathered by the graveside, studying their faces, looking for anyone who might appear guilt-ridden or gleeful. Cavanaugh's death probably had been a drunk driving accident. However, there'd been something about the way his car had drifted right into that lorry…

Listening to the priest drone the standard liturgy of comfort, his thoughts drifted and he wondered who might show up when he packed it in. If his body were recoverable, that is. Some of the places the Nighthawks were assigned… No, his team would be there. Ice, Blueman, Loco Vaquero and Starfish. Men he could count on, who depended on him as well.

Trust had been a foreign concept after he'd lost his parents. Uncle Jack'd had no desire to raise an angry, grieving lad and so shipped him off.

The Gordonstoun School had been a difficult adjustment, putting it mildly. From the time he'd left at sixteen, through his brief SAS career to his recruitment into the Nighthawks, he'd had a pistol in his hand and a mission objective in his sights. He'd learned to quickly assess and place his faith in people upon whom the mission and his life depended.

It was those same instincts that had led him to Stella. He looked at her now, standing quietly at his side.

She'd done up her hair to go with her conservative navy suit. A smile tugged at his mouth, knowing as he did that she wore sexy white lace knickers underneath. They'd spent last night together. They'd spent every night this week that she hadn't tended bar together.

He'd twice replaced the guest room furniture until she settled on something she liked. However, the living room was still a point of contention. English Hunt Lodge—"I don't want dead animal heads on the wall!"; 1960s Retro—"You've got to be kidding"; and Country Farmhouse—"Do I look like a milkmaid?" had all been utterly rejected.

As he'd known they would be. He smiled down at her, anticipating her reaction to French Provincial.

"I don't have a damned thing to say."

Cameron looked over at Frank DiMarco. Apparently he was refusing to give a eulogy for his late son-in-law. The priest stood by awkwardly for a second or two, waiting to see whether anyone else might pay their respects. No one did. Finally, Maria got slowly to her feet and went to the casket.

"Gray was such a wonderful man. We fell in love almost the moment we met and we were happy…right up until the end." Her girlish voice caught on the lie as she drew her fingertips along the glossy mahogany surface. "We were happy…."

He glanced around, checking to see how that statement was received. A few women had sly curves to their lips. Caitlyn's predecessors, undoubtedly. Suddenly his eyes tracked a flash of red, partially hidden behind a tall headstone. Ah, Caitlyn herself, keeping well away from the widow's line of sight.

Maria stood motionless beside the coffin, eyes dull, seemingly lost in thought. Then she abruptly cleared her throat. "Um, thank you for, uh, for coming today."

With that she turned and walked to the waiting limousine, the rose she'd plucked from a casket spray still clutched in her hand. Frank jumped to his feet to follow her. The priest said something or other that no one paid any mind to. The assembly fidgeted for a moment, then began to disperse.

"Well, that has to be the shortest funeral service in history," Stella murmured as she stood up. "I can't believe she didn't have it in church."

He got to his feet as well, but faced the opposite direction. "I'll meet you by the car."

"Where are you going?"

"To talk to someone." He nodded toward Caitlyn.

She looked over, then back. "I'll go with you."

He put a gentle hand on her shoulder. "Not this time, Stella, love. The game isn't called bad cop/volatile cop."

Crossing her arms, she glared at him. "Are you saying I can't do the job?"

"Not at all."

He kept his expression mild and his tone friendly, but didn't give ground. She held his stare, gauging his silence, and then made an exaggerated study of the cars parked along the cemetery road.

"Which one is it again?"

"The Maserati. It's Friday." He gave her a quick kiss on the cheek before moving off.

Gently shouldering his way through the crowd, he caught up to Caitlyn before she could escape into her Mustang. The last time he'd seen her, she'd been full of furious life. Today she appeared so pale that her freckles looked like wounds. He leaned a hand on the driver's door to hold it shut.

"Hey!" She turned tired, confused eyes on him and frowned.

"Miss Folger? Might I have a word?"

She glanced at his hand on her car. "I'll give you a couple of words—"

"You must have cared deeply for Gray to attend his funeral." Taken aback by the question, she blinked twice. "Oh, well, I didn't know him that well. I just thought it was the right thing to do."

"Really? Well, it was a bit of a risk, wasn't it? You might have been seen by his wife." Her eyes widened at his sneering tone of voice. "So exactly how long were you screwing around with Cavanaugh?"

"What? That's ridiculous. I'm not going to answer such a question." Caitlyn forced a laugh.

He shrugged and gave her a relaxed smile. "Fine by me. I didn't walk over to ask about your affair. I'm more interested in the money you stole."

If possible she grew even paler, her eyes darting about for an escape. "I don't—I have no idea what you're talking about."

"You colored your hair or wore a wig, used a different name. However, a handwriting analyst matched the signature on your casino credit and employment applications."

She remained defiantly silent.

"Still not ringing any bells? You remembered well enough the other day at the Vista Buena Inn."

"Have you been following me?" She shouted the question in false outrage, hoping to cause a scene.

Cameron simply stared down the two men who paused and looked over until they kept walking. "Aye. And I'll gladly tell everyone in earshot, why if you don't lower your voice."

A guilty flush darkened her pale features. "I told you, I don't—"

"You're a liar as well as a thief, eh?" He leaned closer, staring into her eyes, using his size to intimidate as he lowered his voice to a whisper. "Are you a murderer as well as a liar, Miss Folger?"

"What? Of course not!" Her words were adamant; however her voice trembled and her eyes flicked to the cemetery workers lowering Cavanaugh into his grave. "Why would you even say an awful thing like that?"

"Other than the four hundred thousand reasons you already had, I can think of one million more."

Comprehension flashed across her expression. She said nothing, however she must have known about the life insurance policy. He saw the pulse jumping at her throat. "What do you want?"

"The money. Where is it?"

"I don't know."

He rested his elbow on the hood of her car and affected a reasonable tone. "Embezzlement is hardly a violent crime, is it? But that won't stop them from locking you away with the worst prison has to offer. I doubt you want to give birth under those conditions."

"Jesus! I don't believe this." Tears filled her eyes and she placed a protective hand over her belly. Caitlyn stared off into the distance, shaking her head slowly.

"Talk to me, then. Mr. DiMarco simply wants his funds restored. You'll lose your job of course, and another casino is out of the question. However, he won't prosecute."

She continued to avoid looking at him. Her expression was pained, as though she were weighing her options and finding all the ways barred. Finally she took a deep breath and bowed her head. "Yeah, I helped him, okay?"

He nodded. "Now we're getting somewhere."

"It was like a game to him, a way to get back at them. But then we started thinking it could be our ticket out, you know? We'd planned to make a fresh start at one of the resorts on the Gulf, live on the money until Gray's divorce came through…"

"What happened?" He only wanted the damned location, and he was certain Stella was beyond impatient sitting back in the car. However, Caitlyn seemed in the mood for a long chat.

She rubbed her belly and gave him a mirthless smile. "This happened. It turned out Gray didn't want the baby. He didn't want the divorce either, not once he found out he'd walk away with his good looks and charm and not much else."

Cameron simply looked at her, keeping hold of his patience whilst she told her story. Perhaps he ought to be more sympathetic, but the situation was of her own making.

"I panicked at the idea of being a single mother." She made a wry face. "So I threatened to tell his wife if he didn't take care of me. He didn't want to at first. But I walked up to them in the Palazzo lobby one day. I just said good morning, but he knew I was serious then. That's how I ended up on the policy."

"You asked for insurance?"

"No, see, that was just a stroke of luck. His wife wanted to increase what they had and gave him the paperwork to fill out. Gray told her he'd take care of mailing it in, so he wrote my name as beneficiary."

He tipped his head and raised one brow. "You realize, of course, that would give you a perfect motive to get rid of him."

Caitlyn's features set. "I didn't force those drinks down his throat and I'm not the one who thought he was worth a million bucks dead. He didn't even show me the insurance papers until the morning he died. It's a whole life policy. He could have borrowed against it when the baby came."

"Let's get back to the matter at hand, shall we? Where is the money you stole from the casino?"

"Gray withdrew every single dollar. Most of it had been turned into traveler's checks and the rest of the cash was in the safe deposit box."

He stepped closer. "You must have some idea what's happened to it."

"I don't know." She stepped back from the look on his face. "I *really* don't. The bank had no record of a cashier's check being drafted or any wire transfer. When I tried to find out what he did with it, he just told me some bullshit story about Maria finding a bank statement so he put it somewhere safer."

Bloody hell. Cameron flattened his mouth into a thin line. He'd been certain the girl could lead him to the cash so he could sign off on this case.

"The money's gone, mister. You'll have to tell Mr. DiMarco that Gray was the only person who knew where it is."

CHAPTER THIRTY-EIGHT

Skeletons

THE EMBOSSED PARCHMENT invitations Maria had sent out directed us to the Canyon Gate estates following the service. The repast was being held not at the Cavanaughs' but at the main clubhouse. In the Petite Ballroom. I guess Gray didn't rate the Grand Ballroom.

After giving the valet the keys, Cameron came around to my door and helped me out of the car. I let him. Something about wearing a skirt makes me want to comply with the courtesies. He lifted my fingers to his lips. "How long must we put in an appearance?"

"Long enough to pick up any information that might help us find the missing money."

"I suppose it's too much to hope that someone will blurt out the location as soon as we walk in?" His lips brushed the tender inside of my wrist.

I gave him a coy smile as a quiver of pleasure traveled along my nerves. "Not in the mood to work, huh?"

He lowered my arm but held on to my hand as we walked toward the entrance. "Let's just say I'm in a different sort of mood."

I gave his fingers a little squeeze along with my promise. "Thirty minutes to an hour, then I'll take you home and race you to the bed. Or the carpet, since that'll be closer."

The Petite Ballroom was decorated for a wedding, not a

wake. Stark-white linen-covered tables laden with bright floral arrangements in crystal vases. The chairs were draped in fabric that tied in large bows at the back. A quartet softly played classical music for the mourners' enjoyment.

Nothing like that personal touch when a loved one dies.

I spotted Maria near the windows and nudged Cameron. We walked over to pay our respects to the "grieving widow." Somehow she'd had time to change into a lighter gray suit and darker pink lipstick. Her full attention was on the good-looking man speaking to her. She smiled at him and took a sip of champagne.

Funny, I'd thought she didn't drink. Then again, it was her husband's funeral and death changes all the rules. I had to stop being so damned cynical.

"How are you doing, Maria?"

"I'm okay, Steele, thank you." She looked at Cameron. "Who's this?"

I turned slightly to make the introductions. "This is Cameron Stone, my...uh, date."

"I'm sorry for your loss, Mrs. Cavanaugh."

"You brought a date to a funeral?" Maria stared at me with an odd little smile, ignoring his condolences. "Well, by all means have something to eat and enjoy yourselves."

As she turned back to her companion, Cameron quietly suggested splitting up to work the crowd. He headed toward a group of self-important-looking men. I headed for the buffet. One thing I'd learned from Aunt Gloria was to stay near the food during investigations like this.

Their mouths are already open so listen up 'cause you never know what might come out.

I picked up a dinner plate and pretended to study the choices. There was so much food it would look like I was counting calories. Three well-heeled and fashionably emaciated women approached. Each of them began filling teacup saucers with seafood-stuffed vegetables as they continued their whispered discussion.

"—Had no family here, Maria didn't know who to call. Gray *said* his people were in Chicago but…"

"I just can't imagine, can you? Two husbands in six years."

"Well, she won't get anything out of this one. She was always complaining about how much he spent—"

They moved off toward a table while I stared at my still empty plate. I hadn't known that Maria was married before. Of course, why would I? But now I was curious about why she'd split from the first husband. Some women unfortunately attracted cheaters.

"Ach. Nobody's-a eating my lasagna."

Hearing the heavy sigh, I looked over at the antique woman who'd come up beside me. She wore understated dignity like a perfume. I glanced from her petulant expression to the table overflowing with delicate hors d'oeuvres and beautifully prepared miniature entrees. Then I saw what had upset her.

Shoved off to the side like primitive art amid masterpieces were two enormous clay dishes of homemade pasta. Hmm. A leaf of endive smeared with a half teaspoon of cold crab salad? Or an aromatic brick of bubbling cheese, meat, sauce and noodles? This would not be a difficult decision after all.

"They look delicious, ma'am."

"What's-a with this 'ma'am'? You a friend of Maria's?"

I offered her my hand. "Yes, I'm Stella. We went to high school together."

"Then you call me Aunt Rosa." She gripped my wrist with a liver-spotted hand and shuffled me toward the lasagna. "This-a one, I put ground sausage and roasted peppers with mozzarella. I make this other one with mushrooms, spinach and provolone."

I pretended to weigh my options while my stomach made its preference clear. "How about a small piece of each, please."

"Now that's-a what I like to hear." A wide smile brightened Aunt Rosa's wrinkled face and she reached up to pat my cheek. "You're a healthy girl, I can tell. Not my Maria, though. I spent all yesterday cooking, but she won't try not one bite. She says she can't-a have the carbs."

Glancing at the trio of skeletons, I lowered my voice as if conveying a secret. "Don't worry. I'm allergic to carb-free diets."

"No, no. Maria, she can't have so many starches. The blood sugar, you know."

I held my plate with both hands as she unloaded a heaping portion of sausage lasagna onto it. "You mean Maria's diabetic?"

"Diabetic, yes." The slice of mushroom lasagna Rosa gave me was thankfully smaller. "There you go. *Mangia!*"

She waited expectantly while I took the first bite, then patted my cheek again when I made complimentary humming noises. It really was good. She'd used nutmeg, of course, but I thought I detected a hint of clove as well. I'd have to tell Papa.

"I'm starved." Cameron walked up behind me and leaned forward to take the next bite. "That's quite good, isn't it?"

Rosa beamed at him. "I'll get-a you a plate."

"You've just made her very happy." He moved around me and tried to guide the next forkful his way but I was faster. "Wait for your own, will you?"

"And here's me thinking we're to be partners. Partners share, Stella, love."

I guarded my plate from further attack. "Why don't you share what you've found out?"

"Not as much as I'd hoped. Cavanaugh did not exactly endear himself to people. The general consensus seems to be that he was tied to his wife's purse strings and took full advantage of being the boss's son-in-law. He was an opportunist at best. At worst…?"

"Nah, it's not wurst. I only use the fresh sausage from Salvatore's *macelleria*. Sal, he's a good butcher. He makes-a the sausage when you order."

Cameron hid a smile as he thanked Rosa for the food. Then he offered her his arm. "Why don't we sit down?"

"Such nice manners. You hold on to this one, Stella."

He gave me a look that said Rosa was the smartest woman on the planet. I stuck the tip of my tongue out at him. Once we were seated at an empty table, Cameron asked, "Are you a friend of the family or family itself?"

"Maria's grandmother is my sister, but she calls me Aunt Rosa. There's-a nothing 'great' about being my age."

I smiled along with him then tried to draw her out. "I'm sorry for your loss. Were you and Gray close?"

Rosa made a wry face. "He's not much of a loss, you ask-a me. Maria, she gave him everything, treated him like royalty. She was such a devoted wife to him. But he wasn't so much of a husband."

"That's too bad."

"I don't think she was very happy." She looked across the ballroom at the sound of Maria's peal of laughter and frowned. "Still it would-a be better to at least pretend to grieve."

Cameron glanced at me before addressing Rosa. "Perhaps she's in shock, or putting on for show. People react quite differently to death."

Rosa sighed again and a poignant expression softened her gaze. "I suppose-a you're right. Maria has seen too many deaths in her short life. First Gina—may God have mercy on her—then the baby and Anthony, and now Gray."

"Anthony?" I carefully modulated my tone to hide my curiosity.

"Maria's first husband, a dear friend of Frankie's. He was so surprised when she finally got pregnant. But then the miscarriage and less than a month later, poor Anthony had a heart attack." Rosa shook her head sadly. "They said if-a he'd only been able to reach his pills, he might have survived."

I SHUCKED OFF my suit jacket as soon as I got home, undoing my blouse while I walked down the hall. Cameron groaned softly behind me. But, instead of going into the bedroom, I headed for my office and started my computer. Waiting impatiently for it to boot up, I toed off my shoes and stripped away my panty hose.

Cameron had followed me. Jacket removed and his tie

hanging loose, he leaned against the door frame. "I'm not racing you to bed, am I?"

"Maria had not only two husbands in six years but two dead husbands? That's incredible bad luck, don't you think?"

"An older man suffers a heart attack. A guy who's been drinking has a car accident. These events are not out of the realm of possibility."

Staring at the monitor, I rolled my shoulders impatiently. "Maybe. But, the timing is kind of suspicious. She loses an unexpected baby and a husband in the same month. Her second marriage and second husband die in the same week. Expedient coincidences? Or something more?"

Cameron waved his hand negligently at the computer. "Go on, then. Do your search so I can finally have you naked."

I opened the Web browser and, after some hunting, I found the August 2000 notice. *Mr. Francis S. DiMarco, widower, proudly announces the engagement of his only daughter Maria DiMarco to long time friend and business associate Anthony Giocondo, 60...*

I stopped reading. Now that I had his name, I ought to be able to find out when he died.

"A classic May-December pairing, eh?" Cameron read over my shoulder then pointed at the screen. "Have a look at this."

The happy couple will celebrate their nuptial mass on Christmas Eve at St. Joseph Catholic Church, Father Samuel Zanti presiding...

"Huh. That's the same priest who did the funeral service this morning. I wonder—" I searched the Web again until I found Maria and Gray's wedding announcement, dated March 23, 2002. "Yep. Father Zanti strikes again."

"When exactly did Giocondo die?" Cameron rested his hip on the corner of my desk.

"Let's find out."

I pulled up the Social Security Death Index and typed in his name. The results came back with three Anthony Giocondos but only one had died in Vegas. That listing also gave his social security number, which would allow me to request a copy of the death certificate.

"October 5, 2001."

Cameron snorted. "Maria barely waited a decent time before getting another ring on her finger, did she? Cavanaugh must have swept her right off her feet."

I was curious about that, but I was more curious about something else. I pushed back from the desk and offered him the chair. "Here. Go to this Web site and find the obituary. The *Review-Journal* keeps them online for six years. I want to check my music collection."

"Beg pardon?"

After dumping my discarded clothes on the bed, I went out to the living room. It took me a minute to find what I was looking for. Somewhere on my shelves was a CD of Santana's *Spirits Dancing* album. When I checked the recording date, I wasn't exactly surprised.

Cameron called out from the office. "According to a newspaper write up, Giocondo died at home."

That didn't surprise me, either. Remembering the photo booth strip I'd noticed the day Maria hired me, I was certain.

She'd been seeing Gray while she was still married to Anthony.

CHAPTER THIRTY-NINE

Dirty Little Secret

THE WORDS I NEEDED to say were crowded on my tongue, decaying from lack of use.

Cameron had taken me out for a great dinner, then afterward we'd gone to his condo where I'd spent the night in his arms. When I woke up, we shared breakfast in bed. Crystal, bone china, roses—the works. He'd somehow arranged for it all to be delivered while I slept.

I hated like hell to break the mood. But now it was time to leave for Sunday dinner at my parents' house. "So, um, what have you got planned for the day?"

"Nothing I can't put off for a bit." He brushed the petals of a rose across my bare chest then followed the touch with a kiss.

A shiver of greedy desire that I should have been too sated to feel skimmed down my spine. I tried really hard to ignore it. "No, don't do that."

"Don't do this?" He moved the flower around to my breast.

"No, not that either. I meant, if you've got things to do, you don't need to change your agenda."

"It's not a problem, Stella, love. I'm sure I can get plenty accomplished…afterward…and before we have to leave. What time do your parents expect us?"

"Um, they're—oooh." I shivered again, distracted despite my resolve. I took a deep breath to clear the lust from my brain. "They're, uh, expecting *me* in about thirty minutes."

The rose stilled in its path along my torso. So did

Cameron's features when I dared to glance at him. He stared at me, utterly motionless, inhaling slowly through flared nostrils, while his pale blue eyes frosted over. The moment stretched out into an unnerving silence. Yet, he said nothing.

I rolled away and slid the three feet from the king-size bed to the floor. Keeping my back to him, I dragged on my panties. I didn't want to feel naked as well as guilty. "You'll have time to do what you need to this afternoon, and then this evening you can, um, do, uh, whatever, and then we can get together later…"

Pulse tap-dancing, I let my words drift into silence. I was being a coward. Squaring my shoulders, I turned around to face him. And felt my heart pierced. Anger or resentment I would have anticipated. I wasn't prepared to see his hurt before he controlled it.

"Cameron…"

He tossed the rose aside and got off of bed. "I do not appreciate being treated like a dirty little secret, Stella."

"Cameron—"

The bathroom door shut firmly between us.

"THEN MR. SINATRA stood up, finished the last of his Jack Daniels and said to us, 'See ya 'round, kids.'"

Normally I would have given my father's favorite anecdote the reverent attention it deserved. But as a seemingly endless stream of food and conversation passed by me, the only sound I heard was a closing door. Cameron hadn't uttered a single word before I'd walked out.

Sitting here in my parents' dining room, surrounded by three generations of family, I felt unexpectedly isolated. And empty. Only my cousin Giada and I weren't paired off. Even Allegra was sitting next to baby Paul. It usually didn't bother me; I wasn't conscious of it. But today? Today I missed Cameron.

"Is something bothering you, *cara?*"

I looked up from toying with the chicken tetrazzini, grilled beef and roasted artichokes on my plate. The Mom Radar was hard at work. She'd been hovering since I walked in the door, sending me furtive worried looks and patting me every time she walked by. So I did what all good daughters did—I lied.

"I'm fine, Mom. Just a little tired."

My youngest brother spoke around a mouthful of pasta. "Yeah? Didn't get much sleep, huh. Where is the boyfriend today?"

"He's not my *boyfriend,* Joey."

Despite the loud and animated chatter around the tables, my father managed to hear the one question I wished he hadn't. "What's this, Stella? You have a boyfriend?"

I cringed as twenty pair of eyes jerked in my direction. "No, Papa, he's not my—"

Mom interrupted with a delighted smile. "*Ammázza!* Why didn't you tell us you had a new boyfriend?"

"He's *not*—"

"What's his name?" Allegra wanted to know.

Aunt Carmella leaned forward so she could see me better. "What's he like? He's Italian, of course."

Santina smiled at me. "Tell us about him. How did you meet?"

Rafe, my uncles and male cousins just rolled their eyes while the women in the family bombarded me with questions.

"Joey, have you met him?"

"No, Ma, *not yet.* I just saw his car still at her house one morning." He ignored the nasty look I gave him.

Papa ducked his head and concentrated on his food rather than acknowledge that his sweet baby girl was having sex. But Mom sent me a cheerful, just-between-us wink. "I guess our little talk at the spa paid off, eh? *Brava!*"

"So when do we get to meet this new boyfriend of yours?" Aunt Julia asked.

I was guessing that "never" wasn't the best answer. But I didn't want everybody getting excited about a relationship that might already be over.

"He's not my boyfriend. Not exactly—"

Papa cleared his throat and cocked his head at me. "Next time, Stella, you bring him, yes? Your *friends* are always welcome in our home."

IT FELT WRONG to use the building pass card Cameron had given me, but I wasn't sure he would answer the intercom. I was just juggling my backpack and two heavy packages, trying to fit the key into the lock, when the door opened a crack.

He was barefoot, his long legs encased in softly faded denim. His shirt was unbuttoned, like he'd just thrown it on, and his hair was tousled and damp. He didn't greet me, just gave me an inquiring look as if I were a door-to-door salesman. He didn't let me in, either.

"Am I interrupting?" I smiled to show how nice I could be.

"Not at all. I've just finished several laps in the stream pool."

He still didn't let me in. I narrowed my eyes and almost forgot my plan to make things up to him.

"I just stopped by to see you."

"Here I stand." He swept a hand up his body, his tone annoyingly composed.

"I was rude and insensitive, okay? I'm sorry. But I think it's way too soon to play Meet the Family. The last guy I took home didn't work out so well. I don't want to rush things any more than they already have been."

Cameron opened the door a little wider and nodded toward the bags I carried. "What's all this then?"

"This," I raised my right arm, "is linguine with red clam sauce and beef *stracotto* with porcini." Lifting my other arm, I said, "This is a container of *minestrone* and some frozen garlic citrus chicken. My mother thought you might be hungry."

Cameron studied me for a moment. I held his gaze and my tongue, sincerely hoping we didn't need to make a big, fat mushy deal about this. Finally he nodded again, the edges of his mouth lifting slightly as he swung the door wide.

"Those look heavy. Come inside."

"You could help, you know." I shrugged to shift the weight of the three bags.

"Certainly not. I've finally accepted that your independence is equally as fierce as your temper."

CHAPTER FORTY

Step Into My Parlor

WITNESSES SAW *Cavanaugh drinking at work. Pretty ballsy. Why? He wasn't sticking around. Maybe a job came through in Mexico.*

I tapped the fountain pen on my desktop to the rhythm of my thoughts as I stared out my office window. How could he have gotten so drunk without anyone trying to stop him? That bothered me. There'd been times when I drank more than I should have; times I drove when I shouldn't have.

But I'd never been wasted enough to aim for a truck…

Could Gray have committed suicide?

Find out Cavanaugh's mind set. Reading too much into his death? Maybe. Accident perfect timing for Caitlyn though. Lying about embezzled money. Motivated by baby? Talk to her again, and again if necessary. Can Maria contest the insurance payout??

What about Maria? Acting really weird. Is it remorse? Maybe just shock. Or could be guilt? Who was the guy with her at the repast? Husband #3? If she cheated on #1, she might cheat on #2. Hired me as a ploy because of divorce?

One woman married to much older man and then to womanizer; two dead guys. Suspicious. Twist of fate or did Maria make her own luck? Find out more about my old "friend."

In the meantime, I wanted to learn what I could about husband number one. After stuffing my notes into the Cavanaugh folder I'd reopened, I got up to grab my backpack. Jon was just switching on the phones when I walked by the reception desk.

He gaped at me, checked his watch and then clutched his heart. "My gawd, you're in the office before me? On a Monday morning? This must be a sign of the Apocalypse!"

"Funny. I'm headed for Shadow Lane, then to follow up on a couple of cases. I've got my cell phone if you need me."

As soon as the Office of Vital Records opened, I handed over fifteen bucks and an application request. The surly-looking woman at the counter eyed me suspiciously. In my Don't Start with Me—You Won't Win T-shirt, I guess I looked like the kind of person who would forge a new identity.

"Death certificate, huh? What do you want it for?"

"A case I'm working on." I flashed her my investigator and driver's licenses as identification.

She squinted at the cards, then back at me, before returning them. "Uh-huh."

I could have smiled to reassure her of my honesty and integrity but I wasn't in the damned mood. Instead I held her stare until she got up to make me a copy of the Giocondo record. After I'd counted the number of fish in the wall art decorating the waiting area—one hundred thirty-six—she finally called me up to get the papers.

Anthony Remiglia Giocondo had died at 10:40 p.m. in his residence on Championship Circle… The same house Maria had shared with Gray. I skimmed down past his family background and work history toward the Cause of Death section, then stopped abruptly and jerked my gaze back to the Method of Disposition.

He'd been cremated?

That was hardly typical for most Catholics, who heartily believed in proper funeral rites. Sure, the Church had lifted the ban back in the 1960s, but it didn't exactly encourage the practice. I was really shocked Maria had chosen cremation. The immediate cause of death had been "acute myocardial infarction." Not much of a surprise.

The sequential conditions were listed as coronary artery disease and hypertension. Since Giocondo had died unexpectedly and at home, the case had been referred to the coroner's office. But, according to the certificate, no autopsy was performed and the Manner of Death was "natural."

I wondered where Maria had been while Anthony lay dying, and decided to go and ask.

"STELLA, what a nice surprise." Mrs. Amalfi answered the door. "Come on in."

Stepping into the cool foyer, I took off my sunglasses. "I was working nearby and thought I'd stop to see how Maria was doing."

"She's resting at the moment. The poor dear has been simply exhausted."

I nodded in genuine sympathy. I knew from experience it wasn't easy picking out all new furniture. "I don't know how she sleeps at night."

Something must have come through my tone, because Mrs. Amalfi wrinkled her brow. "Hm?"

"This must be so hard for her, I can't imagine."

She nodded and sighed. "So hard."

"I didn't know until someone mentioned it at the country club that Maria lost her first husband, as well?" Not exactly subtle. But using a sympathetic tone got it done.

"Ah, Tony. He was a good man, the best." She tugged at her earlobe. "I've always felt a bit guilty about the way he died."

I frowned in confusion. "*You* have? Why's that?"

"I knew he wasn't following his diet, sneaking foods with high cholesterol, drinking caffeinated sodas. Everybody likes to cheat now and again. I—I didn't think it would do any harm…." She wrung her hands. "There was a cola can right next to the bed when Maria found him."

Ding. The cynic sensor in my head went off. "Maria wasn't with him?"

"Unfortunately, no. She'd gone out to a Junior League

meeting. I forget now what event they were planning, but Maria was upset about running late. She told me Tony had turned in early and that she doubted he would need anything." Mrs. Amalfi shrugged weakly. "I'd retired for the evening. I was right here, right downstairs, but never knew anything was wrong until Maria started screaming."

"I'm *positive* there was nothing you could have done to save him, Mrs. Amalfi."

"Did you come to check up on me, Steele?"

We both looked up to see Maria on the upstairs landing. Her voice was pleasant, but her eyes were clear and cold, like the diamonds she wore.

As she came down the steps, the pale pink dress swirled around her calves. Her hair softly framed her face, which had been made up with a light hand. She looked delicate and feminine and almost deliberately innocent. Our gazes met, measured and clashed in the space of a heartbeat.

Somehow, I just knew.

Every instinct I possessed told me Maria had killed at least once, possibly twice. A tingle of anticipation zipped along my nerves. It's the kind of feeling you get when faced with a brainteaser puzzle. This one is going to test you but, in the end, you know you can solve it. Returning her little smile, I held the stare a beat longer before answering.

"I couldn't leave you alone, not after everything that's happened."

"You're good, Steele. A good friend." She remained on the last step so that we stood at eye level.

Unaware of the gauntlet thrown between us, Mrs. Amalfi caught Maria's attention. "I've made your tea, dear. It's in the breakfast nook."

"Thank you, Sarah." Maria looked at me, her eyes warm once more. "Join me?"

I followed her through the house to the kitchen, my boots and her sandal heels clicking on the marble. Heavy white linen curtains diffused the sunlight streaming through the large bay window. I scooted over the booth-style seat while Maria got a second cup. The table was set with nonsugar sweetener, butter and a selection of mini muffins.

"These look great." I reached for one with blueberries. "Are these low carb?"

"No, just smaller portions." She smiled pleasantly as she poured the tea. "You have to be so careful about what you eat and drink, don't you?"

I hesitated with the muffin midway to my mouth, but then defiantly bit it in half, chewed and swallowed. "Delicious."

Maria sat opposite me and chose a miniature corn bread. "So, tell me about Cameron."

"Oh, there's, uh, not much to tell. We're seeing each other, seeing where things lead."

"You two looked great together." She tilted her head with a knowing look. "I got the impression things were leading to something serious."

I laughed. "Define serious? He's seriously hot, I seriously like spending time with him, but—"

"Serious as in marriage."

Matrimony was supposed to be serious, wasn't it? I hadn't been treating it that way because it still didn't feel real. And if it wasn't real, I didn't have to deal with it.

"We haven't been together long enough to consider it. Besides, I'm not sure I'm the marrying kind, you know?"

"I loved being married. Knowing he'd be there, knowing I was cared for, knowing I was wanted. My mother taught me that marriage takes dedication, and sometimes sacrifice…" Her eyes clouded over, momentarily focused on the past. "But it's so worth it. I devoted myself to my man. Until death did we part."

Her features remained soft, her expression impassive, but I sensed I was somehow being tested. "I don't think I'm ready for that kind of commitment."

"You always have to commit, Steele. You have to give everything you have for as long as the love lasts."

I watched her carefully. "What happens when the love dies?"

Maria's gaze held mine, connected. I could sense an uncharacteristic rage just below the surface. Granted, we hadn't seen each other in a long time, but suddenly I felt like I'd never seen her before at all. There was a certain cunning in her baby-blue eyes, a conceit in her smile.

She didn't reply and the silence stretched out.

Finally I answered for her. "You start looking for it again, I guess."

"Yes. That's probably what you should do." She nodded slowly. "And this next time is going to be different."

"Is it already?"

"You tell me. We're talking about you and Cameron."

"I was talking about you."

Maria glanced at my chest then back to my eyes. "Nice T-shirt, Steele. I should get one for myself."

I LEFT the Canyon Gate estates and headed for West Cheyenne Avenue. Cameron had told me about his little talk with Caitlyn, so I figured she wouldn't be going to work today. I got lucky and slipped through the main entrance as someone else was coming out. Caitlyn answered after a few brisk knocks. She didn't look surprised to see me.

Which was odd, considering we'd never met.

"You might as well come in." Her flat tone was completely uninviting.

I arched a brow in response. "Why, thank you, Caitlyn. That's very hospitable of you."

"I don't want you discussing my business in the halls."

She stood aside and I walked past her, down two steps into a small but lavishly decorated living/dining area. The sofas were suede and the dining set looked like solid wood. Oil paintings decorated the walls and she had porcelain collectibles displayed around the room.

"Not bad, Caitlyn. Especially on a hotel desk clerk's salary." The drapes felt like silk when I rubbed the fabric between my fingers. "How *do* you manage?"

She crossed her arms and glared at me. "Stuff the sarcasm, okay? I saw you at Gray's funeral with that blond guy, so I know why you're here. But I'll tell you the same thing I told him—I don't know where the money is."

"How about making a guess? Who knows when—or if—you'll get that insurance money. And I have the authority to offer you a…finder's fee, I guess you'd call it."

She scoffed. "If I knew where Gray had stashed it, why would I tell you instead of keeping it all for myself?"

"You obviously don't know 'Demon' DiMarco at all. He's very protective of what's his. Very protective. Don't kid yourself, Caitlyn. He has proof and you've been damned lucky so far that he hasn't brought charges."

She pressed her lips together and stared at the floor. Okay, time to give "good cop" a try. Just this once.

"Listen, I know this isn't easy for you, Caitlyn." I lowered my voice, slowed my speech and modulated my tone until I perfectly imitated Vivi. "I know what it's like to think your life is going one way, only to get completely knocked off that path. But there's still time to choose another road."

"You sound like my mother."

So much for "good cop."

"Get used to saying that kind of stuff. You're going to be a single mom. *Soon.* That means your only loyalties are to yourself and your child, not to some guy who was ditching you—"

"Gray was *not*—"

"Wake up and smell the reality, honey. He double-crossed you, thumbed his nose at his job and took off in the middle of the day. He had a suitcase full of clothes and cash when he died. That sounds to me like he wasn't planning to be home for breakfast."

Caitlyn stared at me for a moment then closed her eyes and dropped onto the sofa, her head in her hands. I gave "good cop" one last try for the sake of practice and sat beside her. I drew the line at patting her arm though. When she finally looked up and wiped her eyes, they were angry.

"That son of a bitch. It was all his idea, you know. All I did was sign the credit papers he gave me and then cash in my chips at the end of the night. All I asked *him* to do was take responsibility for *his* baby."

"I know. And you trusted the cheating, thieving scumbag. That's why if there's any of that cash left to be found, you really should get a part of it."

Caitlyn sniffled. "But I really don't know where he put it. I mean, maybe he moved it out of state? We'd planned to drive down through Barstow to San Diego, so I don't know why he was heading east unless he hid the money somewhere in Laughlin…"

Laughlin was on the border with Arizona, so I guessed it was possible… And suddenly it hit me. I had an idea where Cavanaugh could have easily stored bundles of traveler's checks and bricks of cash. Men and their mortality. Like Cookie Kingman, Gray must have planned to take it all with him. I'd check my theory when I got back to the agency.

In the meantime, I was wondering about something else, too. "Caitlyn, did Gray normally drink on the job?"

She shook her head. "No, he always waited until his shift was over. Same as he did that day."

"Was he a heavy drinker? I mean, wasn't that unusual for him to get drunk enough to run headlong into another vehicle?"

"I don't know why you're asking me. Obviously, I didn't know him as well as I thought."

CHAPTER FORTY-ONE

Under Pressure

"HELLO?"

The call was answered on the first ring, as if the cell phone had been clutched in anticipation.

"Have you got a minute?"

"For you? Always. What is it?"

"It's Steele. She's asking a lot of questions…."

"She's supposed to—that's her job."

The line was silent, the caller's anxious tension a living thing crawling along the connection.

"What do you want me to do?"

"I want her to mind her own business."

A short pause, and then, "Okay. I think I can arrange a little warning message."

"Thanks. I knew I could count on you."

"Don't worry. I promised to take care of you and I will."

Maria hung up her phone, frowning hard until she remembered the lines and wrinkles the expression would cause. Mama had always said that her job was to stay pretty, to present an attractive image at all times. Pretty girls never have to worry about anything…

Except other pretty girls.

CHAPTER FORTY-TWO

If At First

DAMN, DIDN'T THIS GUY ever go the hell home?

Mick stared hard through the binoculars until he realized he was pressing the eyepieces into his sockets. Resentment burned like acid in his veins. Stone was at her house again, sleeping in her bed, touching her body. In *his* place. He tossed the binocs into the gym bag with his other gear.

He'd been trying for days to get close to her, but she was rarely alone. And he wanted her to be all alone when they finally met face-to-face.

Instead, she either didn't come home or she came home with *him*.

Gripping the prepaid cell phone, he imagined her the way she'd looked that night he'd stood at her window. With her sexy tousled hair, her nipples hard against her tank top, and her long legs bare… His pulse accelerated and he licked his lips.

Staring at the house now in the early morning light, he pictured the change in her expression, from sleepy and confused to wary, when she'd answered. He'd liked it when she got scared. But maybe she wouldn't be, with Stone beside her. That guy was ruining everything.

"You'd better be more careful. You don't want the wrong person mad at you."

CHAPTER FORTY-THREE

Trace Evidence

BESIDE HIM, Stella fairly vibrated with tension.

She'd reached across him to quiet the phone when it woke them, her greeting drowsy and resentful. Then he'd heard the change in her tone. Cameron opened his eyes, instantly alert when her features went taut with irritation.

"Enough with the heavy breathing, asshole. Get a life."

"Give me the phone."

She blocked his hand. "Oh, really? Let me tell you some—"

He pulled the receiver from her grasp, ignoring her protest. "Who the bloody hell is this?"

The only response was a click and the dial tone. His blood pressure rose while latent fury turned his knuckles white. After a few seconds, he rolled over slightly to set the phone down. "What did he say?"

Despite the sheen on her eyes, Stella shrugged and waved her hand. "The usual. Back off, bitch, or else. Blah blah blah."

"Oh, is that all then?" He reached to stroke the back of his fingers along her cheek, admiring her bravado.

"Well, gosh, honey, you went and scared him off before he could finish threatening me." Though her tone was mocking, her hazel eyes were alight with anger.

As much as, if not more than, her fear he hated his own frustration, this feeling of helplessness that he couldn't look after her. He lifted the phone and started punching an eleven-digit number. "I'll take care of this."

She gave him an indulgent look. "It wasn't the same guy as before. The voice was different, even though he made a lame-assed attempt to disguise it. The number was blocked—"

"Jamie, I'm at Stella's. Trace the last incoming call, won't you? No, reach me on my cell."

As he hung up, silence chilled the space between them. She snatched the phone back and slid out from the covers. Looking at the expression on her face, he got up as well and reached for his clothes.

"Before you—"

"Too late!"

She slammed the handset down on the bureau and pulled out a pair of knickers. "You tapped my phone? You tapped my phone!"

He stepped into his khakis, zipping them as he replied. Only an idiot went into battle unprotected. Stella looked ready for an all-out war. "You once mentioned some *stupid phone calls.* I took the necessary measures because I want them to stop."

"So do I, but I can't believe you— Oh my God, you've been listening." She yanked a T-shirt over her head then glared at him once she had it on. "You heard the call to my doctor's office? Oh. My. God. You heard Nikki and I talking about your…"

"Aye, I was quite flattered."

Instead of lightening the mood, his cheek only infuriated her more. Snarling mad, she drew her arm back and hurled the telephone at his head. He snatched it from the air before it fractured his temple.

"I'm sorry, Stella, love. It was a pathetic attempt at a joke. I've no idea what you and Nikki spoke about. The equipment is set up to record the origin of any incoming calls, not the content."

"As if that isn't enough. What else have you got around here? Hidden microphones? Surveillance cameras?"

"The only cameras are set to watch the outside. There are none in the house."

Stella narrowed her eyes. "You didn't answer the microphone question."

His cell phone chirped Jamie's signature ring tone with perfect timing. Pulling it from his trousers pocket, he hit the button. "Yes, Jamie?"

"The call originated at the Palazzo Resort and Casino there in Vegas."

"Are you cer—? Never mind. Of course you are."

"Second-guessing the women in your life is not such a hot idea. Has she ripped you a new one yet?"

He glanced at Stella's shirt, which read *My Measurements? 36-24-.38 mm* across the chest. "No, I'm still intact."

"For the moment… My trace went to the main switchboard number. There's no telling exactly which extension it came from."

"Thanks, Jamie." He snapped the phone closed, already planning a visit to the casino.

Stella gave him an arch look. "Well?"

"He called from the Palazzo. I'll take care of talking to DiMarco, find out whether it was him."

"You're not going to take care of anything else." She crossed her arms. "You listen to me, Stone. Just because you're a duke or an earl or—"

"Only a lord, actually—"

"Whatever! Just because you're some kind of nobility doesn't make me one of your subjects. Christ, don't you see? You can't arbitrarily invade my privacy, force your will on my life or take away my choice. In effect you're treating me no differently than my stalker."

He scowled, deeply offended by the comparison, despite understanding that her personality would always reject any attempt at control. "Don't be ridiculous, Stella. I'm trying to protect you from him. I'll apologize for upsetting you. But if I had it to do again, my decision would be the same."

"Do you not understand how you've betrayed my trust or don't you care?"

"I care, Stella. Very much." He moved to her side. "But I've spent the majority of my life in a man's world, doing work most men don't have the stomach for. I've not had many relationships. Therefore I can only follow my instincts and my training—to protect and defend at all costs."

Her expression softened some. However, she crossed her arms as she looked at him. "I don't know what the hell to do with you, with us. Sometimes it's great and part of me likes how safe you make me feel. Other times, like now, it's all too much, too soon, and I just want to kick your ass."

"You think I don't feel the same?" He scoffed. "You're a handful, you are."

"You're a piece of work yourself, mister." She smirked as she said it, but then the smile slowly faded from her expression. She raked her hair back, combing the long strands over her shoulder. "I think I need some time on my own."

An odd tension clutched his chest and it was a few seconds before he recognized it as fear. If he gave her this time, might she decide not to come back to him? No, it wouldn't do to think that way. He had to trust the connection they both felt. That didn't mean he was happy to let her alone.

"Stella, love, I only want—"

"I know, Cameron. But I'm not sure what I want. Give me a day or two, okay?"

"Not okay, no. There's some lunatic ringing you up and saying lord knows what. What if he decides to deliver his missives in person?"

Though she quickly attempted to cover it, he could hardly have missed the flicker of emotion in her eyes. Yet, damn her stubborn nature, she wouldn't give an inch.

"Then you're only a phone call away."

CHAPTER FORTY-FOUR

Place Your Bet

IT HADN'T BEEN EASY getting Stone to leave. He'd insisted on checking all of the locks first. I guess it's a guy thing. Because, golly gosh, I'm incapable of doing that my pretty little self. Good thing I had a big manly man around to exert his superior intellect and prowess.

I thanked him with a kiss goodbye anyway.

Then the minute he was gone, I did some checking of my own.

I looked along every wall and in every corner for bugs, the electronic kind. But it was quickly obvious that the Guardians were more expert at hiding than I am at seeking. And, just maybe, if I were going to be completely honest, I might admit that I didn't look that hard.

Cameron said the taps were only on my phone. I chose to believe him. Also having the devices in place would help me figure out who the hell had called this morning. Because it wasn't the same guy as before. Despite the effort at disguise, I knew the voice was different.

Since the call had come from the Palazzo, I decided to start at the top. After confirming that Big Frank was at work, I headed for the Strip. When I got to the office suite, his secretary invited me to wait since Frank was on the phone. I wasn't going anywhere without talking to him, so I grabbed a seat on the couch.

None of the magazines interested me so I studied Theresa.

I'm not big on jewelry—I only wear a watch and small gold hoop earrings—but her necklace of pink, beige, amber and bronze beads was gorgeous with her fair skin and red-blond hair. "That looks really great on you."

Theresa explained that she worked part-time selling jewelry at home shows. She'd done a party just the night before, which had run late. "The girls were a lot of fun, but I didn't leave until almost eleven."

"Wow. It must have been hard to get up today, huh?"

She rolled her eyes comically. "You have no idea. But Mr. DiMarco is usually in by eight and he expects me to be here before him."

So, in theory it could have been Frank calling my house this morning. But there's no way I wouldn't have recognized his voice. We chatted until I ran out of small talk and she went for a cigarette, leaving me alone in the reception area. Frank was still on the phone. He wasn't talking that loud but I could hear the strain in his voice.

"Ben, listen to me, will ya? I don't know why Maria contacted ya. Probably just touchin' base, seein' what kinda welcome she's gonna get." There was a brief pause, followed by two thuds that sounded like he'd kicked the desk. "I'm tellin' ya, okay, nothin's gonna change. Maria might be getting Gina's majority shares, but this is still my casino."

Whoa. I got up and wandered closer to the artwork and Frank's office door. My mind raced to process this new information. Maria wasn't happy with the small role she played in the business. Now, with her inheritance, the notes I'd seen at her house made a different kind of sense.

"Listen, this is not gonna be a problem. Her birthday isn't for a few more weeks. And even then, we're family. Maria doesn't have much of a head for business stuff. I'm her father so she'll follow my advice." Another pause then the creak of a leather chair. "Yeah. Yeah, exactly. You don't worry about this, okay? I'll talk to ya later."

I turned and made a leap for the door to the suite, grateful for the thick, sound-deadening carpet. I did *not* want to get caught eavesdropping on that discussion. Big Frank charged out of his office just as I walked back in. He started to smile in greeting, but then his eyes narrowed at the couch.

Dammit! I'd left my backpack on the floor.

Thinking fast, I looked confused for a second then said, "Oh, I didn't want to drag it to the ladies room. I thought Theresa was still here."

"Huh. You've gotta be the only gal I ever met who doesn't haul her purse everywhere she goes. Anyway, good to see ya. What brings you by?"

"I wanted to talk to you, if this is a good time?"

"Sure, Steele. Except I need to get outta this office. C'mon and walk with me."

He waited while I grabbed my backpack, then ushered me down the hall toward the elevator. "What's on your mind?"

I kept my voice down as we walked past the employee work cubicles since I doubted Cavanaugh's theft was common knowledge. "Maria hasn't found any large sums of cash lying around the house and the girlfriend swears she doesn't know where it is. But something Caitlyn said about their plans, along with the road where Gray died, got me thinking."

We were the only two on the elevator so I waited until the doors closed. "Don't he and Maria keep a Hatteras at the Willow Beach Marina? It's possible he stashed that money on the boat."

Frank's dark brows crumpled together then headed for his hairline. "I'll be damned. We just took the *Gina Maria* out two weeks ago for a day trip on the lake. I didn't see a thing."

I shrugged. "It was just a guess. If anyone saw him carrying a bunch of boxes over time, they'd just think he was laying in supplies or something. Anyway, I thought you might want to check it out."

"I will, I will. Thanks, Steele." He let me out first. "So how come you're tellin' me all this? Where's Stone?"

"We're...taking a break."

Frank scoffed and made a face. "Whatever it was, he didn't

do it. Or if he did do whatever it was, he's sorry and he won't do it again."

I laughed. "I'm sure he is."

We reached the lobby and Frank turned to the left. "He'll be real sorry when I hand over the recovery fee to you."

Don't think I wasn't tempted. I was. I had all kinds of bills for the agency and one from a dental procedure my insurance hadn't covered. But it wasn't right and I knew it. Dammit. "That's okay, I just hope I'm right for your sake."

"So do you gotta run off, or have you got a few minutes to keep an old man company?" He raised one hand, his thumb cocked toward the nearest casino, and wriggled his brows.

I'd been wondering how to get more time to talk with him and here was the perfect opportunity. I gave him a smug look, mentally getting into my kill zone. "Don't think I'm going to cut you any slack just because of your advanced age, Mr. D."

He grinned back at me. "Watch yourself, Stella. *I'm* not goin' easy on *you* just 'cause you're a girl."

This early in the day, there were plenty of empty tables to choose from. Big Frank pulled up a chair at one near the middle of the casino and waved a floorman over to act as dealer. His name tag read, *Sergei, Kubyinka, Russia.* Apparently he'd only been in Vegas about six months so his English was limited to phrases like "Place your bets" and "Good luck."

That made him the perfect chaperone to the conversation I wanted to start.

Frank asked for a stack of chips and handed half of them to me. "Your money's no good here."

Since the two of us were going heads up, Sergei dealt us two hole cards each after the initial ante. I lifted the merest corner of mine to see pocket red Queens. Not by so much as a flicker of an eyelash did I show my reaction. But inside I chortled with glee.

In Texas Hold 'Em, fewer players means more folds and fewer wins, but it also means you might take the pot with just a pair. I pushed a ten-dollar chip toward the dealer. "Have you hired a new casino manager yet, Mr. D.?"

"Nah. I got the other three and a coupla assistant managers coverin' for now. I'm still lookin' for the right person."

Frank raised me ten and I called. Sergei burned a card from the shoe and dealt the *flop*. The three cards on the board were the six of clubs and the ace and deuce of hearts.

"Is there any way to make sure this next one's not a heavy drinker? I still can't get over Gray being that lit and no one trying to keep him here."

Big Frank glanced over at me, distracted from his cards and by my implication. "He couldn'ta been that drunk. You remember how it is around here, Steele. The Palazzo don't allow anyone to disturb our guests."

"Sure, Mr. D. He probably had just enough to cloud his head. I can't think of why else he would have hit that truck."

"Yeah. Probably."

He looked back at the *flop* and blinked. I hid a smile and checked my bet. Frank raised twenty bucks, thinking I didn't have anything. But I surprised him by raising another ten. Poker is about thirty percent luck of the draw and seventy percent skill. That skill can be further broken down into thirty percent knowledge and forty percent balls.

"I feel so sorry for Maria, losing two husbands like that. Anthony was a friend of yours, right?"

"I miss him. Like a brother, Tony was."

"Maria must have felt like she had two fathers," I joked carefully.

The twinkle in Frank's eyes turned into a wary gleam. He held my gaze and tossed a hundred dollars in chips. I hesitated, pretending to buy time looking at the *flop* cards. Just as Sergei cleared his throat subtly, I called.

Bluffing isn't the same as lying, unless you're an amateur. Liars always get caught. Their body language and tells give them away. But pros know to tell the truth—just not all of it and not in a believable manner. A good bluff will confuse and misdirect.

Frank had no idea what I was doing. He called as well and Sergei dealt the *turn*. It was the ten of hearts. I didn't breathe. I thought about scrubbing the grout around my bathtub. I thought about my annual pelvic exam. Anything but the fact that I had a chance at a flush.

It's physiologically impossible to hide the dilation of your pupils when you're excited. But living with Bobby had taught me to carefully guard my expressions and suppress whatever emotion I was feeling. I'd had a decent poker face before. After Bobby, you couldn't tell me from a statue.

Big Frank pushed fifty dollars toward Sergei. "How'd you know about Tony?"

"People talked at Gray's funeral. Just commiserating, you know? At least Maria won't have to deal with the same guilt this time." I raised by another hundred.

His brows snapped together. I'd definitely distracted him this time. "What the hell are you talkin' about?"

"When I learned how your friend died… I mean, if it had been me, I'd feel so guilty about not being there, about getting home just too late to help…"

Out of nowhere, a horrible thought occurred to me. My own words echoed something I'd heard a long time ago. For once, I had to struggle to keep my poker face. "Maria was the one who found her mother wasn't she?"

"Yeah." His olive skin took on an ugly ruddiness. "Check."

Sergei dealt the *river*. The final card was another heart, the eight this time. I ignored it, more intent on Frank's reaction. The whole community had been stunned when Mrs. DiMarco swallowed half a bottle of sleeping pills.

"It must have been devastating for Maria to lose her mother so unexpectedly. Miss Gina was always so nice to me when I used to come over…." I sighed heavily and patted his arm. "I'm sorry, Mr. D. I shouldn't have brought that up. I just feel so bad about all the people Maria has lost."

"She still has me." His mouth formed a thin line and he spoke between gritted teeth. He flipped his hole cards to show the ace of diamonds and the ten of spades. Using the cards in the *flop*, he had two pair. "She'll always have me."

"Will she? That's good. When your fortunes change suddenly, you need your family." I slowly turned over my cards. With the *river*, I'd gotten my fifth card in the same suit and a flush will beat two pairs. "Looks like I got lucky."

"Looks like." Frank stared at me hard, his expression inscrutable. Then he forced a smile as he slid off his stool. "Sorry to break up our little party here, Steele, but I don't feel like playin' anymore."

"No problem, Mr. DiMarco. I should be going anyway. I've got a couple things I need to check into."

As I hefted my backpack, he waved at the table. "Don't forget your winnin's."

I smiled and shook my head. "It was just a friendly game."

"Was it?"

Watching him, I wondered if I'd laid it on too thick. "I'll see you around, Mr. DiMarco."

Weaving my way across the casino floor, I had absolutely no proof that Maria had been involved in either of her husband's deaths. And everyone had questioned Gina DiMarco's suicide—it was such a shock—but murder was never a consideration. Maybe my imagination was working overtime and I was wrong about all of this….

At the doorway, I glanced back. Big Frank was watching me and talking on his cell phone. I guess I had my answer.

CHAPTER FORTY-FIVE

Strangers in the Night

AS HEAVY AS Vegas traffic is, I shouldn't have noticed it. Except something about the way the silver BMW was driving caught my attention. Having the same cars travel behind you on the Strip wasn't unusual. But a car that never took advantage of an opportunity to pass or move ahead…?

Kind of odd.

Or maybe it was just one of thousands of people who had more patience than I did. The next time *I* saw a break in the traffic, I grabbed for it. Man, I love my Harley. No one made a move to follow me and the rest of the commute to the agency was uneventful. So were the hours I spent there.

I left work ten minutes later than I'd planned, making me only twenty minutes late for my shift at Mezzanotte's. Pulling out of the parking lot and onto Paradise Road, I looked for a break in the traffic. I made the turn and that's when I caught sight of something in my rearview mirror.

I'd seen that silver BMW before.

Damn. Now I wished I'd noted the license plate earlier. I couldn't be sure it was the same car. I tried to get a look at the driver, but the windows were tinted. Just as I was starting to get a shiver of suspicion, though, the Beemer turned off at Tropicana Avenue and I didn't see it again.

That night, things were as dull at the bar as they'd been in the office, leaving me entirely too much time to think about Cameron. I'd asked for some time alone and he'd graciously given it to me. But was that what we really needed? Something Maria, of all people, had said about commitment kept haunting me.

My marriage had been a hormone-induced impulse. In Nevada, you can get a no-fault divorce on the grounds of incompatibility in as little as two weeks. If ever two things were totally mismatched, it would be steel and stone, right? But I hadn't made even a token attempt to file the papers locked in my desk drawer. So what was I waiting for?

It was hard to lie to myself the way I'd lied to him when he'd reappeared. I wasn't really better off without him.

There are few things I hate more than having to apologize and it seemed like I was doing a lot of that lately. All of my customers were taken care of, so I picked up the phone and dialed Cameron's number. He answered before the first ring had finished.

"Have you called to admit I'm the perfect man for you?"

I grinned, knowing that whatever we were doing together would somehow work out. "Not even close."

"You're ringing to declare your everlasting affection?"

"Uh, no."

"Then why on earth are you pestering me, woman?"

I twisted the phone cord around my index finger. "I'm calling to say I've had all the time I needed."

In the brief pause that followed, I sensed his pleasure. When he spoke, his brogue was low and seductive. "Ah, Stella. I'm glad you told me. And sorrier than hell I can't see you tonight."

Something in his tone went beyond sorry to real regret. That's when I became aware of other male voices talking over a rumbling noise. I massaged my forehead and stared at the floor. I wanted to demand details, to know everything he couldn't tell me. "I won't even ask where you're going."

"You can ask. However, I'm afraid I can't tell you." He exhaled sharply. "I hate to leave, truly, what with all that's happening—"

"I took care of myself before you and your white steed rode into my life. I'll take care of myself now." I closed my eyes as I said it, infusing my voice with all the enthusiasm I could muster. "When do you think you'll be back?"

He hesitated and I knew I wasn't going to like his answer. "When we accomplish what we've set out to do."

I hated that he had to leave while our relationship was still so undefined. Not to mention while I was in some kind of nebulous danger that he alone made me feel safe from. My chest felt tight with inexpressible fear and resentment.

But also a little pride. Reminding myself that he'd bailed on the last "mission," and of the story he'd told me about Jamie, I set my selfishness aside.

"Bring everybody back safe, Cameron."

"I fully intend to, love."

I hung up, but left my hand on the receiver as if I could hold on to him as long as I didn't break the connection. I stood there, lost in a jumble of thoughts, until I felt a prickle of awareness on my neck. Like someone watching me...

Thinking of whoever had been in that silver BMW earlier, I spun around. The guy two seats down seemed to be looking at me intently. It was hard to tell, though. He'd been propping up the bar for the past couple of hours without ever taking off his baseball cap or sunglasses. He'd only said one word—the name of his beer of choice.

Now I was getting some sort of weird vibe from him and my stomach clenched as he opened his mouth to speak. "Boyfriend left yeh, huh?"

His voice sounded almost familiar but his flat drawl wasn't hitting my ear right, like maybe he was faking it. I crossed my arms and glared at him. "Is that any of your business?"

"Yeah, if yer love life's gonna keep me from getting another beer."

"Sorry." I offered him a smile to go with my terse apology.

"Sure, sure. No prob."

I poured him a draft and set it in front of him. He didn't

say anything else, not even thanks. A few minutes later, I had to deliver a tray of Cosmopolitans to a table of undergrads celebrating the end of exam week. When I went back to the bar, the guy in the cap was gone.

"YOU OUGHTA BE more careful."

The cool, menacing voice came out of the darkness to my left. Way too close behind me for comfort. Startled, I turned my head to see who'd gotten the drop on me. I'd looked around when I left the bar for the night. Really, I did. So where the hell did this guy come from...

Enough light shone from a streetlamp for me to see a good-looking guy, average height with dark hair. His clothes were casual but still managed to look expensive. I didn't remember seeing him in the bar—he would have stood out from the locals and frat boys.

I kept walking. He followed.

"Sexy girl like you shouldn't be all alone this late at night."

Oh, good. A threat with a side order of flattery. What a great deal.

"Yes, you never know who might be around."

At the sound of a second voice—the smooth, almost alluring one I'd heard on the phone this morning—I whipped my head to the right. This other guy was the size of a tank, with a thick neck and huge hands. But just as nicely dressed.

That next sound? Fear plunging into the pit of my stomach. Because one guy accosting me in the empty parking lot I could handle. Two, I was nowhere near so sure about.

I slowed my steps, trying to act casual. Meanwhile, though, my thoughts were racing. I didn't think I had much chance of making it over and onto the Harley, my pepper spray was buried at the bottom of my backpack and I doubted these guys were going to just let me go back inside.

So the best defense is a good offense, right?

I dropped my backpack and spun around to confront my

self-appointed safety advisors. Shifting my weight onto the balls of my feet, I prepared to either fight or flee. Probably flee. I'm not stupid and I was counting on them not having track ribbons in their parents' attics.

"What do you want?"

"Simply to deliver a message. Your interference is unwelcome and further involvement could result in considerable harm." Tank was the one who'd answered. It was weird hearing such well-modulated speech from a guy who didn't look like he could put more than two words together.

"You could have called. Again."

He gave me a pleasant smile. "You didn't seem to listen this morning. Therefore it behooved us to deliver the message in person."

"Behooved?" I stared at Tank, thinking he seemed familiar.

"Behooved?" Cool stared at Tank, scratching his head.

Tank stared back at us. "*Behoove*. To benefit, to be necessary or advantageous."

Cool frowned. "Can you use it in a sentence?"

"I already have."

The lightbulb went off when he crossed his arms in annoyance. The last time I'd seen Tank was the night the girls and I had gone to Element. He was one of the bouncers. Which meant somebody from the Palazzo employed him. Somebody from the Palazzo had sent him here.

"I appreciate the vocabulary lesson. Really. But it's been a long day, guys."

"We could make it a long night. A very long night." Cool made the prospect sound ominous and perverted at the same time.

Tank tilted his head. "Far be it for us to keep you any longer. Let me leave you with this thought, though. There are 206 bones in the human body. The majority of them are not that difficult to break. Have a pleasant evening."

My heart shuddered in my chest as I stood rooted to the spot, more shaken than I wanted to show.

"Hey, babe?" Cool tipped his head in the direction of the Harley. "That was your cue to get outta here."

I lifted my backpack but shook my head. "I'm not leaving until you do."

"Well, we're not leaving until you do."

"Forget it, guys. I don't want you following me home."

"We don't want you running our plates."

"Enough." Tank interrupted without raising his voice. "We don't intend to follow you home, Ms. Mezzanotte. We already know where you live."

On that less-than-reassuring note, I backed toward my motorcycle. I kept them in sight until I had no choice but to turn around and start the ignition. When I glanced over my shoulder, they were gone. All the way home I constantly checked my mirrors but the trip was blessedly uneventful.

That night, I stayed in the guest room under the magenta paisley sheets rather than sleep in "our" bed without Cameron.

Not that I slept much.

CHAPTER FORTY-SIX

Bad Medicine

THAT LOOKED REALLY, really heavy.

From my crouched position down the street in another one of Anna's cars, I held my new digital camera at the ready and grinned. I'd made arrangements with a local florist to send a well-established potted ficus tree to Kenny Asher's house at exactly 10:00 a.m. They were even attaching a nice Get Well Soon card, supposedly from the office at Rose Trucking.

The delivery guy hauled the tree to the front door on a handcart and rang the bell. I checked my camera again, determined not to miss this shot. After a minute, the driver knocked a couple of times. Kenny finally answered the door, scratching his head and his balls at the same time.

Gee, there's a nice Christmas card photo.

The driver got him to sign the tracking sheet, confirmed Asher's name and started to push the cart away. Kenny called him back, but the driver just shook his head and shrugged. Kenny gave him the finger. The tree looked lovely sitting on the top step, blocking the entrance. Kenny looked like he was considering leaving it there.

But then, just as I hoped, he leaned over at the waist to test how much the thing weighed. I snapped two good shots and mentally crossed "no bending" off the note from Dr. Oldenberg, a notorious claimant's hack. Kenny's lawyer must not have warned him about tricks like this. Or maybe he just liked ficus trees.

They say that clothes make the man. So I guessed Kenny's wife-beater tank shirt and baggy sweatpants inspired him to squat down and plant wrestle. Good stuff, let me tell you. I crossed off "no pushing or pulling" and "no lifting." The ficus ended up a few feet into the yard and Mr. Asher would end up losing his workers comp benefits.

I waited until Kenny had smeared the sweat off his brow and shuffled back inside before I got out of the Toyota. I figured while I was here I'd say hello to Mrs. Sharp. There was no answer when I knocked, but then I noticed the little side gate was open. I stayed on the path, careful not to step on her precious grass.

"Mrs. Sharp?"

My voice escalated to a squeal as I called her name. She was in the side yard, swaying a little on her feet. I watched in confusion while she ripped the flowers off one of her prized rose bushes and tossed them into a wicker basket. I walked toward her and called again.

"Mrs. Sharp, what are you doing?"

She spun around, almost losing her balance, and clutched her chest. "What? Who are you? What do you want?"

I slowed my approach, worried by the glassy look of her eyes, and wary of the pruning shears she wielded in one gloved hand. "It's me, Stella. Remember? I helped you mulch the flowerbeds last week."

"Stella? Oh, yes! Stella, I know you, don't I?" She giggled so crazily that I had the astonished suspicion she was drunk. "Now that you're here, you can help me with the weeding."

"Um, those aren't weeds, Mrs. Sharp. You're cutting off your roses."

She blinked at me a few times and then slowly turned her head to look at the wrecked bush. Tilting her head, she looked at it like she didn't understand what she was seeing. Then, without warning she came at me. "What did you do? What did you *do?*"

Her movements were uncoordinated and I caught her

wrists before she could hurt one of us—most likely herself. That's when I noticed her skin felt clammy. The fight abruptly went out of her and she slid out of my arms to the ground. Mrs. Sharp was sweating despite the dry heat and she was muttering incoherently.

Something was seriously wrong. I laid her back as gently as I could and felt for a pulse. It was kind of sporadic. Then I pried open her mouth. Her airway looked clear to my inexpert eyes, so I made a run for the house—I'd left my damned cell in the car.

I gambled on the back door being open and burst into the kitchen. Rushing to the wall phone, I wondered what the hell had just happened. It might have been the heat, but maybe she'd had a different kind of stroke.

"9-1-1. What is your emergency?"

"I don't actually know. She's an older lady and she was acting weird then she collapsed and I don't what's wrong but—"

"Miss, slow down. Slow down. First tell me the address and the victim's current condition?"

After telling the dispatcher what little I could, I went back out to stay by Mrs. Sharp's side. Thank God the phone was cordless. Time slowed to a crawl when I realized she'd lost consciousness, making it seem like a year before the paramedics arrived. In reality, it was probably only four to six minutes since the fire station wasn't far away.

"Are you her daughter?" One of the guys—his shirt said Bank—nudged me aside to place a stethoscope on Mrs. Sharp's chest.

"No, I'm just… I'm a friend." I stood there helplessly, thinking that Mrs. Sharp looked too pale and way too still.

The other EMT, Lippman, secured an oxygen mask on her face while the third, a woman named Chaplin, went into the house. While the first paramedic was taking her blood pressure, she raced back out holding something in her hand.

"She's hypo, guys!"

Whatever that meant, it wasn't good. Lippman hurried to

the ambulance and came back with an IV bag and a couple of needles.

"What's wrong with her?" I didn't want to interfere, but I had to know if she would be okay.

Lippman stuck a tiny needle into Mrs. Sharp's finger and Bank inserted the IV needle into her elbow while EMT Chaplin explained. "The lady is a diabetic. Apparently her blood sugar took a dive and she went into insulin shock. My guess is she forgot to eat and didn't take her medication."

She opened the prescription bottle and poured the few remaining pills into the cap. I counted only five pale yellow tablets… With a tiny blue logo on them. My pulse jumped in recognition. "What are those?"

"InsulOr RA tablets. Oral insulin."

"I thought most diabetics took insulin shots."

"This is for people who don't want to give themselves the needles. The pills are a pretty expensive alternative, though. That's probably why Mrs. Sharp didn't take them like she's supposed to."

"What do you mean?"

"A lot of older people on fixed incomes hoard their meds so they don't have to refill them as often."

I looked over at Mrs. Sharp's supine body. "When I first got here, I thought she'd been hitting the cooking sherry."

Chaplin nodded. "That happens all too often. Somebody who's diabetic starts 'going low' and the people around them will mistakenly think they're drunk."

I felt a rush of excitement knowing, *knowing,* I was on the verge of figuring out what bothered me about Cavanaugh's death. "What would happen if somebody took diabetic medicine by mistake?" When she gave me an odd look, I explained, "I'm a private investigator and this might help with a case."

"Well, it would be the same situation as this lady. There'd still be too much insulin in the body and not enough glucose. InsulOr RA is the rapid-acting version—that's why you have to eat right away."

"And if the person actually had been drinking?"

Chaplin shook her head and snorted. "Then, in just a short while, that unfortunate person would drop like a rock."

As soon as Mrs. Sharp had come around and been taken to the hospital, I'd headed straight back to the agency.

"Hey, Steele. Maureen Ridenour called. She needs—"

"To wait. I've got some research to do."

I strode back to my office, threw my backpack at the sofa and launched my Internet browser. I typed *InsulOr* into "Google search" and quickly got the CliniTech Pharmaceuticals Web site. I clicked on the tab for the product description page. My eyes glazed over most of the medical stuff.

Type 2 Diabetes is a metabolic disorder resulting in the body's inability to properly utilize insulin... Insulin is an essential hormone secreted directly into the liver via the hepatic portal vein... The high acid content and enzymes of the digestive tract can degrade some drugs before they can be absorbed...

CliniTech's synthetic chemical compound delivery agents allow therapeutic macromolecules to be transported across biological membranes... InsulOr is available in both regular absorption and rapid-acting forms...

Okay. Enough of that. I went back to Google to see the other results. The one that caught my eye had to do with steroid abuse, insulin and bodybuilding.

Anabolic steroids have long been the choice of bodybuilders wanting to bulk up... Insulin, however, is so virtually undetectable that it doesn't show up in blood tests, making it the better choice... Athletes need to consume at least 100mg of carbohydrates or risk hypoglycemia...

Severe hypoglycemia from mixing alcohol and other drugs can cause a person to stop breathing or make their heart stop.

I leaned back in my desk chair and stared blindly at the computer screen. That must be how it happened. Somehow

Gray had been given the insulin pills not long before drinking those last gin-and-tonics. Except, Mrs. Sharp's tablets were a different color than the ones I'd seen Maria take and InsulOr wasn't the only product that might carry the company logo.

I had to be sure.

"Jon?" I held the intercom button on my phone. "Can you come back here a minute?"

When he stepped into my office I explained what I needed him to do. While he dialed the number I gave him, I closed my eyes and concentrated hard. I focused on the necessary vocal inflection, cadence, accent and diction. Jon hung up and I gave him an inquiring look.

"You're good to go, Steele."

I nodded but didn't say anything. I wasn't ready yet. This had to be right, better than right. It had to be perfect. When I thought I could do it, I took a deep breath. Then I picked up the receiver and placed the call.

"Cavanaugh residence."

"It's me, Sarah."

"Yes, Maria? What can I do for you, dear?"

Closing my eyes again, I kept her image in my head. "I think I'm low on my InsulOr. Can you check for me?"

"Of course, let me just run upstairs and I'll call you back."

"I'll wait. I need to stop by the pharmacy anyway."

"Just a minute, then."

My heart knocked hard against my ribs while I waited for her to return. A bead of sweat trickled between my breasts. What if the real Maria returned home while I was on the line?

Finally Mrs. Amalfi came back to the phone. "Maria? I found a full bottle in the medicine cabinet and another in the vanity drawer. You should be fine."

"Thanks, Sarah."

"You're welcome, dear. Now about dinner—"

"I've got to go. I'll see you later." I hung up before she could engage me in a conversation that might give me away.

I dropped my head into my palms as a burst of adrenaline made my hands shake.

Jon whistled in admiration. "My gawd, you sounded *exactly* like her."

"Luckily, Mrs. Amalfi thought so, too. And she told me exactly what I needed to know."

CHAPTER FORTY-SEVEN

Kiss Today Goodbye

WHEN THE BELL RANG the next night, my heart skipped a clichéd beat. I broke out in a big grin as I ran for the door. Cameron had only been gone for two days, but it felt like longer, eating dinner by myself then later lying alone in the bed we'd shared.

I wanted to yank the door open and throw myself into his arms. But, I didn't. I slowed my steps instead and decided to play it cool. There was no reason to let him know how worried I'd been, how I'd prayed he was safe wherever he was and whatever he was doing. A girl had to have some secrets.

However, my welcoming smile ratcheted down a few notches when I saw who was actually on my front step.

"I take it you were hoping for somebody else?" Maria eyed my camisole, jeans and bare feet. "Cameron, perhaps?"

Involuntarily, my gaze went over her shoulder. "He's out of town, but I thought maybe…"

"Sorry to disappoint you."

"Oh, it's not that." I held the door wider and stepped back to let her in. "I just wasn't expecting you."

"You should have been." Her voice had a certain edge that put me instantly on guard.

She followed me back to the kitchen where I'd left some chicken on the stove for dinner. Missing Cameron, I'd prepared enough for two. Maria settled onto one of the stools at the breakfast bar while I turned the meat over to brown the other side. "So what brings you by tonight?"

"Right to business, huh, Steele? This is a friendly visit. Aren't you going to offer me a drink?"

"Sure. How about that vodka you gave me?" I nodded toward the bottle on the far counter. I'd polished off the one in the freezer but had yet to open her "gift." "I was going to save that as evidence, just in case. But help yourself."

Maria gave me a patronizing smile. "Evidence of what?"

Good point. Besides, why would she want to poison me? I wasn't married to her. Still, I didn't grab for the bottle.

"Look, Steele, the original seal is still intact." She held it for me to see before she cracked it open. "Where do you keep your tumblers?"

I handed her a single glass from the cabinet near the sink then watched her pour about half an ounce. "You told me you didn't drink, but I saw you with champagne after the funeral."

She waved a dismissive hand. "I told you I don't drink *this* stuff. A celebratory glass of bubbly doesn't count."

"A celebration isn't what one expects from a recent widow."

Maria gave me a deadpan look. "I was celebrating Gray's *life* and accomplishments."

I just looked back at her. I wasn't buying it, and I wasn't touching that booze. Shaking the pan, I made sure the chicken wasn't sticking.

"It's fine, okay? I'll prove it." She lifted the shot, her gaze never leaving mine. Then she swallowed the clear liquid and shuddered. "Uckh. That's strong…"

Suddenly her eyes widened and she started to gag. Holy, shit. I took an automatic step toward her, my hand raised to offer my help—

Then Maria laughed abruptly and shook her head. "You should have seen your face, Steele. Now can I have a Coke to wash this vodka taste away?"

"Is caffeine the antidote?" I set the vodka glass near the sink and got two fresh tumblers.

She gave me a brittle smile. "You've been playing detective too long. You're getting paranoid."

"Unless you really are out to get me." After filling both glasses with ice, I handed her the soda.

"Oh, for heavens sake, why would I be?"

"Because I think you murdered your husband. Maybe both of them."

She didn't seem to react at all. I watched her carefully, but Maria just took another sip of soda with the same impassive expression. Then she tipped her head as if in admiration and her smile took on a wry slant.

"That was very clever of you to trick Sarah. You must have improved since we were kids—she couldn't tell our voices apart. You probably would have gotten away with it if I hadn't called a few minutes later."

I bowed with a showmanship flourish. "It's a gift, what can I say? But then I'm more interested in what you have to say." She gently twirled her glass so that the ice cubes circled the sides. And kept giving me that freakin' smug Mona Lisa smile. "What I don't understand, Maria, is why. How could you do that to someone you loved?"

"I don't know what you're talking about, Steele." She set her glass on the bar top. "I never loved Anthony."

"So that made it okay to kill him?"

She ignored my question. "I wanted to get out of the house, out from under Daddy's thumb. But he wouldn't let me marry the man I really loved—"

"Gray, right? The guy in the photo booth strip." I went to the fridge to get the asparagus, washed it and then began to peel the stems.

Maria smiled again, but didn't answer directly. "Anthony seemed like a good solution. He was rich enough to indulge me, old enough to understand I needed my own set of *friends*. And he treated me like a fairy princess. I used to sit on his lap while he brushed my hair…"

Okay, there was a mental image I didn't need. I turned off

the flame under the chicken and plated it to rest while the potatoes roasted. Drawing out the moment, I drank half of my Coke. "So, did you actually poison him that night, or did you just withhold his medication?"

"What happened to Anthony was a tragedy, it really was. But he'd lived his life and I won't apologize for being glad I was out of a loveless marriage. Mamma taught me how devastating that situation could be."

"Do you think that's why she…?"

"I *know* that's why she died. She was so unhappy, Steele. You have no idea how much it hurts to have to live with a man you no longer love, who smothers you and never lets you be your own person." Her blue eyes gleamed with a combination of anger and unshed tears, making them look a little wild.

An image came to mind of that day at the Palazzo, of Maria trailing behind the group of executives. I spoke quietly and with genuine empathy from my experience with Bobby. "That must have been hard for you growing up. You must have hated him."

"I hated how depressed Mamma was. She was never that strong. I wanted to help her, but I didn't know how."

"So, since divorce wasn't an option… You took the solution right from the wedding vows."

Maria focused on something behind me, a moment in her past no doubt. "She looked so peaceful at her funeral, even though we couldn't have it in the church. I have to believe that in the end she was better off."

"Is Gray better off, too?" I crossed my arms and rested my back against the counter.

She stared me down. "I have no idea."

"I know *you're* better off without him. You don't have to give up half of your Palazzo shares in the divorce now, do you?"

Her pupils dilated and her features tightened for just a second. But, instead of answering, Maria finished off her soda and reached for her purse, fishing around until she found a small pot of gloss. She casually slicked it over her pink lipstick, as if I'd asked about giving some insignificant donation to charity.

"Come on, Maria. It's just us." I taunted her, making my disdain clear. "All I've got is suspicion and circumstantial facts, not even evidence. I think you knew Gray's habit of ordering gin-and-tonic after work. I think you somehow slipped your insulin into his drink. It's only you and me here, so tell me I was right."

"About what? That Gray was unfaithful? That he betrayed the faith I had in him and in our marriage? I *loved* him, Steele. I loved him with all my heart. I never abandoned him, not even when I lost my b—" She slid off the stool and stood with her hands flat on the bar top.

Her voice had risen with each sentence, soaring into a crescendo of rage. "I supported him emotionally and financially. I was devoted to him. I worshipped him. I gave him everything I had, but it wasn't enough! He *stole* from me!"

Shaking, she closed her eyes for a second. Then her outburst was over as abruptly as it started, the dim-witted, innocent mask back in place.

Stunned by her violently rapid transformation, my voice was only a whisper. "Tell me I was right, Maria."

"The only thing I came to tell you is thank you and goodbye." She turned her back to pick up her purse.

"Thank me for what?"

"For your help, of course. Without you, I wouldn't have proof of exactly when I found out about Gray's affair. I wouldn't know about the money Gray and his pregnant girl-friend stole." Her expression became wistful, her eyes unfocused. "Oh, Gray's baby is going to be so beautiful."

I blinked a few times. I never told her about Caitlyn's involvement and I sure as hell didn't tell her about the baby. "Maria…"

"You've really turned out to be a worthy opponent. Then again, you always have been." Her eyes darkened with something that almost looked like hatred. "You were the smart one, the bold one. The only one anyone saw when we were together.

My father has always wished you were his daughter instead of me. You never knew that, or how I really felt about you."

What the hell was I supposed to say to that? A part of me could sympathize, but I wasn't going to excuse what she'd done. I pushed away from the counter and walked toward her. "I'd waste my breath saying 'you won't get away with this,' but I think you need help, Maria. You need—"

"I'm about to get everything I need." She suddenly reached up and grabbed me by the back of the neck. Maria pulled me to her with surprising strength, then kissed me full on the mouth. "Look who turned out to be the smart one after all."

Shocked, I could only stare at her. Completely at a loss for how to react, I tried to play it off. I rubbed my lips together and attempted a casual smile. "Oh, good. I was all out of mint-flavored gloss."

"It's been a pleasure, Steele. Maybe I'll see you when I get back from my...vacation. We decided we'd celebrate my birthday on a white sandy beach."

"We, huh? You've replaced Gray already?" Her only reply was an arrogant grin. "Where are you going?"

Maria tossed me a sly look over her shoulder as she headed for the door. "Wouldn't you like to know?"

I didn't bother trying to stop her.

It was much too late for that.

CHAPTER FORTY-EIGHT

The Mick of Time

THAT KISS HAD BEEN *smokin'* hot! If his dick got any harder, it would bust through his jeans.

He'd waited for some more girl-on-girl action, but the blonde had walked out, leaving Steele alone. And horny? Mick sure as hell hoped so. He was loving the way she kept stroking her bare arm. One girl getting off was better than nothing and he wanted to watch.

Stone was gone; he'd heard her say so that night at the bar. Once it got dark, he'd hopped the wall again, figuring to catch Steele by herself for a change. No such luck. But that kiss had been worth the price of admission. Maybe later she'd be in the mood for a naked moonlight swim in the pool....

He reached down to adjust himself.

Peering through the French doors, he saw her cover the vodka glass with a plastic sandwich bag and seal it up. That was weird, but whatever. He took a step forward, careful not to get too close in case the alarm had been set. Groaning softly, he watched her lick her lips as she carried her dinner plate into the living room and flopped onto the couch.

Maybe she was feeling horny after all. He should walk right in and touch her. He could stroke his fingers over her mouth the way she was doing, rub his hand along her throat and down her... The plate fell to the floor. She jolted forward clutching her throat, a worried look on her face.

Frowning, he moved even closer to the door. Too close this

time. She jerked her head around, her eyes widening when she saw him, but he didn't think he'd been the one to scare her. She tried to get up and stumbled across the room, her chest heaving like she was having some kind of attack.

Even through the dark glass, he was sure she'd gotten a clear view of him. He had to go before she called the cops. But she didn't look right. The mouth that turned him on so much was gaping like a goldfish. Knowing he was going to regret it later, he reached for the door.

"What's the matter?"

"Heh-help." She answered with a wheezing gasp.

"Sure, sure. No prob."

Her eyes widened as she backed away from him, her gaze darting around frantically. Mick knew he was made. But her face was turning red and if he didn't do something, she was going to quit breathing altogether.

"Are you asthmatic or something? Where's your inhaler?"

She just shook her head and dragged in another labored breath. Then her eyes started to roll back in her head and she buckled to the floor. He was no Boy Scout, but he couldn't leave her like this. He needed her alive.

Reaching for her with one hand, he pulled his cell phone from his back pocket with the other. "Hold on, Steele. Hold on."

CHAPTER FORTY-NINE

Everything We Have

"YOU CAME BACK."

At the sound of Stella's raspy voice, Cameron closed his eyes on a rush of gratitude so profound it left him weak. He'd been sitting by her hospital bed, useless to do anything except watch her sleep and fixate on how he'd almost lost her. The anaphylaxis episode could easily have killed her.

Her face still lacked color and her eyes were dull from whatever medications she had been given. Seeing the smile brighten her pale cheeks, he offered a silent prayer of thanks and reached for her hand. "I came back."

And there'd be the devil to pay for leaving his team as he'd done. She was worth the price.

"I wasn't sure—"

"Always be sure, Stella. I can't tell you that I won't leave again. I will. But I swear on all I hold dear, as long as there's breath in my body, I'll come home to you."

"Oh, Cameron." He saw her eyes well before she ducked her head. "You know I hate that mushy crap."

"In that case I'll let my actions speak." He pressed the object he'd been holding for the past hour into her hand. "This is—"

"Your mother's." Tears spilled from her lashes as she looked at the filigreed cross lying on her palm. "It's just beautiful."

He gave her a quizzical look. "I thought you'd fallen asleep that night on the phone."

"I still heard your story. Thank you very much for making me cry. I hate that, too." She swiped at her eyes then raised up on one elbow and leaned toward him. "Help me put it on?"

As he fastened the delicate gold chain behind her neck, he wondered what his parents might have thought of Stella. Thinking on their similar personalities, he figured she and his mum would have clashed a bit then become friends. Dad, on the other hand, would have adored her from the start.

As her fingers gently brushed the pendant, her voice was tinged with uncharacteristic emotion. "I guess this means committing everything we have for as long as the love lasts."

The word sliced through him, laying his soul bare, leaving him vulnerable. It was all he'd ever wanted, all that had never been right before now. Despite what she'd said, though, he knew the effects of post-trauma. Given their lightning-fast relationship, he wanted to take the time to court her properly.

He wanted her to be as sure as he was.

Cameron leaned back in the chair, relaxing for the first time since he'd arrived. "Who said anything about love, Stella?"

"Not me, no way. All I want from you is great sex and some decent living room furniture." Her words were playful but she'd yet to let go of the cross, pressing it to her heart. "So, how long have I been here? I thought I remembered a different room."

"I asked that you be moved. I knew you'd appreciate having privacy." Not to mention it made it easier to guard her safety. "Do you remember what happened?"

She frowned and rubbed her forehead. "Not really. Maria paid me a not-so-friendly visit last night. After she left I wasn't feeling well and then this guy came out of nowhere to help me."

He nodded brusquely. "A man called to report an injury at your address."

"It was him, the guy who's been calling."

Cameron held his tongue, but he was not bloody pleased at all. He'd wait until she left hospital before lecturing her that the damned security system didn't work unless it was activated.

He was absolutely furious that someone had gotten into the house, despite the measures he'd taken. However he also had to be grudgingly thankful. Apparently the man had performed CPR until the paramedics arrived, thus saving Stella's life. Then he'd slipped away without anyone seeing. But Cameron planned to make it his life's mission to find him.

"How in the world could you have ingested the penicillin do you think?"

"I didn't drink the vodka. So Maria must have somehow slipped it into my Coke."

"The paramedics brought the glass you'd bagged, along with the other two, for testing. There were traces of antibiotic on one cola glass but the lip color wasn't yours."

"Well, then, how could—?" Stella sat bolt upright. "Oh, that bitch! It had to be in her lip gloss. Geez, don't Italians have to deal with enough stereotypes without her giving me the Corleone kiss of death?"

He raised one brow. "Should I inquire as to why she kissed you?"

She gave him a baleful look. "Don't get excited. It was her way of telling me to kiss off when I accused her of murder."

"I don't suppose she offered you a full confession."

"Not, not in exact words. But I'm sure your spyware got a recording, right?"

It took him a second to realize what she meant. "I'm afraid not. I told you only the phones were tapped."

Her face finally took on some color as she shrugged in embarrassment. "Sorry for not believing you. I guess Maria's confession, such as it was, couldn't have been used against her in court anyway."

Cameron twisted his mouth into a wry smile. "Before any kind of trial, we'd have to locate her first."

"She left for 'vacation' already, huh?"

"Aye. And according to the housekeeper, she took her new personal assistant along with her."

Stella snorted. "Some good-looking stud muffin no doubt."

"Actually, according to Mrs. Amalfi, a 'very nice young lady' named Caitlyn."

"What?!"

Cameron shrugged. "She was hired this past March. However Mrs. Amalfi said she'd only seen the girl once before the night she and Maria left."

Stella merely stared at him, apparently struck speechless. Finally she shook her head in tempo with her words. "I. Don't. Believe. This. The whole affair was a setup? What the hell?"

"Only Maria knows the why of it. But I'd hazard a guess that this way she got rid of a cheating husband and gained the baby she'd been wanting, while Caitlyn gets her big payday. I've got Jamie tracking her credit card expenditures. It's only a matter of time before Maria's found."

"Are you going after her personally?"

He nodded grimly. "Frank DiMarco's feeling horribly guilty for not seeing what his daughter had become. He's asked me to bring her back, if possible. I expect he'll have her committed, rather than risk police involvement."

Stella flopped back against the pillows, a look of disgust on her face. "Like that's going to do any good. She'll probably marry her shrink."

He cleared his throat. "Speaking of marriage, we have a bit of a problem—"

"You're awake. Thank God!" Vivian Mezzanotte burst through the door, her lovely face crumpled in concern. "We've been so worried!"

"That would be the problem." Cameron let go of her hand and backed away from the bed.

"Oh, *cara,* my poor girl. *Tesora mio.*" She spoke in the high-pitched tone women used around infants. Bending down for an embrace, she rained kisses all over Stella's forehead. "How are you, darling? Are you okay? Do you feel all right?"

"Yes, Mom. I'm really tired and my throat's sore. But other than that I feel fine." Stella appeared guilty and embarrassed, but Cameron found himself more amused than sympathetic.

"Good." As her mother straightened, her voice went sharp with anger. "Stella Gail Mezzanotte, you have got a lot of explaining to do! Most everyone is here—waiting for *hours,* worried to death."

"I'm sorry, Mom—"

"Only we can't see you, your own *family,* because," she looked over to point at him, "*this man,* who *claims* he's your husband, told his hired henchmen not to let anybody in!"

Stella had developed a sudden fascination with the pattern of her hospital gown. But she jerked her attention to him. "You have henchmen?"

"Singular, not plural, and he's actually a professional bodyguard. I asked that he watch over you until I could get here."

Mrs. Mezzanotte waved her arm about. "Hello? Can we get back to the husband claims being made, please? You just told us you had a boyfriend last weekend!"

He braced for the denial, willing himself not to feel rejected when Stella shot him an apologetic glance. Then she briefly looked at her mother before dropping her gaze. He saw the shame burned onto her cheeks and knew she wasn't ready. Intent on protecting her, he began to offer her mother an excuse that would put the blame squarely on his own shoulders.

However, Stella surprised them both. "Um, he's not claiming anything, Mom. Cameron actually is my husband."

CHAPTER FIFTY

Reflections

THE MOMENT I'd been dreading with every fiber of my being went pretty much the way I'd expected. Mom had stared at me while the color drained from her face, then burst into angry tears. She wasn't sure which was worse—the elopement or the pretense—and I was on her shit list until she figured it out.

Oh, she'd eventually forgive me. But she wasn't ever going to let me forget.

Her new son-in-law was another matter. With a dignity and grace I could only envy but not emulate, she had turned to Cameron and held out her hand.

"I'm Vivi. And you are?"

"Very glad to meet you."

Luckily, the nurse who'd come in for the next series of vitals and fluid checks had kicked them out before Mom could interrogate me. The two of them had left so Cameron could meet my family and left me with a sinking feeling in my gut. Once the Mezzanotte tribe knew about him, there'd be no going back.

You can't hide a secret once it's out, and you can't end a marriage once it's common knowledge to a family of Italians.

Now it was ten o'clock, blessedly after visiting hours ended, so I had a reprieve until midmorning. When the phone rang, I tried to ignore it. Until I realized the hospital didn't provide answering machines and that it might be my mother, whom I needed to make very happy right now. I picked up on the sixth ring.

"How are you feeling, Steele? Better, I hope."

I closed my eyes. Even though it was dark on the room, all I could see was red. Damn, I hate being played for a fool. "Better than dead. Hello, Maria."

"I'm very glad you're all right." Her words seemed sincere, but, now that I knew what to listen for, I detected the deceit in her voice.

"There's one thing I've learned about you recently, old friend. You're a lying bitch."

She laughed. "Right now I'm *lying* on a beach chair, watching the sun rise."

"Yeah? Is it rising over the water?"

"Nice try, Steele. I'll give you that one. It's over the water. But I'm not telling which hemisphere or which continent."

My thoughts turned to Gina DiMarco, who had been given no choice, and to Anthony Giocondo, who'd apparently just been an inconvenience. And to Gray, who'd been a schmuck, but who still didn't deserve to be roadkill. "I'll be at the airport to welcome you home. There's no statute of limitations on murder."

"But there are limitations on evidence. As in, you need to have some."

"How about the penicillin-laced lip marks you left on the glass? I think that will count, don't you?"

Her voice was all sweetness and innocence. "I don't know what you're talking about."

"You tried to kill me with a kiss! I'd call that evidence."

"Steele, you're exaggerating. I was taking antibiotics for a minor infection. I had no idea that you were allergic."

And there it was—the bottom line. I would never be able to prove any of my suspicions, never prove that she'd intended to harm me. And really, what had I expected? It was my first murder, but her third.

"You win, Maria. Dammit, you win."

"Oh don't be a sore loser, Steele. You were never really in the game."

AT TWO O'CLOCK in the morning I still wasn't sleeping. Instead, I lay in a restless tangle of darkness, wondering if lies really do always follow you. I'd been dreaming, relentless recurring nightmares so real that I'd woken up sweaty and in imagined pain. The long healed fractures on my ribs throbbed with the memory.

I thought about the night Bobby died, about my choices and my ultimate decision. My reasoning might have been justified, more acceptable, than Maria's. Hers had simply become twisted along the way. And, really, who the hell was I to judge Maria for getting away with murder when, once upon a really bad time, I had too?

In the real world, there's plenty of judgment. And, for some, there's punishment. But all too often there is no justice.

Just before she died, Gloria gave me one final bit of her wisdom. In a voice that sounded like rock grinding against metal, she said, *Remember what's really important in life, kiddo. You gotta be able to look yourself in the eye and be okay with the things you've done.*

It's good advice. So I tried to do what I thought was right in any given situation. And when I couldn't, I just avoided mirrors.

Sighing deeply, I closed my eyes. Tomorrow would be soon enough to face the world with guts and grace. And I would.

Because, after all, they don't call me Steele for nothing.

* * * * *

AUTHOR'S NOTE

Currently, insulin is only available in an injectable form. While there are several oral anti-diabetic medications that control diabetes by stimulating the pancreas, the essential hormone insulin cannot be taken orally. InsulOr and the pharmaceutical company that makes it are fictional.

Silhouette® Romantic Suspense
keeps getting hotter!
Turn the page for a sneak preview
of Wendy Rosnau's latest SPY GAMES *title*
SLEEPING WITH DANGER

Available November 2007

Silhouette® Romantic Suspense—
Sparked by Danger, Fueled by Passion!

Melita had been expecting a chaste quick kiss of the generic variety. But this kiss with Sully was the kind that sparked a dying flame to life. The kind of kiss you can't plan for. The kind of kiss memories are built on.

The memory of her murdered lover, Nemo, came to her then and she made a starved little noise in the back of her throat. She raised her arms and threaded her fingers through Sully's hair, pulled him closer. Felt his body settle, then melt into her.

In that instant her hunger for him grew, and his for her. She pressed herself to him with more urgency, and he responded in kind.

Melita came out of her kiss-induced memory of Nemo with a start. "Wait a minute." She pushed Sully away from her. "You bastard!"

She spit two nasty words at him in Greek, then wiped his kiss from her lips.

"I thought you deserved some solid proof that I'm still in one piece." He started for the door. "The clock's ticking, honey. Come on, let's get out of here."

"That's it? You sucker me into kissing you, and that's all you have to say?"

"I'm sorry. How's that?"

He didn't sound sorry in the least. "You're—"

"Getting out of this godforsaken prison cell. Stop whining and let's go."

"Not if I was being shot at sunrise. Go. You deserve whatever you get if you walk out that door."

He turned back. "Freedom is what I'm going to get."

"A second of freedom before the guards in the hall shoot you." She jammed her hands on her hips. "And to think I was worried about you."

"If you're staying behind, it's no skin off my ass."

"Wait! What about our deal?"

"You just said you're not coming. Make up your mind."

"Have you forgotten we need a boat?"

"How could I? You keep harping on it."

"I'm not going without a boat. And those guards out there aren't going to just let you walk out of here. You need me and we need a plan."

"I already have a plan. I'm getting out of here. That's the plan."

"I should have realized that you never intended to take me with you from the very beginning. You're a liar and a coward."

Of everything she had read, there was nothing in Sully Paxton's file that hinted he was a coward, but it was the one word that seemed to register in that one-track mind of his. The look he nailed her with a second later was pure venom.

He came at her so quickly she didn't have time to get out of his way. "You know I'm not a coward."

"Prove it. Give me until dawn. I need one more night to put everything in place before we leave the island."

"You're asking me to stay in this cell one more night...and trust you?"

"Yes."

He snorted. "Yesterday you knew they were planning to harm me, but instead of doing something about it you went to bed and never gave me a second thought. Suppose tonight you do the same. By tomorrow I might damn well be in my grave."

"Okay, I screwed up. I won't do it again." Melita sucked in a ragged breath. "I can't leave this minute. Dawn, Sully. Wait until dawn." When he looked as if he was about to say no, she pleaded, "Please wait for me."

"You're asking a lot. The door's open now. I would be a fool to hang around here and trust that you'll be back."

"What you can trust is that I want off this island as badly as you do, and you're my only hope."

"I must be crazy."

"Is that a yes?"

"Dammit!" He turned his back on her. Swore twice more.

"You won't be sorry."

He turned around. "I already am. How about we seal this new deal?"

He was staring at her lips. Suddenly Melita knew what he expected. "We already sealed it."

"One more. You enjoyed it. Admit it."

"I enjoyed it because I was kissing someone else."

He laughed. "That's a good one."

"It's true. It might have been your lips, but it wasn't you I was kissing."

"If that's your excuse for wanting to kiss me, then—"

"I was kissing Nemo."

"What's a nemo?"

Melita gave Sully a look that clearly told him that he was trespassing on sacred ground. She was about to enforce it with a warning when a voice in the hall jerked them both to attention.

She bolted away from the wall. "Get back in bed. Hurry. I'll be here before dawn."

She didn't reach the door before he snagged her arm, pulled her up against him and planted a kiss on her lips that took her completely by surprise.

When he released her, he said, "If you're confused about who just kissed you, the name's Sully. I'll be here waiting at dawn. Don't be late."

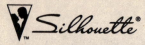

Romantic
SUSPENSE

**Sparked by Danger,
Fueled by Passion.**

Onyxx agent Sully Paxton's only chance of
survival lies in the hands of his enemy's daughter
Melita Krizova. He doesn't know he's a pawn in the
beautiful island girl's own plan for escape. Can
they survive their ruses and their fiery attraction?

*Look for the next installment in the
Spy Games miniseries,*

Sleeping with Danger

by **Wendy Rosnau**

Available November 2007 wherever you buy books.

Visit Silhouette Books at www.eHarlequin.com   SRS27559

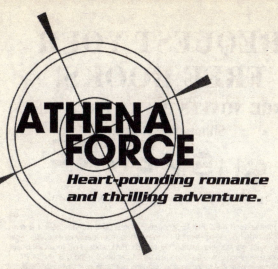

ATHENA FORCE

Heart-pounding romance and thrilling adventure.

History repeats itself...unless she can stop it.

Investigative reporter Winter Archer is thrown into writing a biography of Athena Academy's founder. But someone out there will stop at nothing—not even murder—to ensure that long-buried secrets remain hidden.

ATHENA FORCE

Will the women of Athena unravel Arachne's powerful web of blackmail and death...or succumb to their enemies' deadly secrets?

Look for

VENDETTA
by *Meredith Fletcher*

Available November wherever you buy books.

Visit Silhouette Books at www.eHarlequin.com   AF38975

REQUEST YOUR FREE BOOKS!

2 FREE NOVELS PLUS 2 FREE GIFTS!

Silhouette® Romantic

SUSPENSE

Sparked by Danger, Fueled by Passion!

YES! Please send me 2 FREE Silhouette® Romantic Suspense novels and my 2 FREE gifts. After receiving them, if I don't wish to receive any more books, I can return the shipping statement marked "cancel." If I don't cancel, I will receive 4 brand-new novels every month and be billed just $4.24 per book in the U.S., or $4.99 per book in Canada, plus 25¢ shipping and handling per book plus applicable taxes, if any*. That's a savings of at least 15% off the cover price! I understand that accepting the 2 free books and gifts places me under no obligation to buy anything. I can always return a shipment and cancel at any time. Even if I never buy another book from Silhouette, the two free books and gifts are mine to keep forever.

240 SDN EEX6   340 SDN EEYJ

Name	(PLEASE PRINT)
Address	Apt. #
City	State/Prov.	Zip/Postal Code

Signature (if under 18, a parent or guardian must sign)

Mail to the Silhouette Reader Service™:
IN U.S.A.: P.O. Box 1867, Buffalo, NY 14240-1867
IN CANADA: P.O. Box 609, Fort Erie, Ontario L2A 5X3

Not valid to current Silhouette Intimate Moments subscribers.

Want to try two free books from another line?
Call 1-800-873-8635 or visit www.morefreebooks.com.

* Terms and prices subject to change without notice. NY residents add applicable sales tax. Canadian residents will be charged applicable provincial taxes and GST. This offer is limited to one order per household. All orders subject to approval. Credit or debit balances in a customer's account(s) may be offset by any other outstanding balance owed by or to the customer. Please allow 4 to 6 weeks for delivery.

Your Privacy: Silhouette is committed to protecting your privacy. Our Privacy Policy is available online at www.eHarlequin.com or upon request from the Reader Service. From time to time we make our lists of customers available to reputable firms who may have a product or service of interest to you. If you would prefer we not share your name and address, please check here. ☐

SRS07

HARLEQUIN Romance®

New York Times bestselling author

DIANA PALMER

Handsome, eligible ranch owner Stuart York knew Ivy Conley was too young for him, so he closed his heart to her and sent her away—despite the fireworks between them. Now, years later, Ivy is determined not to be treated like a little girl anymore…but for some reason, Stuart is always fighting her battles for her. And safe in Stuart's arms makes Ivy feel like a woman…his woman.

Winter Roses

Available November.

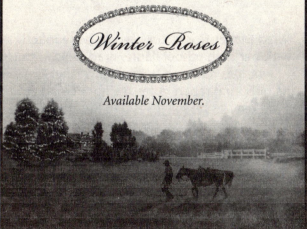

HRIBC03985

Silhouette®

SPECIAL EDITION™

**brings you a heartwarming
new McKettrick's story from**

NEW YORK TIMES BESTSELLING AUTHOR

LINDA LAEL MILLER

THE McKETTRICK
Way

Meg McKettrick is surprised to be reunited
with her high school flame, Brad O'Ballivan,
who has returned home to his family's
neighboring ranch. After seeing Meg again,
Brad realizes he still loves her. But the pride
of both manage to interfere with love...until
an unexpected matchmaker gets involved.

— McKettrick Women —

Available December wherever you buy books.

Visit Silhouette Books at www.eHarlequin.com SSEIBC24867